The Enchanter's Flame

The Ellwood Chronicles I
Michele Notaro

ISBN: 9781719957434

The amazing book cover was done by:
Soxsational Cover Art

http://www.soxsationalcoverart.com/index.html

Table of Contents

Prologue

A hooded figure in a black robe walked through a long, dark tunnel, hunched over, protecting something in her arms. She kept her hood up, hiding her face as she walked through a small passage to the back of a cave and pulled out an old wooden box covered in etchings. She ran her fingertips over the etchings, then carefully lifted the lid and gently set the small bundle inside. Placing her hand on the bundle, she knelt and began to chant.

"Elita le mehi elmirai sel eh. Elita le mehi elmirai sel eh," she said over and over and over.

A loud bang came from the cave entrance, and the robed woman cut herself off, then shut the box and carefully placed it in a crevice in the rocks. She swiped her arm over the crevice and the hole closed, leaving only rock in its place as if the hole and box had never been there.

"Where issss it," a man in red hissed as he entered the cave. His voice sounded more reptilian than human, and his face was hidden from view.

"In a place you'll never think to look," the robed figure said.

"It belongs to me!"

"Not anymore." The robed woman swirled her arms in a circle, and the air began to whip around her. "Leave this place. You do not belong on sacred ground."

The man in red threw his head back and laughed. "You really believe that, don't you, old wench?" He lifted his arms and inky black smoke poured out of his hands, filling up the cave and shrouding the woman in complete darkness.

The woman screamed in pain as the smoke filled her lungs, her veins, her bones. She coughed out. "You'll... never... find it."

The red man hissed. "You led me straight to it, old wench."

The woman screamed in agony as the smoke finally reached her heart.

I sat up in bed, sweat dripping on my forehead as I looked around my apartment, blinking myself awake. Where was I? What just happened?

I shook away the foggy aftereffects of sleep and blew out a breath.

It was just a dream. A weird, crazy-as-hell dream that made no sense, but a dream nonetheless. I'd never had a dream feel so real before. *Maybe that's what I get for watching a scary movie before bed last night.*

I blew out a breath and looked at my alarm clock. Three-twelve a.m. I still had a few hours before I needed to wake up, but there was no way I'd be able to sleep after that dream, so I got up and walked into my kitchen to fix a glass of water.

As I filled my glass, I couldn't help but wonder if the woman was okay. But I was curious what that bundle was, and if that weird, red man had found it or not. I had a feeling that if he had found it before I woke up, my dream would've gotten even darker really fast.

I took a sip of my water and tried to shake the weird feelings off.

Chapter One

I was sitting at my desk going over a file when I heard yelling coming out of the chief's office, followed by a door slamming and more yelling. I looked up from my file to the open doorway just in time to see some guy in a leather jacket rush past, mumbling under his breath. I somehow got the faint scent of rosemary as the dark-haired man ran by.

My coworker, Darren Thompal, walked past my door calling after the man, "Fucking asshole."

I got out of my chair and walked to my door to see what the hell was going on. I joined the crowd of other detectives right in front of my office.

Leather Jacket yelled back, "Bite me."

Suddenly, a stapler flew through the air—even though I hadn't seen anyone throw it—Thompal jumped back in surprise, but still managed to get hit with it in the chest. When the stapler clanked to the ground, Thompal yelled, "Real mature, Ellwood!" *Did that guy really throw a stapler at him?*

I couldn't hear what the reply was, but I did see Leather Jacket flip Thompal off with both hands above his head as he walked away. The front glass door slammed loudly—a feat I didn't think was possible—and for a split second, I thought the glass looked cracked, but I blinked and it was whole, so it must've been my imagination.

Through the door I saw Leather Jacket jump on a motorcycle and take off before he even put a helmet on.

Thompal turned his snarled growl on me, "What the fuck you lookin' at?"

I held my hands up, not wanting to get involved in the office drama. I'd only been working here at Central for two months, so I didn't have a clue who or what that was about. Darren Thompal wasn't the friendliest guy in the office, and he was also a huge meat-head—shaved head and all. I didn't want to get in a confrontation with him, even though I wasn't small by any means, and I figured I could hold my own if it ever came to a fight, it wasn't worth it.

Another coworker, Anita Long, walked over to Thompal, placing a hand on his elbow. "You better calm down before the chief kicks your ass."

"Me?" Thompal exclaimed. "It was that asshole's doing." He gestured toward the front doors.

Long rolled her eyes. "Doesn't matter. You know who he is. Come on." She pulled a grumbling Darren Thompal away to his office.

I turned to Detective Walter Madler, who had watched the scene beside me, and asked, "Who was that guy?" Madler was a decent looking guy with sandy blond hair and brown eyes. He was around six feet tall with a firm build, though not as muscular as me, it was still clear that the guy worked out. He was usually pretty happy and pleasant to talk to. We'd gone out for a few beers since I started here, and we'd occasionally partnered up since neither of us had a permanent partner at the moment.

Madler eyed me for a moment before blowing out a slow breath. "His name's Ellwood. Some big-wig that you don't wanna get involved with, Fitz." He seemed unusually tense and pissed, like maybe there was a history there. "He's a complete dick." With that, he turned and headed to his office.

As I walked back and sat at my desk, I shook my head a little; office politics and drama were so not my thing. I absentmindedly scratched the tattooed chain around my wrist. It'd been there so long I hardly even noticed it, but for whatever reason, the coffee-colored ink that was only a few shades darker than my brown skin itched every now and then. So weird. I took the hair tie out of my small ponytail and ran my fingers through my curly hair for a second before tying it back up. Growing up I'd had to keep it short, and in the military, they were even stricter, so once I'd left the Special Forces, I'd decided to let it grow.

With a sigh, I looked back at the file on my desk. The case had only come in yesterday morning, though the crime scene had been found almost two weeks ago. The local police department was apparently slacking on their duties. *Typical.*

I pulled out the crime scene photos to examine them for the hundredth time since yesterday. I spread the photos out on my desk, taking in the poor eighteen-year-old girl that was covered in blood and bruises. She was found naked near the bay by my old town covered in gashes with marks on her wrists and ankles that indicated being tied up. The freakiest part was she'd been completely drained of blood, although there was blood all over her body, none was left inside it. The medical examiner I talked to yesterday actually remembered the case even though it was two weeks later, probably because he'd never seen anything like it before. Unfortunately for me, I'd seen all kinds of fucked-up shit.

I shook off those thoughts and picked up a close-up of one of the more peculiar marks on the body. The mark was burned into her skin right in the center of her throat; like a brand. When the body had been found, the brand was still covered in blisters so the image was difficult to decipher. There was a fairly clear circle surrounding the whole image, but inside, the only thing I could make out was a straight line in the center with a small circle on the bottom. The rest of the lines were blurred together by blisters.

I got a strange chill thinking about it, but I didn't look away. There was something about the image that seemed oddly familiar, but I couldn't seem to grasp where I'd seen it before.

After examining the evidence for a while longer, I grabbed my jacket and headed out to interview the family members of the victim.

***

Two weeks after getting that strange murder case of the branded girl, I still hadn't turned up any new leads. The victim was a straight-A student from the university and didn't seem to have any enemies. I was starting to believe that it was more of a wrong place, wrong time kinda thing, and that the branding was the key. Too bad all my research looking into that symbol had turned up nil.

I looked up from my desk when I heard someone knocking on the doorframe—as usual, I had left my office door open.

Detective Madler was standing in my doorway with a file in his hand and a small smile. "You came from the Strimville Station, right?"

"Yeah, why?" I asked. I'd gotten the promotion to detective and transferred to the Brinnswick Central Agency here in Arronston City—the central part of the country of Brinnswick. Before that, I'd worked as a police officer in Strimville.

His smile grew. "Great. You can take this, then." He walked the three steps into my office and dropped a file on my desk. "Straight from Strimville PD."

I sighed as I reached for the file and opened it. "Another murder? What the fuck? This is the second one this month." Strimville wasn't exactly known for its crime rate. The entire five years I'd worked there I'd only come across two murders. Strimville was pretty much the complete opposite of the city I now lived in. Even though Strimville and Arronston were both in Brinnswick and only separated by about twenty miles, it was like they were two completely different worlds.

Walter shrugged. "Don't know, but since you know the town, you get the case."

"Gee, thanks," I grumbled with a sigh.

His smile grew larger. "Getting frustrated already, Fitz? I'll have to take you out again soon. Maybe we can find you some ass." He walked away chuckling to himself. Idiot.

I snorted at him, then examined the file. I read the report before looking at the crime scene photos. It was a young woman, early twenties, murdered in what appeared to be a very bloody way. She was covered in cuts and bruises. There was a close-up picture of her throat, so I grabbed it, half expecting to see the same brand as the other murder case, but it looked like the girl's throat had been cut without any sign of it being branded.

I flipped through the next few photos, then came across a picture of the living room the body had been found in. There was a large, brick fireplace behind the victim, who was lying on a hardwood floor. There were a few pools of—according to the crime scene analysis—the victim's blood. As I looked closer, it almost appeared to be in a pattern... small pools of blood arranged in a circle.

I flipped to the next picture which was a close-up of the blood. In the center of the circle, a symbol was drawn... also in the victim's blood.

I gasped as recognition hit me. I knew that symbol. I remembered it well from my tour in Gauhala when I was in the military—Special Forces. My unit had come across some crazy-ass, old-school witch doctor. In a clusterfuck of events I'd spent the last five years trying to forget, I ended up stumbling across a vile witch doctor's shrine. All over his shrine was the same fucking symbol.

I ripped open my filing cabinet and pulled out the file from the young girl with the branding. I found the picture of the brand and decided that it most certainly could be the same damn symbol. *Fuck.*

I immediately looked into the database on my computer for any related cases, here or in any of the surrounding towns and cities. I didn't really expect to find anything, but I wanted to cover all my bases before taking this to my boss. Unfortunately, I found a case with a description of a symbol drawn in blood near the victim. I scoffed as I looked it over. The photos definitely matched, and the fucking case hadn't been handed over to us even though the body was found months ago.

I packed up both files and headed out of my office and straight for the printer where copies of the case I just discovered were waiting for me before heading to the chief's office. Of course, his door was shut, so after taking a deep breath, I tentatively knocked.

"Come in," a deep husky voice called out.

I opened the door and stepped in, shutting it behind me.

"Fitz." Chief Gillman nodded to me. "Have a seat. What can I help you with?"

I sat in one of the chairs across from him and placed two files on his desk, taking out a picture from each and passing them over to him.

As he looked, I explained, "Both these cases came in from the Strimville PD in the past month." I pointed to the second one. "This one just came in today, though the body was discovered over a week ago. If you look at the brand on the other victim, you can see that it could be the same symbol. The blistering on the victim makes it difficult to match." I cleared my throat before pulling out the last file. "I also looked up old cases and found one more match from Owentine." The town between here and Strimville. "Also a young victim, early twenties, female. The, um, the case was never handed over to us. I just found it earlier, but the body was found six months ago."

A flash of anger showed on his face before the chief made a noncommittal sound in his throat and looked down to examine the photos. He took each file and reviewed them for a long moment before he looked up at me. "Good catch, Fitz. I need to make a few calls. Meet me back here in thirty minutes." He nodded at the door, obviously dismissing me.

"Yes, sir." I stood and walked out of the room.

"Shut the door behind you," he called out, even though I was already shutting it.

I walked back to my office to try and research the symbol that was burned into my memory. I didn't find anything useful which wasn't surprising, even when I looked up witch doctors in Gauhala—not that I expected that to be posted anywhere, but I had hoped. With no new information to go on, I made my way back to the chief's office and knocked on the door.

He yelled for me to come in and motioned for me to sit down as he finished up a phone call. I shut the door behind me, sat down, and tried to ignore his conversation. After he hung up, I was surprised by the amount of stress I could see on his face. It seemed like his stress grew with each passing second, and he rubbed a hand over his face and sighed. I fidgeted in my seat a little, unsure of why he was reacting that way. I just figured we had a serial killer on our hands, but he was acting like it was an even bigger deal than that.

Finally, the chief looked at me. "I have a specialist coming in. He should be here any minute."

My eyebrows rose to my hairline in surprise. "A specialist? Like an informant?"

He sighed again. "No, he works for a different department, but we're going to need his..." he seemed to think over what word to use, then settled on, "particular set of skills to deal with this."

Before I could ask what exactly he thought *this* was or what kind of *specialist* he meant, the door to his office burst open and a man came in without knocking or being invited.

I turned my attention to the man who so casually walked into the chief of the BCA's office, and I was hit with a strong spicy smell with a hint of rosemary. He had very dark hair—black, really—that hung down to his shoulders and contrasted with his pale skin. His hair was parted on the left side, but the left side was braided back from his temple to behind his ear with beads or something braided into it. He was pretty short, maybe five-eight, and thin—I could probably snap him in two pretty easily—and when his bright green eyes assessed me, I was surprised that I wanted to squirm. He looked young, maybe mid-twenties at most, especially since he was dressed in black jeans, combat boots, and a black t-shirt with a leather jacket over it. He seemed to have that Goth bad-boy thing down pat. He even had a bunch of black leather cords around his neck, although they were tucked under his shirt.

Despite myself, I still found the little punk sexy, even though I was pretty sure he was the guy that fought with Darren Thompal and stormed out of the building a few weeks ago. *Fucking great.*

The newcomer looked past me to the chief and glared at him. I followed his line of sight only to find the chief glaring right back at the guy. I looked back and forth between the two for a tense minute until the chief finally cracked saying, "You wouldn't dare." I had no clue what he was talking about.

Goth Guy raised one brow. "You wanna take that chance?"

Chief Gillman narrowed his eyes before finally grinning. "Asshole." He threw his pen at the guy, and it bounced off his chest as the guy snorted.

He unceremoniously plopped down in the chair next to me, leaned back and put his feet up on the desk. Ignoring me, he spoke directly to the chief, "How's Aspen?" It took me a second to place the name, but I soon remembered it was the name of the chief's wife, though I'd never met her before.

"It's been two weeks," the chief replied, looking decidedly put-upon.

Goth Guy sighed. "I know."

"Do you know what it's been like?"

Goth Guy grimaced. "I can imagine. I'll call her tonight."

"No, you'll come for dinner."

My eyebrows shot into my hairline for a second time. Wow, I guess the chief was good friends with this guy, or at least his wife was.

Goth Guy sighed again. "Fine."

"Good. Now get your stinky-ass feet off my desk."

"Make me." Goth Guy grinned at Chief Gillman.

The chief snorted, but reached across his desk and knocked his feet off before gesturing to me. "This is Detective Sebastian Fitz." He gestured at Goth Guy. "Ailin Ellwood."

Goth Guy—Ailin—turned his head to me, looking unimpressed. I almost held out my hand to shake his, but decided against it and ended up just nodding at the guy. He didn't do anything back; he just turned his head back to look at the chief. *What a dick.*

Ailin flapped his leather jacket. "Fuck, it's hot in here." As soon as he said it, it felt like the temperature in the room dropped fifteen degrees. The sudden change actually made me shiver.

"Knock it the fuck off." Chief Gillman shot Ailin a look I couldn't interpret. "Just take off your jacket like a normal person."

"Where's the fun in that?" Ailin looked like he was going for an innocent look, but he failed miserably because he just exuded mischief. The fact he was in the BCA, and not in handcuffs, was a mystery. The guy was trouble.

The chief glared at him, then Ailin sighed and the temperature seemed to slowly rise. *I must be going out of my fucking mind.*

Ailin tilted his head a little and stared at the chief, still completely ignoring me. "So, Alec, why'd you call me down here? You know I've been busy."

The chief—apparently *Alec* to this Ailin guy—grinned and shook his head. "I know exactly what you've been up to."

"With that grin, I very much doubt it, Al." Ailin looked him up and down with a smirk. "I didn't think you swung that way."

The chief laughed at that before sobering and throwing the three files at Ailin, who caught them effortlessly. He took a moment to review them, then looked up at the chief. "You're thinking demonic?"

Well that doesn't sound ominous at all... I held in a snort at the thought.

The chief nodded. "Looks like it to me, but figured you should take a look."

"I'm guessing the crime scenes have been cleaned," Ailin mused, barely looking for the nod from the chief. "What about the bodies? Can we dig them up?" I was sure my eyes were as wide as saucers at that suggestion. We didn't typically go around digging up dead bodies, at least, not unless we absolutely had to.

"All three were cremated," I finally said something as I scratched at my wrist tattoo.

Ailin didn't even acknowledge me, he just mumbled under his breath, "Of course they were." He read over the reports for a few more minutes. "You need to find any other cases where the body was drained. I'm gonna need an office to start compiling everything together. There was a four-month leap between the first body and the second which means there are a lot more we either haven't found yet or haven't linked to this case." He looked down at the papers again and furrowed his brow. "Wait a minute. This body was found six months ago, yet you weren't given the case until today?"

"Actually, Fitz pulled it from Owentine PD earlier today," the chief told him.

"Dammit. I'm gonna kill Ed." Ailin pulled out his phone.

"I already took care of it," the chief said.

"This isn't the first time that dumbass messed with us," Ailin reminded him.

The chief smiled at him. "I sent Avery over twenty minutes ago. I don't think we'll be having anymore issues with Owentine PD."

Ailin grinned back and I couldn't help but agree with the sentiment that Ed, of the Owentine PD, was a dick and deserved whatever punishment my chief sent his way.

Ailin finally looked over at me. "How far did you search? Just locally?"

I nodded. "Just here and the surrounding towns."

Still looking at me, he said, "We need to start a global search for anything or anyone with this symbol and for any bodies drained of blood in the last five years."

Global? Five years? Really? Should I mention...? I know the chief has clearance, but...

I took a deep breath and directed my question at both of them, "How high is your security clearance?"

Ailin simply looked back at Chief Gillman with that damn raised eyebrow again. The chief sighed. "His clearance is higher than mine, Fitz. What's this about?"

That was extremely surprising to me. The guy looked younger than me and was wearing a leather jacket and necklaces for fuck's sake. But I knew the chief's clearance was even higher than mine, so I took a deep breath. "When I was deployed in Gauhala, my unit ran into a witch doctor. I came across his shrine, and this same symbol was etched into the ground. I remember because..." I looked down and took another deep breath. "I remember because the bastard cut open one of my... teammates and was trying to fill the ingrained symbol with his blood."

When neither of them said anything, I finally looked up and found them both staring at me. Ailin had actually turned all the way in his seat to face me fully. With wide, shocked eyes he asked, "Did he finish the ritual?"

Huh? "I don't... what?"

"Did he fill the etching completely with blood?"

"Uh... no? My captain got there before the witch doctor finished."

"Are you sure the symbol wasn't completely filled with blood?"

I thought about it for a moment. That night had been a crazy fucked-up mess that I tried to forget at all costs, especially the part after my captain came in. I took a shaky breath before answering him, "I remember my captain kicking the dirt and saying something about 'breaking the circle', so I don't think there was blood over the whole thing, but I can't say for sure because I was focused on..." I trailed off, deciding not to go into any more detail about that. I couldn't afford to go down that road again.

"What was your captain's name?" Ailin asked, still looking intense.

"Robert Greenleaf."

Ailin immediately looked relieved. He glanced at the chief and gave him a slight nod which seemed to relieve him as well. Then Ailin focused on me again. "What happened to the witch doctor?"

"He was killed. Captain Greenleaf shot him." That part I didn't mind sharing. The world was definitely better off without that crazy asshole in it.

"Good. How long ago was this?"

"Uh... about five years ago."

He nodded at me, then pulled his cellphone out of his pocket, making a call. He held the phone to his ear for a long time before finally saying into it, "Hey, Rob." Pause. "No, I don't." Pause with a chuckle. "Yeah, yeah, yeah. Okay... five years ago, Gauhala, witch doctor." Long pause. "Good. How far in was it?" Pause. "Yeah, possible demonic." Pause. "Alright, I'll let you know. Keep an ear out and call if anything comes up." He snapped the phone closed.

Before I thought better of it, I opened my mouth. "Was that my old captain?" *Who in the hell is this guy and how does he know every-freaking-one?*

He glanced at me with a curt, "Yeah." Then refocused on Chief Gillman. "You know what this means, Al. I need to get to the most recent site. You can make the appropriate calls, right?" Half this conversation made no sense to me, but they clearly had a strong history.

"Of course." The chief waved it off. "You're gonna have to use Fitz's office, and I want you to keep him on the case with you."

Ailin immediately protested, "But—"

"Look, Ailin, I know it won't be easy bringing him up to speed, but he was brought into this department for a reason."

Ailin growled. "It didn't work out so great the last time."

"Stop acting like an asshole and maybe it'll go better this time." Ailin opened his mouth again, but Gillman held his hand up to stop him. "Please just do this, okay?" *Really? The chief is actually* asking *for permission to assign him a partner? Again, who in the hell is this guy?*

Ailin eyed him tensely, then groaned. "Argh, fine, but you owe me, Alec."

Chief Alecander Gillman grinned at him. "Two weeks."

Ailin gave him a dramatic eye roll before jumping up to his feet. "Come on, then, Fitzy. Lead the way." *God, I hated when people called me that.* "We'll set up, then head over to the last known crime scene."

I almost protested, too, but one look at the chief's face, and I snapped my mouth shut. I stood up, grabbed the files off the desk, and walked Ailin down to my office getting a bunch of sympathetic, surprised, and amused looks from my coworkers along the way.

Before he walked in, he said, "I gotta piss. Get the files ready so we can start when I'm finished."

I didn't have time to remind him that I didn't take orders from him because the asshole walked to the bathroom without waiting for a reply. With a heavy sigh, I went in and got the damn files out.

I wasn't surprised that the guy literally started taking over my office as soon as he walked in. He brought a second whiteboard in that he stole from someone else, started hanging shit on my walls, and even moved my fucking desk to the side of the room. I wanted to punch him, even if I did get a nice view of his little ass when his leather jacket raised a bit as he reached up to hang something. And even if he somehow made my whole damn office smell like rosemary, I still didn't appreciate it.

When he took off his leather jacket and revealed these black leather arm bracers, I was confused for a moment. Did people really wear those things? What was he planning on doing? Going into battle?

After I hung a few pictures, and he ended up taking them down and rehanging them differently, I just sat down and let him do his thing. He was irritating me beyond belief. I was pretty sure he only did it to piss me off, so I didn't give him the satisfaction of seeing my reaction. I sat in my chair and watched his little ass move around the room with my hands behind my head.

After a while, he must've realized I wasn't going to react because he eyed me up and down. I smiled sweetly at him just to piss him off.

His eyes narrowed. "Let's go." He dashed out the door.

I chuckled as I grabbed my jacket off the back of the door and followed him.

When we got outside, he seemed irrationally angry. "You'll have to drive. I rode my bike."

"Fine." I pulled my keys out of my pocket. "This way."

I led the jerk to my car, unlocked it, and got in. He got in the passenger seat, and we were off to my hometown of Strimville. I knew where I was going because Strimville wasn't a very big town to begin with, and I'd lived there for years.

The drive was met with silence, except for the radio. I was actually surprised that he hadn't tried to change the station on me, but he either didn't mind or wasn't paying attention. It took about a half hour to get there. I pulled up to the curb right in front of a house that still had crime scene tape blocking the front door.

Ailin immediately got out before I even turned the car off, and I followed him up the path. He seemed to have no problem ripping the tape off the door and somehow opening the door without a key. I'd thought we were going to have to break in, but it looked like the idiotic police in this town hadn't bothered to lock the door at all. I hoped everything was still inside the house.

Right before he crossed the threshold, I asked, "Do you want gloves and stuff? I have a kit in my trunk."

He waved me off, clearly distracted. "Not necessary. It's been compromised already."

I didn't know how he knew that, but I just shrugged and followed him in. I'd studied the crime scene photos and knew this neighborhood, so I was pretty sure I knew the layout already. There was a staircase right inside the door and a dining room to the immediate right. We had to walk a few feet down a small hallway to get to the living room where the body was found. I was surprised there was still some blood on the hardwood floor, although it was hard to see since it was dried on the dark wood.

Ailin walked right over to the symbol on the floor, and before I could figure out his intention, he had both bare hands lying on top of the sticky goo. I wrinkled my nose at him, wondering what in the fuck he could possibly get out of touching old blood. It was disgusting, so I looked away and walked the perimeter of the room. Every single photograph and frame was facing down, as if the killer couldn't stand to look at them. That made me think it was personal; that the killer had a hard time dealing with it.

I walked further in to the fireplace where ashes still remained. I glanced over my shoulder at Ailin—he still had his bare hands in the old blood—and his lips were moving. I turned around to fully face him, and I squinted at him. *What in the fuck could he possibly be doing now?*

As I silently watched him, I realized that he was chanting. *Oh shit.* I took a step away with wide eyes. He was chanting... just like that fucking witch doctor had... and he was doing it over that same fucking symbol. *Oh shit. Shit. Shit. Shit. Shit.*

Ailin's eyes snapped open to look right at me. "I'm not going to hurt you." Then he closed his eyes and resumed his chanting.

Ice cold fear ran through my body. His declaration did absolutely nothing to make me feel better. *Oh god... what the fuck am I going to do?* I eyed the distance to the hallway. I'd have to run past him to get there, but it was only ten feet away. I looked at the window in the room, also about ten feet away, but I'd have to break the glass to get out, so that'd have to be a last resort. Or I could shoot him if I had to, but I'd probably go to jail for it. Unless he attacks me. *Then that asshole is going down.*

I took a step toward the hallway, but was immediately blocked by Ailin, who'd jumped in front of me with a scowl. *He's small, I can take him.*

As if he could read my thoughts, he snorted before saying, "I'm not going to hurt you. Considering your background, I probably should've explained what I was doing." He pointed to the symbol he'd been touching. "I was trying to sense who drew that."

I furrowed my brow. "How could you possibly 'sense' that?" Before he could answer, I said, "Move."

He looked at me curiously before stepping out of my path. I practically ran out of that room and out the front door. I heard him mumbling behind me, but I didn't give a shit at that point. There was no fucking way I was going to let some witch doctor, or anyone else for that matter, ever hold that power over me again.

When I got outside and a few feet away from the house, I took a deep, calming breath.

"I'm not a witch doctor." Ailin's voice made me jump. *Jesus, did he just read my mind?*

I turned around to face him, but stepped back so there was a good distance between us. "Then why were you chanting?"

"I told you, I was trying to sense who drew the rune on the ground."

That didn't make sense, so I stepped back to further the distance between us.

"I'm not a witch doctor, I swear."

I squinted at him, studying him. I was pretty sure he was telling the truth.

"I was just seeing if I could sense anything. I was trying to follow my... gut."

Again, I thought he was being truthful. "Did it work?"

"No, you were thinking too loudly in there."

I rolled my eyes. "You're such an asshole." Why was he being such a dick?

He waved me off. "Been called worse. I may be an asshole, but I'm not some evil witch doctor." He looked right into my eyes. "You have nothing to worry about from me. I promise I would never hurt you."

I had no freaking idea why, but I believed him. I was usually pretty good at reading people—part of the job—so I didn't think he was lying. He was a conceited dickhead, but I didn't really think he wanted to hurt me. If he did, he probably would've done it already, right? We'd been alone in the car for a while, and we were alone out here, and he hadn't even touched me once. I took a soothing breath and accidentally breathed in his rosemary smell which somehow made my cock twitch in my pants. *What the fuck? This guy is such an asshole and possibly evil—but apparently my dick didn't get the memo.* I cleared my throat at the strange and sudden lust I felt. "Okay."

He nodded, unaware of my predicament, thank god. "I have an idea of where to start. Let's go back to the station." He walked past me and bumped into my shoulder. He didn't even apologize. *Dickhead.*

Again, the car ride went by in silence... at least until Ailin rolled down his window a little and lit a fucking joint in *my* car.

"What the fuck do you think you're doing?" I clenched my teeth in anger.

"Oh, you want one?" He sounded like he didn't have a care in the world.

"You cannot smoke in my car." I ground my teeth.

I could feel his eyes on me as red-hot anger filled me, and I knew he had to see it on my face and probably on my skin since I was most likely turning red.

He jabbed at the button to roll down his window all the way. "Fine." Then he unhooked his seatbelt and leaned his entire head and arms out of the window with the joint still between his lips.

"What the hell?" I yelled at him.

"It's no longer in your car, asswipe, so chill the fuck out. I just need to take the edge off after the shitshow you threw in my lap today."

I glanced at him, but held my tongue. I didn't exactly like the fact that he was hanging out the goddamned window, but at least my car wouldn't stink. Though maybe that would've covered up his spicy scent and given my insane cock a break. I sighed. *What the fuck is happening today?*

He hung out the window for a couple minutes, then sat back down—without the joint—and we rode in silence for the rest of the drive. I hoped to god we figured this case out soon so I wouldn't have to endure his torturous company for much longer.

Chapter Two

Out of the corner of my eye, I swore Ailin's pen was floating over his hand, but as soon as I turned, it was in his palm. I shook my head at myself. I was seriously losing it. I'd been seeing shit like that—or thinking that I was seeing it—since that guy started working with me. And he was so weird. So, so, so weird. And rude. I didn't know what to do with his... oddness.

I looked at the strange man in my office again—the man that'd been working this case with me for the last three days. All we'd done is look over old cases, and occasionally, Ailin would make a phone call and *not* share whatever he'd discovered with me.

What was with this guy? He looked like a punk, but was high enough on the chain that my boss had to answer to him. And he was a *specialist*. But a specialist of what? What could he possibly be a specialist of when he barely looked to be twenty years old?

"I'm a specialist in... cult crimes and serial murders," Ailin said from his place on the other side of the desk.

How did he...? Had I accidentally said that out loud? I winced and cleared my throat. Well, shit. "Okay, but... do you think this is a cult crime?"

Without looking up from his file, he replied with boredom in his voice, "Don't know yet, but I think so. I'll know more once we finish looking through these files."

"You really think we're going to find something in the cold cases from five years ago?"

"Probably not."

"What makes you think that? Why are we looking this far back, then?"

He huffed out a put-upon sigh. "It's just a feeling I have, but we need to be sure this is what I think it is and not something... bigger."

"A feeling that specifically told you to go back that far in time?"

He finally put his file in his lap and looked at me. "I've run into something similar in the past. Just put it down to a feeling I have. And I'm usually right about these things."

"Okay, well, I couldn't find anything from the Strimville files, so I guess I'll move on to Almahast."

"Sounds good."

I opened my mouth to ask him another question, then snapped it closed again and looked down at my file.

"Sebastian?"

"Yeah?" I glanced up to find his bright green eyes observing me.

He tilted his head and examined me. "You can ask, but that doesn't mean you'll like the answer you get."

I narrowed my eyes. "How old are you?"

He snorted and shook his head. "Wouldn't you like to know."

I sighed and looked at my file. He was such an arrogant asshole. There was no way he was much older than twenty. So how did he become such a highly ranked specialist so young? Was he one of those child geniuses that graduated college when they were like thirteen? That had to be it, right?

He snorted again and I looked up to see what he was laughing at, but his eyes were focused on his file again. I wrinkled my nose—*how can he find a murder case funny?*

"How long have you been working with the department?"

"A few years."

I held back the urge to roll my eyes. This guy was going to drive me crazy with all his vague answers. "How many years, Ailin?"

"Not sure."

"For fuck's sake. Can you just give me a straight answer for once?"

He looked up at me with pursed lips. "Fine. I guess it's been about six years since I started consulting, but I... *worked* with the department for about eight years before that."

I blinked at him. That long? Seriously? "What did you do with the department before you were consulting."

He smiled, but it wasn't really a nice smile, it was more of a *I'm-a-huge-troublemaker* smile. "Mostly, I got arrested for doing shit to help your precious little system out. But they eventually saw the error of their ways and decided to hire me instead of working against me."

I stared at him for a long time. "Are you one of those genius kid hackers that hacked into the most secure government systems, so they hired you to make stronger firewalls or some shit?"

He chuckled. "Something like that."

I sighed and went back to my file. He still never told me how old he was. I had trouble believing he was anything but a young kid. He was probably lying about how long he'd worked here, too. I glanced at him. No way was he old enough to even drink. Definitely a young kid.

"I'm twenty-six, Sebastian. Hardly a young kid."

I quickly did the math. "You got arrested when you were twelve?"

He shot me that shit-eating grin again. "Yep."

"For what?"

"Wouldn't you like to know."

"I could just look you up in the system."

"You won't find anything. My records were sealed, then a few years ago, we erased everything to do with my identity. According to your precious system, I don't even exist."

For a split-second, I thought he was joking, but then I realized he was completely serious. "Great. So I'm working with one of those ghost people?"

"Sure, if that's what you wanna call it. Although, I'm clearly here and not a spirit, so..." he shrugged.

"You know what I mean."

He waved me off, and we both went back to our files. After another half hour of finding nothing, I found an old case from sixteen months ago in Almahast county that could possibly match our profile. "Hey, look at this." I threw the file toward him on the desk, and he swiped it up. "Eighteen-year-old girl found murdered in the woods, drained of blood. The report mentions strange symbols drawn on the ground with her blood."

"Son of a bitch." Ailin flipped through the file and stood up, pacing my office. "Son of a bitch." He continued pacing as he studied the crime scene photos. "Son of a bitch!"

He suddenly stormed out of my office with the file, so I stood and scrambled to follow him. He marched over to Chief Gillman's office and burst through the door without knocking again. I walked in behind him, just in time to see him throw the file on Chief Gillman's desk.

"Another from sixteen months ago, Alec. Sixteen months. What the fuck has this department been doing? I only agreed to these terms because you promised you'd help keep an eye on things from your end. This has been happening for at least sixteen months." Ailin crossed his arms over his chest and glared at my boss. "You better hope it doesn't go further back than this, Al. I'm going to have to notify the Supreme Assembly about this." *Supreme Assembly?*

"Ailin, you know I can't get in trouble with the assembly, man. What if they—"

Ailin held up his hand to stop him from talking. "Not my problem. We have a serious issue on our hands. I don't know if I'll be able to take it out on my own. I'm going to have to get the assembly to send in reinforcements."

Chief stood from his desk with wide eyes. "The last time they sent reinforcements, you and Aspen were almost killed! You can't go to them, Ailin. You don't know what they'll do this time."

Ailin ran his hands through his hair and started pacing. "I know, man, but I don't have the reinforcements I need here. I'm going to have to bring in more people to cover more ground. The kuma mali demon has been gaining strength for sixteen months. It's going to be too powerful for me to handle alone." *What in the hell is he talking about? Did he say demon? Gaining more power? That makes no sense.*

"Can't you call Emrys?"

Ailin groaned. "The last time I did that, he tried to burn me alive." *What? Someone tried to burn him alive!?*

The chief visibly winced, but shrugged a shoulder. "That's better than what the assembly will do."

Ailin sighed and rubbed his face with his hands. "I don't know. Dammit! Why didn't you catch this sooner? I can't believe this thing's gone unopposed for sixteen months. And it's been in my territory this whole time. Do you realize how this makes me look, Al? They're going to try to sweep in like vultures again. I can't go through another co—" he cut himself off, "—another war."

"You're getting ahead of yourself, Ailin. Calm down. Let me call Aspen. Maybe she can help."

"No, she can't get anywhere near this thing. Not with a baby on the way."

"Emrys is your only hope, then. And maybe Basil and Thayer."

"They're so young, I don't know if that's a good idea."

"You might not have a choice."

Ailin put his hands on his hips and stared at the chief for several tense seconds. "If this goes south, you're taking the fall for this one."

Chief held up his hand. "Fine."

Ailin nodded, then turned and as if just remembering I was standing there, he stopped in his tracks to look at me. He stared into my eyes for a second, then grabbed my sleeve and yanked me out of the office. "I need you to drive to the place of the first murder."

"Are you serious?"

"Yes, I might be able to find something."

"It's been sixteen months."

"I know."

"It's over two hours away."

"I know."

I sighed. "You're going to be stuck in the car with me for over two hours straight. You sure this is a good idea?"

"No, it's a terrible idea, but we don't have a choice. I can't take my bike right now."

"What happened to your bike?"

"My little brother happened. It's incapacitated right now."

"Of course, it is," I muttered under my breath. "How did you get here?"

"I got dropped off."

Fuck.

"Unless you'd rather I drive your car without you in it?"

Picturing Ailin driving my baby made me wrinkle my nose.

Ailin laughed. "Yeah, I didn't think so."

I rolled my eyes. "Alright, let me grab my shit. We'll have to stop for some food because I'm starving."

"Does that mean you're buying me lunch?"

"Only if it'll stop you from acting like an arrogant asshole."

He surprised me by letting out a laugh that actually sounded amused, for once, instead of the condescending laugh he'd been doing.

I grabbed everything I needed from my office, along with the rest of the files from Almahast County and carried it out to my car with Ailin following me. Once we were inside the car, I said, "Why don't you go through the rest of the files from that place so we can check out any other locations while we're out that way."

"Good plan." He settled in his seat and put his feet on the dashboard in front of him, then grabbed a file out of the box I'd set on the back seat.

"You know, it's really rude to put your feet up on my dash like that without, at least, asking."

He didn't say anything, so I glanced at him before I pulled out of the parking lot. He was leaning back with his eyes closed. *What the hell? Is he fucking sleeping already?*

"I'm not sleeping," he muttered. *How the hell does he keep doing that? It's like he's reading my mind.* "I was concentrating on something. I need to make a call, do you mind?"

The fact that he'd even asked was surprising. What wasn't surprising was the fact that he started dialing a number on his phone before I even acknowledged his question.

After a few seconds, he said, "Yeah." Then he paused. "Yes, human." I furrowed my brow at that, but figured that maybe he was referring to the case and someone wanted to know if it was a human body or something. Ailin sighed. "Yeah, I know. Okay. See ya." He hung up, then asked me, "Can we stop to pick something up before we get on the highway?"

My brow furrowed. "Yeah, I already said we could stop for food."

He waved me off. "That's not what I mean. I need to pick something up."

"Um... okay. Where to?"

He rattled off some directions, so I headed that way into a part of the city I hardly ever went to. Actually, I'd never stopped in that area at all; I'd only passed through on a rare occasion. It was the rich neighborhood that sat on the outskirts of the city and right along the Brinnswick Forest. There were huge mansions on huge acres of land. Most of the farmlands and wooded areas had several large mansions on the property. Each family owned a piece of the land, and the homes were divided up between the family members. It was weird, but apparently that was how it'd always been over here. Although, I wouldn't really know because I'd never even stopped to look. The whole area gave me the creeps.

There was this one property that was completely uncrossable. I'd been warned my whole life not to set foot on the property, and when I began working for the department, I'd been reminded of it. We weren't even allowed to drive over this one bridge that led to the large piece of land. I had no idea why or who lived there, but I assumed they paid the government some big dollars to keep their land off limits.

I pulled up to a random corner of streets where Ailin told me to go. On one side of the road there were woods, on the other there was flat farmland. But there weren't any houses in sight. *Why the hell did he want to stop here?* I looked around, wondering if Ailin asked me to drive out here to kill me and hide my body in the woods so he could steal my car.

Ailin suddenly snorted and shook his head, muttering under his breath. I could've sworn that he'd muttered, "humans," but I wasn't positive. Plus, that made no sense at all. *I think I'm hearing things.*

I practically jumped out of my skin when there was a knock on Ailin's window. A girl, no older than eighteen, stood beside my car. Where in the hell had she come from?

Ailin rolled down his window. He reached out and grabbed a bundle from the girl. "Thank you, Honey." *Honey?* I didn't think Ailin was capable of pet names.

"No problem, Ailin. When will you be home?"

"I probably won't make it back tonight, Honey. I'm really sorry."

The girl frowned at him, and I frowned back. Was this girl his girlfriend? She was so young. I wrinkled my nose at that thought. Why did that make me feel so weird? I didn't give two shits who Ailin dated. It was none of my business.

"I thought you'd be home this week?" The girl bit her bottom lip.

Ailin sighed. "I know. But... something came up."

"You always say that."

"I know, Honey, but if I don't take care of it—"

"The end of the world and everything I hold dear. Yeah, yeah, yeah, I've heard the speech a million times before, Ailin. Just be careful, okay?"

"I always am, Hon."

She leaned in and kissed his cheek. Then skipped off—to where, I had no idea because I lost track of her after a few seconds. Did she go into the woods or something?

Something meowed and I jumped in my seat, finally looking at the bundle in Ailin's lap. "What the fuck is that?"

"It's a cat, Seb. Obviously."

I opened and closed my mouth several times, completely at a loss of what to say. "I... I... I... I thought you had to pick something up?"

"I did." He gestured to the cat in his lap.

"But... but that's a cat!"

"Yes, I know."

"Why the hell did you need to pick up a cat?"

"Because she would've gotten lonely at home by herself."

"But... it's a *cat*!"

"A kitten, actually. She's a baby."

I stared in shock for a few seconds. "Ailin! You can't have a cat in my car!"

He huffed. "What is with you and all these rules in your car? You should tell a person all the rules before they get in or accept a ride from you!"

I shook my head at him. I mean, wow. Just... wow. "Dude, you can't just go around smoking and bringing animals inside a person's car. That's not something I should have to tell you about. It's common courtesy."

"Are you allergic to cats?"

"What? No." I blinked at him.

"Then what's the problem?"

"What if it shits in my car or something?"

The cat suddenly hissed, and I jumped, moving back and staring at it. If a cat could glare, the black thing staring at me was glaring at me like I'd just offended its precious ego or some shit.

Ailin snorted again. "I assure you that Seraphina will not shit in your car. She's very polite."

"Sera-what-now?"

"Seraphina."

"Sera-phina." I tried the strange name out on my tongue.

"Or Sera for short."

I looked at the black cat again. It was kinda cute, actually. I sighed. "At least tell me why you needed to bring your kitten with us?"

Ailin pet the cat. "I told you, she was getting too lonely at home. I wanted to bring her in case we end up staying overnight."

I huffed in defeat. I supposed he had a point. By the time we got there, it'd probably be dark, so we'd need to wait until tomorrow to look at the wooded area where the body had been found. "Maybe I should turn around and pack some clothes or something."

Ailin waved me off. "You have clothes and a toothbrush in your trunk. Anything else, we can buy there."

I gaped at him. "How the hell do you know that? Did you go through my things?" He ignored me. "Ailin, did you go through my things? When did you go through my stuff?"

"When I told you I was going to the bathroom the first day we worked together. I had to make sure there wasn't anything demonic in your car before I agreed to go somewhere with you."

Demonic? What the actual fuck? What does he mean by demonic? "What's that supposed to mean?"

He waved me off and concentrated on the cat in his lap. "Don't worry, I didn't find anything."

Could've told you that, asshole.

"Unless you call that Santa Claus underwear you have in your bag demonic. I mean, really? Does all of your underwear have cartoons of evil demons on them?"

"Evil demons? You think Santa Claus is evil?"

"Not important. Now let's get going."

I clenched my jaw. "Don't give me orders. I don't work for you."

"Actually, you do, but that wasn't an order, it was a suggestion."

"Actually, I don't work for you, asshole. We're partners, which means we're equals in this case and in everything that comes with it. Now knock it off with the orders before I make you leave your cat on the side of the road."

The cat hissed and Ailin covered her ears with his hands, looking at me with wide eyes. "Do not *ever* offend my cat again."

My brow furrowed as I looked at him. For a split-second there, I thought I saw smoke float through his eyes, but it was gone in an instant, so it must've been my imagination. But he did look mega pissed. Dude was serious about his cat. "Fine, I won't offend the cat as long as you stop treating me like one of your little soldiers or whatever. You're not my boss. I don't take orders from you." I put the car in gear. "Let's go. And... don't go through my shit ever again without permission."

Ailin sighed and leaned back in his seat, pulling the random cat up to his chest. Who the hell stops in the middle of a dirt road to pick up their pet cat from their girlfriend? I mean, really? Who the fuck does that?!

"That wasn't my girlfriend."

"What?"

"That wasn't my girlfriend."

How does he always know what I'm thinking about? "It's none of my business." *You sounded awfully close with her... calling her* honey *constantly.*

Ailin snorted out a laugh. "Honey is her name, you dumbass."

I gaped at him, then shook my head. "Her name is Honey? Who the hell names their child Honey?"

"The same ones that named her siblings Peach and Pear."

"You're shitting me."

He chuckled. "Nope. She has twin sisters named Peach and Pear. I bet you'll never guess what her twin brothers are called."

"Um... Pineapple and Cantaloupe?"

He laughed. "No, but I'll make sure to call them that the next time I see them. They're named Pepper and Pumpernickel."

I burst out laughing. "That's seriously awful!" I laughed a little more. "That's weird that she has two sets of twin siblings."

"Actually, she's a twin, too. Her sister's name is Sugar."

"Wow. Those poor kids."

"Right? And my brother thinks he has it bad with Basil."

"Your brother's name is Basil?"

"Yep."

I opened my mouth in shock for a second. "How do you know so many people with foods as names?"

"Honey is my cousin."

"Oh."

"Yeah."

I cleared my throat. This was the most normal conversation we'd had, so I wanted to keep it going, even though I didn't understand why I did. "Is your brother older or younger?"

"Younger. All my siblings are younger than me."

"How many do you have?"

"Three. Opal, Aspen, and Basil."

My brow furrowed. "Aspen, as in the chief's wife?"

"One and the same."

"So... my boss is your brother-in-law?"

"Yep. Do you have any siblings?"

I cleared my throat. "Um... no. I was orphaned as an infant, so I grew up in the system."

Ailin turned completely in his seat. "You grew up at Eastbrook Youth Academy?"

"Yeah."

"Uh... do you mind if I ask... how was it there? I've heard many horror stories."

I took a deep breath. "Most of those stories carry some truth to them, but many are exaggerated. It was..." I thought about what I wanted to say. "Lonely. It was lonely."

"I... can't even imagine living such a life. I grew up with siblings and cousins running around the house with me, so I can't picture what it's like being alone like that. I'm sorry you had to go through that, Sebastian. I'm very, truly sorry. No one should grow up feeling alone in the world."

I shot him a glance, but he was looking out the window, still petting his kitten. I couldn't see his facial expression, but I was pretty sure that he'd been serious just now. For some reason, my loneliness growing up seemed to be affecting him more deeply than anything else we'd talked about—including the murder case we were working.

"Um... thank you. It's... fine. I'm okay."

Ailin shot me a sad smile, then looked out the window again, so I refocused on the road and the GPS. After a few seconds, something cold touched my hand, and I was completely surprised that the kitten had made her way over to me. She nudged my hand, so I began petting her and before I knew it, she climbed onto my lap. *I hope Ailin doesn't mind his cat hanging out with me.*

"Seraphina likes you."

"Huh?"

Ailin cleared his throat. "Sera likes you. She doesn't like many people, so I'm surprised she crawled over to you on her own. I figured I'd have to drop her on your head or something to get her used to you, but she's content already."

I gave the cat an extra scratch after that.

Chapter Three

Traffic was horrible and it was already dark when we arrived, so I drove straight to a motel. Ailin went in to get the rooms situated while I waited in the car with Seraphina. The cat hadn't moved from my lap since she'd sat there. Even when we stopped for food, Ailin had gotten out of the car to grab us both something, and she'd slept in my lap while I ate. It was actually really cute, and I was enjoying her company.

Ailin hopped back in the car. "Room one-oh-four."

I waited for him to announce the other room number, and when he didn't, I looked at him. "Just one room?"

He shrugged. "Does it matter? It has two beds."

I gaped at him for a moment, then rolled my eyes and drove the car across the parking lot to park in front of *our* room. Ailin picked up Seraphina, we got out, I grabbed my bag from the trunk, and we walked into the shitty motel room. Okay, it wasn't *that* bad, but it wasn't that nice, either.

Ailin went to the bed closest to the door. "You good if I take this one?"

I shrugged. "Sure." I walked over to the bed farther in the room and set my bag on top, then pulled my handgun out of its holster, checked it and set it on the nightstand before shrugging the holster off. I startled when Seraphina jumped from Ailin's bed to mine. I heard

Ailin sigh, but he didn't say anything. I pet the cat and she purred at me before walking to the top of the bed and settling on a pillow.

"I don't think she's leaving your side. You okay with that?" Ailin asked. He had an edge to his voice that I didn't like. Was he seriously jealous of the cat staying near me?

"Um... yeah, it's fine."

He sighed and flopped down on his bed, then looked over at Seraphina and said, "It's really gonna be like that, huh? You *know* I couldn't come home early." He narrowed his eyes at her for a long moment, then said to the cat, "Really? Don't pretend you don't understand. I *know* you, you know?" He waved her away, then looked at me. "I'm hungry."

My eyebrows were up high on my forehead. *Who talks to their cat that way? He's so fucking weird!* I licked my lips. "Uh...what?" Did he ask me a question?

"I'm hungry. You want to order something?"

"Uh... I guess?"

He puffed out his cheeks, then pulled out his phone. "I'll get a pizza. Are you okay with a veggie pizza?"

I tilted my head at him as I realized something. "Are you a vegetarian or something?" I hadn't seen him eat meat at all.

"Yep. Always have been."

I nodded and shrugged. "I'll eat whatever, so sure." I grabbed my clothes. "I'm gonna change in the bathroom. I think I have some cash in my wallet I can give you."

He waved me away. "No worries, Seb. I got it."

"Sebastian," I corrected.

He lifted one eyebrow at me. "Really?"

I nodded.

"I like the way 'Seb' sounds."

I rolled my eyes and grabbed my wallet.

"I said I got it… Seb."

I opened my mouth to complain about the name *and* him paying because he'd bought me food when we'd stopped earlier. He hadn't taken my money then, either, but he cut off my complaints, "Seriously, it's not a big deal. I'm sure you'll buy me a meal eventually."

I nodded. "Thanks."

"You're welcome."

I walked into the bathroom to change. While I was in there, I heard Ailin's voice. He ordered a pizza, but once he'd finished, he was still talking. It sounded like a one-way conversation, so I figured he'd made a phone call, but when I walked out of the bathroom, his phone was on the nightstand and he was facing Seraphina, who lay on my bed staring at him. Was he seriously having a conversation with his cat again? What the actual fuck? Why did Chief Gillman think this guy would make a good partner for me? He was a freak.

Ailin turned sharply to me and glared as if he'd heard my stray thought. He sorta looked almost hurt, but I hadn't said it out loud. I mean, I didn't think I had. *Oh god, did I call him a freak out loud? Shit. Shit. Shit. Shit. Shit. Fucking fuck.* I might've thought he was a strange guy and a jerk most of the time, but I didn't want to hurt his feelings.

Ailin took a deep breath as he stared at me, then he sat up abruptly and grabbed the TV remote, flicking the television on. "Want to watch something while we wait for dinner?"

I cleared my throat. I didn't know what to say. I didn't think I'd said it out loud, but Ailin's body language was telling me something different. Should I apologize even though I didn't actually do anything? I took a deep breath. "Ailin, I'm sorr—"

He cut me off, "Can we watch the news? Maybe we'll pick up a random crime that's related to our case."

So maybe I hadn't said it out loud. Ugh, I dunno. "Yeah, that's fine."

He nodded and flipped to a local station, so I sat on my bed, leaning against the headboard. As soon as I settled, Seraphina climbed onto my lap. I heard Ailin sigh again, but he didn't say anything, so neither did I.

We didn't say much to each other for the rest of the night. We watched the news while we ate, and when we finished, he turned off the tv and the light, so we both settled down. Seraphina wrapped her body around my head.

***

I woke up with fur in my face. I pushed it away. *What the hell's in my face? And where the fuck am I?* It took a few seconds for yesterday's events to register, and I groaned when I realized Seraphina's ass was in my face. I

51

pushed the little kitten over a bit so I could breathe and rub my eyes, then I sat up and looked around.

The sun was just starting to come up, and Ailin was still sound asleep in the other bed. I looked around, trying to figure out what had woken me. I wasn't typically a person that would wake up before my alarm unless I needed to piss really bad or something, but that wasn't the case.

I didn't see anything in our room that could've been the cause, so I figured that maybe it was the cat ass in my face that did it. I only had a few minutes before my alarm was set to go off, so I didn't bother lying back down. I rubbed the sleepiness from my eyes and yawned before looking over at Ailin again. He was lying on his side facing me on top of his blankets with his hands near his face, so I took a moment to examine him. He'd taken off his jacket, bracers, boots, and socks, so he was barefoot with some tattoos showing on the skin of his exposed arms, but he hadn't changed his clothes. Maybe I should've asked him if he needed something to sleep in. I hadn't thought about it last night.

Ailin's eyes were closed and his face looked almost peaceful. He was actually sort of pretty for a guy. He had a light speckle of freckles over his nose, and his lips were plump and soft-looking. His black hair was still braided back on the left side with a bunch of beads in it. His pale skin was such a contrast to my own golden brown that I couldn't help but wonder what it'd look like if we were both shirtless together—or god, completely naked. Thinking about seeing Ailin naked had my body heating up, and I knew I was blushing even though he wasn't even awake, and it wasn't like he'd know what I was thinking about even if he was. God, why was I even picturing him naked? He was such an arrogant asshole. But he *was* really pretty, and hot, and hella sexy. Not that I'd *ever* in a million years tell him that. His head was big enough as it was.

But for some reason, I couldn't stop thinking about what it would be like to have him naked and writhing underneath me. He was so much smaller than me in stature, but he wasn't tiny by any means. He was short, but muscular and strong, and the thought of having all of that power under me was... exhilarating.

Ailin stirred and I froze with wide eyes as if I'd been caught doing something I shouldn't be. But luckily, he remained asleep, so I was able to keep up my creepy fantasizing. What would it be like to take that condescending man down a few pegs by fucking his brains out?

My body responded to that thought of its own accord, and I held in a groan.

"Do you always stare creepily at your roommates or am I just special?"

I startled at the sound of his voice. His eyes were still closed, so I had no idea how he knew I'd been staring at him. I opened my mouth, but no words came out.

Ailin grinned as he opened his eyes and focused on me. "Keep staring at me like that and you won't know what hit you." His voice was low and husky and... *sexy.*

I opened my mouth again, then slammed it shut as I just stared like a deer in the headlights. Was he flirting with me? Did Ailin just hit on me?

He chuckled lightly. "Relax, Seb, I'm not going to jump you." He turned to lay flat on his back. "But I wouldn't be opposed to the idea."

I sucked in a breath and my eyes widened. There was no way in hell that Ailin just suggested we sleep together, was there? I mean, right? He wouldn't want to… no. *No.* No, we couldn't possibly.

He waved me off. "I'm going to shower before we leave, but I need to get some fresh clothes. I'm going to run to that little corner store. I'll be back in a few. Is Sera good to stay with you?"

It took me a few seconds to regain my composure, but I cleared my throat and shook myself out of it. He was obviously just messing with me. "Sure, she's fine."

He nodded and hopped out of bed, walking through the door within seconds.

I flopped back on the bed and blew out a breath. Sera came over and rested her head on my neck. I pet her and willed my heartrate to slow back down. After a minute, I got up to stretch, then walked around a little before sitting at the small table. It only took a few seconds for the cat to jump on my lap, and I couldn't help but smile. I'd never had a pet before. We weren't allowed to have pets in Eastbrook Youth Academy, and I couldn't have one when I was in the military and traveling all the time. Maybe I could get one now, though. That'd be nice. I kinda liked the company.

I needed to pee, so I set the cat on the floor and went to take care of business. The thought of jumping in the shower while Ailin was out crossed my mind, so I pulled the shower curtain back, but yelled out in surprise. Holy shit! There was a fucking snake in the tub! "What the fuck?" I ran out of the bathroom and scooped up Seraphina so she wouldn't go investigate the bathroom and wind up hurt, then I ran straight for the phone to call the front desk to take care of it. I had no idea what kind of snake it was or how it'd gotten in there or whether or not it was venomous or whatever. But I didn't want to take the chance of trying to grab it myself. If it was venomous, I could end up in the hospital.

I picked up the phone and dialed the front desk, but just as the girl picked up on the other line, Ailin slammed the door open and boomed, "What's wrong?"

I blinked at him as a huge rush of wind came in through the door, blowing the loose side of his hair. I lowered the phone a little and answered, "There's a snake in the tub."

He narrowed his eyes at me. "Who are you calling?"

He looked... terrifying. It was like the wind coming through the door was playing off his emotions. I knew that wasn't really happening, but he looked as stormy as the weather behind him. "I-I was calling the front desk to come get it."

"Hang up the phone, Seb."

"Wh-what? Why?"

"I'll take care of the snake. They'll probably just kill it. I can grab him and release him outside."

I stared at him for several seconds before hanging up the phone. I could see how serious he was, and I knew he was right, that the front desk girl would likely just kill the animal. It seemed like Ailin's love for animals knew no bounds.

He glanced at me, then noticed the cat in my arms, and his gaze softened a little. "You saved Sera."

"Of-of course I did. I didn't want her to get hurt."

Some of the wind died down. "Thank you."

He headed straight into the bathroom, so I got up and followed him, holding the kitten tight to my chest. I stood in the doorway to watch him. He made a few sounds, like hissing, and I swear the snake hissed back, then Ailin spoke under his breath, but I couldn't understand what he was saying.

"How are you going to get—"

I cut myself off when Ailin reached a hand into the tub, and a second later, the snake was slithering up his arm. I took a step backward and stared in disgust. *What the fuck is he doing? That thing is going to bite him!* Ailin stood and the snake wrapped around his arm, then around the back of his neck.

"Ailin, it's going to bite you," I whisper-yelled.

Ailin shot me a cocky smirk. "It's nice to see that you care, Sebastian, but I guarantee he won't hurt me."

"How can you possibly say that?"

He shrugged and I frowned as the movement caused the snake to shift so its head was near Ailin's throat. "He's just lost."

I blinked at him. "Okay, well, go... throw him in the parking lot or something."

Ailin frowned at me. "I'm going to help him find his home. I think he comes from the same woods we're heading to, anyway."

"That thing is not coming in my car!"

Ailin huffed. "You and the car rules again! How can I possibly keep up when you keep adding more and more rules?"

I closed my eyes and my nostrils flared in irritation. "I'm not changing the rules. I told you before I didn't want a cat in my car, so it's the same rule... it applies to *all* animals." Sera hissed a little at me, and I mumbled down to her, "You don't count. I like you." *Okay, so I guess Ailin isn't the only one that talks to her.*

"But you changed your mind and let her in. Why would it be any different with George?"

"Did you seriously just name that snake 'George'?"

"No, that was his name already."

I had no words for that. "You... you're not bringing *George* into my car!"

"Then I guess I'm walking to the crime scene." He clenched his jaw, then shouldered past me out of the bathroom as I tried to scramble away from the snake. "And you think *I'm* the mean one."

I just stared at him for several long seconds, then shook my head and announced, "I'm taking a shower, and

I'm taking Sera into the bathroom with me so she doesn't get hurt by your new best friend, George."

"She's perfectly capable of taking care of herself. And George would never hurt her, anyway."

"She's a kitten, a *baby*. She needs protection."

Ailin eyed me for a moment, then waved me away. "Whatever, Seb. We can take turns in the shower, and I'll keep George with me, you keep Sera with you. She seems to like you better than me, anyway." *Is he actually mad about that?* "I'll order us some breakfast, and before you say it, I got it covered."

I sighed and grabbed my clothes out of my bag with one hand so I didn't have to put Sera on the ground. I was afraid she'd go up to George and try to smell him or claw him or something. Once I had everything, I said, "Don't open the door in there."

Ailin rolled his eyes.

I walked into the bathroom, shut and locked the door, then set Sera on the floor and stripped down, hopping into the tub. I washed myself and kept peeking out the curtain to make sure the little kitten was okay. That made me think about the fact that she didn't have a litter box or food or even a water bowl. Shit. I hurried as fast as I could, then got out, dried off, and dressed before scooping up the kitten and exiting the room.

"Hey, did you bring some of her food with you? And what about a litter box and water and everything?"

"I fed her and took her outside in the middle of the night. She's fine." Ailin wasn't looking at me. He was staring at George, who was slithering around Ailin's arm.

That was... odd. "Okay. Can I give her some water, at least? Maybe I can use one of the cups over by the coffee pot."

"That's fine. Thanks."

"You know, I've never had a pet before, not that I think Sera is *my* pet or anything, but..." I trailed off as I made a cup of water for the cat.

"Sera isn't anyone's pet."

"What do you mean? I thought she was yours. You said she'd get lonely at your house by herself, so I know she's not a stray."

"She's a... companion."

I held in a sigh. "Right, that's what a pet is."

He looked at me and narrowed his eyes. "She's more than just a *pet*, but you can think whatever you want."

I shook my head at that. "Whatever, man. The bathroom's free, just make sure you take that slimy thing in there with you."

"Snakes aren't slimy."

"Oh my god, Ailin, will you please stop arguing with every single thing I say?"

"Probably not."

I groaned. "You're the most frustrating person I've ever met."

He didn't respond to that, but he did get up, grab a bag that must've held his new clothes, and walk into the bathroom carrying George with him. I let out a sigh as soon as the door clicked shut, then fell back on my bed to blow out a breath. That guy might've been the hottest guy

I'd ever laid eyes on, but he sure as hell was also the most annoying. Jesus.

Sera laid on my chest and licked my chin. At least putting up with his annoying ass came with the kitten benefit. She was such a sweetheart. I kissed the kitten's nose and chuckled when she sneezed on me. "You're such a cutie pie. I know I complained about you being in my car at first, but you can come in there anytime you want." Okay, seriously, what was with this cat making us grown-ass men talk to her like she could understand us?

Seraphina stared me in the eyes, and I could've sworn I saw a deep intelligence in her gaze. I scratched behind her ears. "You understand a lot more than us humans give you credit for, don't you?"

She licked my chin in answer and I smiled.

***

How in the hell did I wind up in my car with an asshole, a cute kitten, and a creepy as fuck snake? That sounded like the beginnings of a bad joke.

"George isn't going to hurt you, me, or Sera," Ailin said from the back seat. I'd forced him to sit as far away from me as possible because I didn't want that *thing* that was wrapped around his shoulders to strike out at me or Sera, who was on my lap again. If Ailin was going to be a dumbass, I could at least protect the kitten.

"You don't know that, Ailin. It's a wild animal. Wild is right there in its name."

I glanced in the rearview mirror and saw Ailin lift the snake so its head was right by his face. "You're not going to hurt anyone, are you, little Georgie? You're such a good snake."

I shook my head and ignored him as I followed the directions to the edge of the woods where they'd found the first body. Or at least, I hoped it was the first. It would suck some major donkey balls if there was another body from more than sixteen months ago.

I pulled off the road and parked the car at the edge of the tree line, then hopped out with Seraphina and the crime scene photos in my arms. I'd suggested leaving the cat at the motel while we were out, but Ailin said he didn't trust the motel manager to leave our room alone. When we'd walked past the guy on our way out, I was inclined to agree with him, so Sera was coming with us. At least Ailin would be getting rid of George so we could take turns holding the kitten while we examined the crime scene.

"Alright," I said, "we're here. You can release your snake."

Ailin frowned at me, then lifted the snake's head up to his eye level, staring into its creepy eyes.

"Do you really have to keep putting that thing in your face? It's going to bite you."

"*It* is a *he* and *he's* not going to bite me."

"You don't know that, Ailin." He ignored me and continued his weird stare off with the snake. I shook my head. "You know what? If that *thing* bites you, I'm not driving you to the hospital. You can just suffer and die from *its* venom."

"You and I both know that's an empty threat." He didn't even look at me. "Okay, George needs a ride farther into the woods, so let's head toward the crime scene. Hopefully, he'll recognize our surroundings soon."

I didn't even bother to argue with that because I knew Ailin wouldn't listen. I shook my head and followed behind him so I could keep an eye on George. As we walked, Sera climbed up on my shoulder and wrapped around the back of my neck. I let her stay there; I figured I'd be able to feel her getting ready to jump down and could grab her if need be.

"We're almost there," Ailin said after we'd been walking for a good ten minutes.

"Aren't you going to let... *George* go now?"

Ailin looked over at the snake, who looked like he was sleeping with his head on Ailin's shoulder. "No, he's still not ready."

My nostrils flared. "How are we supposed to examine a crime scene when we each have an animal to carry?"

"Well, I don't really have to hold George, he's just along for the ride, and you can always put Sera on the ground and ask her to stay out of the crime scene area."

I closed my eyes and shook my head a little. "She's a kitten. What if she takes off? And how the hell could you possibly think she'd be able to understand where the edge of the crime scene is? Even if she did understand, she's a cat. Cats go wherever the hell they want. And we can't risk her running away, she wouldn't survive out here on her—"

"Okay, okay. Good Mother of All. She would be fine, but by all means, hold her while we examine the area. Mother knows you won't let me hold her while George is on my shoulders." *Mother of All. What religion is that?*

"No, I won't let you."

He sighed and muttered what sounded like "humans" again. What the fuck. Does he think he's an alien or something?

Ailin snorted out a little laugh before stopping in his tracks. "We're here."

I pulled out the crime scene photos and began setting them in place where each item was found. We had some closeups of the woman's body, so I was able to put down the photos of the markings they'd found on her, as well as the closeups of the symbols that'd been drawn around her. Sera had really good balance and managed to stay on my shoulders. Once everything was set, I stepped back and frowned. The crime scene was nearly identical to the ones back in Strimville and Arronston. We had a serial killer on our hands. One that'd been killing young girls for at least sixteen months. There was no way this was a coincidence.

Ailin kneeled in the center of where the circle would've been drawn and put his hands on the ground, closing his eyes and chanting under his breath. I swallowed down my nerves. I'd been working with him for several days; he wasn't going to hurt me. We'd been alone a million times before, including when I was sleeping in the same room as him last night, so he'd had plenty of opportunities to kill or maim me already. He was just one of those weird people that tried to solve crimes with their guts and all that weirdo mumbo jumbo. He was getting a sense of the crime scene again. I mean, right? *That's what he said the last time he did this. I'm fine. This is fine.*

"I'm not going to hurt you, Seb. I'm just checking for residual energy." His eyes remained shut.

"O-okay." I licked my lips and took an involuntary step back.

Ailin opened his eyes and looked straight at me. For a second, it looked like he had green smoke in his eyes again, but it was gone in an instant. "I would never hurt you, Sebastian. You know that."

I blew out a breath and nodded. I somehow *did* know that.

His lips curled into a tiny, almost-not there smile before he closed his eyes and resumed chanting, so I ignored him—or tried to. I slowly walked around the whole scene, trying to see if looking at it from a different angle would reveal any new information.

Unfortunately, the only thing I could tell was that this was some kind of ritual. A sacrifice. So we were looking for some crazy zealot. What I needed to do was research what these symbols meant. Then maybe I could determine what religion this was based on, and that could help us locate him or make an estimated guess of his next move.

Ailin suddenly stood up and brushed his knees off with no regard for the snake in his face. George slithered around Ailin's neck, and the guy actually laughed like it tickled him or something. *So fucking crazy.*

Ailin frowned at me. "This was the first site, so we should go to the local station and see if we can connect any other open cases with our perp." He started walking away. "I might have a few books at home with some of these symbols, so I'll bring them to your office when we get back. Maybe we can figure out his next move."

I followed behind him lost in thought with Sera still on my shoulders.

When we reached my car, I looked up to find George on Ailin's shoulders. *Still fucking there.*

I narrowed my eyes at them both. "You need to set George free."

Ailin started petting the snake. "He wants to stick with us."

I closed my eyes and blew out a breath. "Ailin, he's a wild animal. You don't know what he wants. Wild animals are meant to live in the wild. Set him free. He'll be okay. It's better for him to be free."

Ailin frowned at me. "He wants to stay with us."

"Set. Him. Free."

He glared at me. "Fine. But he's not going to go anywhere."

I rolled my eyes, then leaned my ass against the car so I could watch him. Ailin walked into the trees a few feet, whispering to the snake the whole time. He set George on the ground, and the snake slithered in a circle around Ailin, then started heading toward me.

"Ailin."

Ailin stood with his hands behind his back and a smirk on his face.

The snake kept coming at me.

"Ailin. Get your snake!"

Ailin ignored me, so I jumped on the hood of my car, pulling my feet up and holding onto Seraphina. George came right over and slithered up the side of my car and onto the hood as I scrambled backward. I could hear Ailin laughing in the background, but I didn't spare him a glance because the fucking snake kept getting closer. The snake slithered over my ankle as I screamed out and kicked, then jumped off the hood on the opposite side of the car. The snake kept coming, so I ran to the trunk and popped it open with my key fob.

The snake followed me, so I opened the trunk, put Sera on my shoulder and pulled out the shotgun I kept back there because the handgun I had on me might not get the job done.

"Woah, woah, woah!" Ailin yelled as he suddenly jumped in front of me with his hands out. "Do not shoot the snake, Sebastian."

"It's attacking me." I lifted the gun and tried to aim under Ailin's arm. "Move before you get hurt. I don't want to shoot you."

Ailin stepped closer to me and put his hand on the gun, pushing it lower so it was pointed at the ground. "Seb." His voice was quieter than I'd ever heard it, which caught my attention.

I looked into his green eyes that were surprisingly soft considering the situation.

He smiled a little. "He's not going to hurt you or Sera. I promise."

A big part of me wanted to believe him. "He's a snake, Ailin. A wild animal."

"A wild animal that has no intention of hurting you. He was just messing around. I told him to."

I shook my head. *What the fuck is he talking about?* "Do you seriously think you're the Snake Whisperer or something? You can't talk to animals, Ailin."

Ailin's brow furrowed in confusion. "Anyone can talk to animals. I heard you talking to Sera earlier."

"That's not what I mean. I can talk all I want; that doesn't mean she'll understand me, and it doesn't mean that George understands you. You don't speak snake."

He opened his mouth to argue, but seemed to think better of it because he snapped his mouth shut and sighed. "George isn't venomous. Even if he bites you, it wouldn't matter."

"What if he was trying to get to Sera just to *eat* her?"

Ailin pinched the bridge of his nose. "He's not going to eat her, and even if he tried, he'd probably get hurt in the process. Sera has claws, you know."

"But she's a baby."

He sucked in a deep, annoyed breath. "I'm aware."

"Whatever. Let's just get in the car and go to the local station."

He narrowed his eyes. "Fine." Then he turned around and picked up the fucking snake.

"Ailin! He's not coming in my car! This is where he lives. You did your duty to return him home. Now leave him the fuck here!"

"I know you find this hard to believe, but he doesn't want to be here anymore. I've been trying to convince him all morning, but he wants to stay with us. He likes you."

I snorted out a humorless laugh. "Right. He *likes* me, that's why he tried to *eat* me."

"He wasn't trying to eat you; he was just messing with you because we both think it's funny that you're scared of a tiny snake."

"That thing is not *tiny*, and I'm not scared of him."

Ailin suddenly stepped forward and brought George up to my face, so I scrambled back as fast as I could and accidentally let out a little yell. Ailin laughed so hard, he bent over with his hands on his knees as he cracked up. I stood back and glared at him with my arms crossed over my chest.

"That wasn't funny."

That made Ailin laugh harder, and if I didn't think it was crazy, I would've sworn it looked like the fucking snake was laughing at me, too. At least Sera was on my side; she kept rubbing against my neck and purring.

After I calmed a little, I shouted—since I'd scrambled away so far, it was the only way he'd hear me, "George is *not* welcome in my car!"

Ailin waved me off, then walked over to the front passenger side and opened the door. "Whatever." He got in with George wrapped around his shoulders.

"Son of a bitch," I muttered under my breath as I walked to the car and placed the shotgun back in the trunk, slamming it shut. I yanked the door open and glared. "At least get in the back seat so I can concentrate on driving and not the fucking snake in my car."

Ailin grinned at me. "I knew you'd see it my way."

I clenched my jaw in anger and refrained from saying what I was thinking out loud. *Asshole. You're a fucking arrogant little shithead.*

Ailin tensed a little before getting out and sitting in the back seat with George still wrapped around him. I reluctantly drove them to the station. When we got there, Ailin said, "I'll just leave George here while I run in to get access to the files. I know Captain Hildan, so it'll be easier if I run in since, based on your reaction, I don't think George would be welcome here. Hopefully, everything is digital, and we can just go back to the motel to work. If not, I'll snag a conference room."

"I'm not sitting in the car with George." I got out and leaned against the side of my car, holding Sera to my chest, but I left the car on for the stupid snake even though he'd probably be fine without it.

Ailin hopped out. "I'll be right back."

I pet Sera while I waited, but luckily, he didn't take long.

He carried a box out. "I have complete access, so we'll go through everything they have in the system. If we find something, we'll come back to go through the evidence. In the meantime, I snagged the evidence box for the Charlene Thomas murder."

"I thought the file said the evidence was lost in that fire at this station a couple months ago?"

"Turns out, they were full of shit." He clenched his jaw and looked at me over the hood of the car. "Someone here was covering for this asshole. I've already called Alec to start an investigation."

I blinked at him. He may have been an asshole, but he was on top of this shit. He'd barely been gone five minutes, and he'd already found "lost" evidence, got access to the system, *and* called my chief. Totally on top of it. At least he was good at what he did, and not an incompetent asshole.

We both got in the car, and I momentarily forgot about George, but luckily for me—and him, since I had my handgun on me—he slithered onto Ailin's lap in the passenger seat. I glared at both of them and almost told Ailin to move, but he pulled the snake closer to him and farther away from me. Sera rubbed her face against my cheek. I blew out a breath and drove back to the motel. We hadn't checked out yet since we weren't sure if we'd be coming back, so I parked in front of our room and we hopped out.

"I know you don't like him, but George will stay on my side of the room. Actually, I'll just tell him to stay on my bed while we're going through the records."

"Whatever you say, Snake Whisperer." I shook my head and went inside with him following behind me.

Sure enough, he set the snake on his bed, and George curled into a ball in the middle, looking up at Ailin. *Jesus, maybe he really is the Snake Whisperer.* I pulled my laptop out of my bag and sat at the table with Sera around my neck. George may have curled up on the bed, but you never knew when a wild animal would strike, and snakes were fast as hell. I wasn't sure I could get to Sera before she got eaten or injured if the snake decided to attack.

Ailin sat across from me with his own laptop and stared at me for several long seconds before he spoke, "I appreciate that you're helping with Sera."

I stared at him for a few seconds. I hadn't expected that. "Um... no problem."

He smiled before focusing on his laptop.

I looked him over for a few seconds. He was such a contradiction. At times he was this hard, angry, argumentative asshole of a man, and other times he was kind and even... nice to me. I never knew what I was going to get.

Chapter Four

We went over file after file for nearly eight hours.

And believe it or not, that damn snake stayed right in the center of the bed the whole time. Maybe Ailin had drugged it. Maybe he had tranquilizers in his bag or something.

"We haven't found anything yet. What's our next move?" I shut my computer and rubbed my eyes because they were hurting from staring at the screen for so long without a break.

Ailin looked at his phone before focusing on me. "I have the clearance to access the files of the whole Brinnswick area, so we can head home and start going through everything from here to Arronston over the past sixteen months."

"If you had access, why'd you go in to talk to Captain Hildan earlier?"

"I needed to remind him of who he was messing with by keeping this from me." He shrugged when I gaped at him. "And I wanted to check for any physical evidence left. I had a feeling he'd been lying to me when I talked to him on the way up here. Figured I'd get a better sense of him face to face."

I nodded. I didn't really know what reminding him who he was messing with entailed, but I had a feeling that a threat from Ailin would be... terrifying.

Ailin tilted his head at me. "Why are you afraid of me?"

I blinked at him. "I... I... I'm not."

He licked his lips, and I couldn't help but stare at the wetness left behind on his pink mouth. My cock twitched in my pants as I thought about what those lips would look like wrapped around me. After a second, one corner of his mouth lifted, and I knew I'd been caught staring. I cleared my throat and started packing up my laptop. *Stop thinking about what the sexy guy across from you would look like naked... spread out on the bed right over there. Buck. Naked. No! Stop it, Sebastian.*

"We could stay another night if you wanted?"

My eyes widened as I snapped my gaze to him. "Wh-what?"

He smirked and licked his lips again, then played with his bottom lip with his teeth. "We don't have to leave right away. We could... *take advantage* of the room. The beds are pretty comfortable."

I swallowed down my momentary fear of actually being with someone so... full of himself. I took a deep breath and fanned my shirt a few times against the sweat suddenly covering my body. "Is it hot in here?" *Oh god, why did you say that out loud?*

"I'm okay, but you can always take your shirt off if you're hot."

I stood so abruptly, Sera had to claw my neck to avoid falling off. I hissed at the sting, then put my hand up to help her balance. "Um... uh... um... I.. I-I.. I'm going to the bathroom." I ran into the bathroom and slammed the door shut, then leaned back against it and dropped my chin to my chest. *You're a fucking idiot. Such a damn spaz. Like someone like Ailin would want you like that, anyway. He's just messing with you. He doesn't like you. And even if he did—which he doesn't—he's your work partner. You can't sleep with a colleague. A one-night stand could mess everything up. Unless he'd want more than a one-night stand.* I shook my head. *No, that's ridiculous. He just might want to have sex, to fuck me, or maybe be fucked by me. Not that Ailin would ever in a million years want me, but no... just no. He doesn't even like me because I'm nothing. No one has ever wanted me in their life long-term. Not that sleeping with him would mean anything, but—*

"Hey, Sebastian?" Ailin's voice was soft and sounded like it was close, like maybe he was standing right on the other side of the door.

I cleared my throat. "Y-yeah?"

"Can I take you out to dinner?"

What? Is he asking... "Um... I guess? I'm kinda hungry."

"Good. And look, I know you're worried about Sera, so maybe we can lock George in the bathroom and let Sera stay out here."

I cringed a little and looked at the cat that'd been rubbing against my cheek the whole time we'd been in here. "What do you think? You think you'd be okay with George in here?" I yelled to Ailin, "What if George gets out?"

There was a long pause before he said, "We can leave George in the car if you want?"

"No, you're not supposed to leave animals in a vehicle by themselves. Maybe we can just push something in front of the bathroom door, just in case?" I opened the door quickly, and Ailin fell a little, but caught himself before faceplanting into me.

He grinned at me. "That'll work. Come on, partner, lets get some food." He walked over and picked up the snake, then carried him into the bathroom, placing him on the floor. "You'll be okay, George. I promise we'll let you out as soon as we get something to eat, okay? And Sera will be right on the other side of the door, so you're not alone." Ailin stood up and looked at me. "He has bad memories of this bathroom. He's afraid he's gonna get stuck in the tub again."

I rolled my eyes and waved him off. He shut the door, and we pushed the armchair in front of it, then I set Sera down on the bed. Ailin pulled out a couple bowls of food and water, and I did a double take when I noticed a litterbox in the corner of the room. *When in the hell had he gotten all of this stuff? Did he have a bag in my car or something?* I shrugged it off, happy that the kitten had what she needed, and after giving her a kiss on the top of her head, we both headed out the door.

"Can I drive your precious baby? Or would you rather I give you directions?"

I chewed on my cheek for a moment before passing Ailin the keys. I didn't know why, but I trusted him. "Just be careful."

"I promise not to crash or even scratch your baby."

"Thank you." I was pretty sure he was making fun of me, but whatever.

We got in and Ailin drove us to a place ten minutes away. As we were walking in, I asked, "Do you think we should get on the road after dinner? Maybe we can get an early start at the office tomorrow."

"Uh, it's up to you. We can eat and see how we feel afterward. This place has a delicious tofu parmigiana that you should try."

I wrinkled my nose. "Do they have real meat on the menu?"

"Yes, but..." He looked at me with squinty eyes. "I'm not sure I can be friends with someone that eats dead animals."

"Ew, Ailin." That brought up an unwanted and super gross picture, but my insides did a weird flutter when he called me his friend—or kinda called me his friend. Not that I should care.

He shrugged, held the door open for me, then told the hostess we needed a table for two before picking up our conversation as we waited. "It's true. You eat dead animals all the time. What were you thinking about getting tonight? Dead cow? Dead chicken? Dead pig? Oh Mother, you better not eat dead deer around me."

"Okay, okay, okay. Stop saying 'dead' and talking about dead animals. If you were trying to get me to change my mind, it worked. I'll get the damn tofu."

"Right this way, gentlemen," the hostess interrupted.

He grinned and made a goofy face as we started to walk. "I knew you'd see it my way."

I rolled my eyes and followed the hostess to our table.

After we ordered, Ailin kept looking at me with this strange expression on his face. I couldn't tell if he was annoyed, pissed, upset, concerned, or what. Finally, I said, "What's up?"

He pursed his lips. "What happened to you in Gauhala?"

I sucked in a breath and shook my head.

Ailin looked around the room and muttered under his breath, then tilted his head. "Was it your... partner that was killed?"

I closed my eyes as I pictured his face, as I pictured Zane's broken and bloody body and his pale skin as that *thing* bled him dry. I pictured him reaching for me, I remembered how I couldn't reach him, I couldn't do anything, I couldn't save him, I couldn't—suddenly I was there again, there in that awful place.

"Zane!" I yelled as I walked through the sand. "Zane, where are you?"

I heard a yell from my right, so I took off, my feet pounding on the sand. "Zane!" I heard another yell, and finally saw a small hut hidden in the dunes. "Zane!"

I aimed my semi-automatic rifle in front of me and kicked the door in. It only took me a few seconds to survey the scene, but as soon as I did, I wanted to vomit. That insane motherfucker! The hut was a perfect circle with dirt-packed walls. The place was covered in symbols; they were painted on the floor, the walls, the ceiling. There were twigs weaved together and hanging around the one-room hut. But the worst thing I'd ever seen in my life was splayed right in front of me in the center of the floor.

Zane lay on his back with those same symbols carved into his skin and painted in blood on his chest. He was filthy with dirt and sweat and blood all over him. His blond hair was covered in blood, and he had tear tracks on his cheeks. I took a shaky breath when he looked at me with only one eye—the other had been carved out.

The evil motherfucker was standing over him with a bloody knife, chanting. Chanting, chanting, chanting.

"Back up and drop your weapon before I blow your brains out, motherfucker!" I yelled.

The witch doctor didn't even glance at me, he just kept chanting. When he lowered his knife toward Zane, I pulled the trigger without hesitation. He would not be hurting my partner anymore. But the bullet never made it to him. It ricocheted off something and up into the ceiling.

"Fuck." I pulled the trigger again, but the bullet hit the wall instead of my target. "What the fuck?" I glanced at Zane, he was looking at me as he yelled out in pain while the witch doctor carved another symbol deep in his chest.

I yelled and unloaded my weapon on the evil bastard, but the bullets kept shooting in every other direction. Zane cried out, so I ran farther into the room, lifting my rifle over my shoulder so I could knock the asshole out, but before I could reach him, I got knocked back. I tried to step forward again, but ran into something... some invisible shield.

"Fuck, fuck, fuck." I looked down at the man I loved and tried to keep my panic at bay. "I'm coming, Zane, I'm coming for you."

He cried out again as the witch doctor pulled his torn-up arm out. I banged on the barrier over and over and over, but I couldn't get through. The witch doctor spread Zane's fingers out and sliced off his thumb. Zane screamed in pain, and I yelled out for him as tears fell freely from my eyes.

The witch doctor cut off another finger, then put his hand over a bowl, collecting his blood. He set the other fingers on a plate on Zane's stomach.

"Get the fuck off of him! Get off! Leave him alone!" I banged and banged, but nothing worked.

Zane reached his other hand out toward me. "S-S-Seb. 'S'kay."

I fell to my knees crying and pounding on the barrier. "Zane, I'm right here. I'm right here."

His breathing grew more and more labored as the witch doctor kept slicing him open and cutting him apart. I couldn't get to him. I couldn't get through. He was right there, and I couldn't reach him.

"Zane," I cried. "Just hold on. The others are coming. Just please hold on."

His eye clouded over, blood dripping from it and from his mouth. "Love... you."

"No, you... you can't say that now. You have to hold on."

He took a deep breath, and I knew it'd be his last one.

"I love you too, Zane, I love you too."

His chest didn't move again, and I screamed and wept.

I had no idea how long it was before my captain got there, but as soon as he broke the barrier, I pulled Zane to me. I tried everything I could, but he was gone... he was gone... he was gone.

"Sebastian?" Ailin's quiet voice got my attention. "Hey, Seb?"

I blinked at him.

"I'm sorry, I didn't mean... I didn't mean to send you back there, I'm so sorry." He took a deep breath. "I don't want to upset you, but I-I'm here if you need to talk."

"Why?" My voice had more bite to it than I'd meant.

"I'm sorry, detective, I didn't mean anything by it."

I narrowed my eyes at him and ground my teeth together. "Zane and I had been sleeping together for a couple of years. I wouldn't exactly call him my boyfriend, but... I..." I glanced at him, then looked away. "We loved each other."

"I'm so sorry you lost him."

"He was tortured and killed right in front of me. That witch doctor had some kind of... shield or something around him and Zane, but I could... I could see everything. No matter what I did, I couldn't get through. I couldn't... he reached for me, and I couldn't even hold his hand as he took his last breath. Nothing worked until Captain Greenleaf came in. I don't know how he did it, but he broke through and killed the witch doctor, but... but it was too late for Zane. I tried... I tried to bring him back, but he was just... gone."

"Seb, I'm so—"

"Can I order a beer? Do you mind?"

Ailin looked a little sad, but he simply nodded and allowed me to change the subject. I pushed away all the old feelings and tried to stop picturing Zane bloody and carved up.

Luckily, Ailin was good at distracting me, so I was able to push my grief and pain to where it belonged—far, far in the back of my mind. I couldn't let myself go down that dark path again. I'd barely made it back the last time.

Every time my mind wandered during our meal, Ailin brought me back to the present.

***

"Oh my god, I'm stuffed." I held my stomach as we headed back into our motel room. "That tofu parmigiana was delicious." As soon as I stepped over the threshold, Seraphina meowed and started rubbing on my legs. "Hey, sweet girl. Did you have fun while we were out?"

"I knew you'd like it." Ailin walked past me and pat the cat on her head before walking to the bathroom and opening the door. "Tofu is amazing." He kneeled down and whispered into the bathroom, then stood up with the snake around his neck again. "George is going to go hunting tonight. Do you want to stay here another night and leave in the morning?"

I was surprised he was even bothering asking me. "Uh, sure. That sounds good."

Ailin nodded and walked over to the door, opening it and letting George slither away. "He'll be back in the morning."

I bit back the response of *Yeah, right, he's a freaking wild snake and will slither away and never come back.* "Uh huh."

Ailin rolled his eyes at me, then plopped back on his bed. I followed suit and laid on my bed. Sera stayed on my chest.

We lay there for a while in silence, but Ailin broke it when he looked at Seraphina. "What are you gonna do? Move in with Seb when we get home?"

Sera purred and kneaded my chest, then rubbed against my cheek before she stared at Ailin. Ailin's eyes flashed with something I didn't recognize and I cringed, then cleared my throat. "Do you want me to pass her over?"

Sera made a hissing sound and Ailin sighed. "You're fine. She's just never been so... all over another person before."

I frowned at him because he sounded like his feelings were hurt. I sorta felt bad, but there wasn't really anything I could do about it. After a while, we turned off the lights and went to sleep. I fell asleep with Sera curled by my head again.

***

I woke up with a cat ass in my face again. Ailin was already in the shower, so I pet Sera while I waited for my turn. Ailin walked out of the bathroom without a shirt on, and I found myself looking him up and down—he was covered in tattoos, like completely covered. I wanted a closer look, but I took my fill from where I lay. He had on his normal black cargo pants and a bunch of necklaces hanging over his chest. I had to look him up and down one more time before meeting his cocky eyes that'd obviously noticed my lazy perusal of his body. It wasn't like I could help that he was hot. Honestly, what did he expect coming out here all wet and shirtless?

"You have a lot of tattoos," I blurted, then snapped my mouth shut as my cheeks heated with embarrassment.

He smirked and ran a hand down his chest. My eyes naturally followed the movement and I swallowed audibly. Ailin walked closer to me, and I couldn't remove my eyes from his muscled chest. When he was right in front of me, he leaned down so his face was in front of mine, forcing my gaze up to his green eyes. "Eyes up here, Seb." He pointed to his own face; his eyes dancing with mischief. "The shower's open, so it looks like it's your turn to take off your clothes."

I felt my cheeks heat further as I quickly jumped out of the bed, grabbed my clothes and headed into the bathroom. The last thing I heard before turning on the water was Ailin's soft chuckles.

After showering and dressing, I walked out of the bathroom and stopped in my tracks staring at Ailin's bed, then I shook my head. "That thing came back?"

Ailin glared at me from his place on the bed with George. "He's not a *thing*, he's a snake. Show a little respect, Seb."

"What the hell is it doing here again?"

"He decided he wants to come home with me."

"Do you seriously expect me to be okay with George riding in my fucking car for over two hours?"

Ailin threw his hands in the air. "You and the car! He's been a perfect gentleman in your car every time he's been in it, so what the hell is the problem this time?"

"I don't like snakes!"

"Could've fooled me. You've been such a wonderful friend to George since you found him, I thought for sure you loved snakes!" *Hello, Mr. Sarcasm.*

"I don't want to be worried about being bit the entire time we're in the car."

Ailin sat up and looked me in the eyes. His green eyes were intense. "I promise you he won't hurt you or me or Sera. I promise you."

"How can you make a promise like that?" I whispered.

He sat up straighter and looked right at me. "Do you trust me?"

"What?"

"Look, I know we don't know each other very well, but do you trust me to have your back? Do you think I would ever let someone or something hurt you if I was able to prevent it?"

I just stared at him as I thought about it. It wasn't like I believed that Ailin was evil, or even a bad person at all. He drove me crazy, but... I didn't think he'd purposefully hurt me. Picturing Ailin doing something so malicious didn't sit well with me, but did I truly believe that he'd protect me if the time came?

I thought about that for a few moments. I thought about how despite his rough exterior and general rudeness, he'd been gentle with his cousin, he'd been caring and tender with Seraphina, and with George. He seemed to really care. But that wasn't the question. Ailin had been nothing but a complete asshole to me since the moment I'd met him, but underneath all that macho bullshit he put forward for everyone to see, I'd also had a glimpse of his caring nature. Despite my grievances, I was pretty sure he was actually a good guy. If he cared that much about animals and nature, did I really think he'd ever hurt me? No, I didn't. But that didn't mean that he'd choose to protect me over protecting his snake or any other animal.

"Seb?"

I looked at him with a lifted brow.

"I will always protect you, no matter what I have to protect you from, just like I know you'd protect me. We're partners, right?"

I blew out a slow breath and nodded.

"Do you trust me?"

I *felt* in my gut that I could trust this guy, and I had to follow my gut. "Yes."

Ailin smiled widely, the biggest smile I'd seen on him yet. "Good. That's... good."

"So I guess George is riding in the car. Just... keep him away from me."

Ailin chuckled. "I will." He picked up the snake and spoke in a baby-voice, "Don't bother grumpy old Sebastian while he's driving, okay?" He kissed the snake on the head and I wrinkled my nose. "That's a good snake. Who's a good snake? George is a good snake."

Oh my god. He's seriously insane. Who talks to a fucking snake like that?

The drive back home was uneventful, and I found myself content with our times of companionable silence. I'd never been one of those people that felt the need to fill the silence with nonsense, and it seemed that Ailin wasn't either.

Growing up, I'd spent a lot of time alone, so being lost in my own thoughts was something I was accustomed to.

When we pulled into town, I asked, "Where should I go? Do you want me to drop you off at your house so you can leave George and Sera there?" The cat rumbled in my lap, so I scratched behind her ears.

"Nah, just go straight to the station."

"But... the animals...?"

"Alec won't mind. Sera's been there before." He grinned at me as he pet the sleeping snake in his lap. Ailin, of course, had his feet up on the dash.

I was about to argue, but thought better of it. If I'd known where he lived, I'd drive there and insist he leave the pets there, but I had no idea where he lived. Although, I assumed it was in the rich part of town since that was where we'd picked Seraphina up from the other day.

When I parked at the station, I turned in my seat to Ailin. "Are you sure this is a good idea?"

"Look, I know Alec is your boss or chief or whatever, but he's my brother-in-law, and honestly, I've been working here as long as he has. Technically, he can't tell me what to do."

I stared at him for several seconds. "So basically, you just like to push everyone's buttons all the time."

He barked out a laugh that turned into a chuckle. "You know me so well already." He shot me a grin before jumping out of the car and wrapping George around the back of his neck.

I shook my head and held Sera against my chest, then got out and followed behind him. "If he gives us shit, you better cover for me. He might not be able to fire you, but he sure as hell can fire me."

Ailin stopped in his tracks on the front steps and turned to look down at me. "I won't let that happen." He turned and kept going.

I nodded and took a deep breath because I believed him. God help me, I trusted and believed him, even if I couldn't put my finger on why I did. I followed him inside.

About five seconds after we'd entered the building, Chief Gillman came charging out of his office, bellowing, "What the fuck do you think you're doing, Ailin?"

I flinched. I'd never seen him look so pissed before.

Ailin absentmindedly pet George. He looked like he didn't have a care in the world—he probably didn't, really, at least not past caring about George and Sera. Ailin glanced at me for a split-second before looking at the chief. "I'm taking care of a problem you should've found months ago, Al, that's what I'm doing."

Chief Gillman's jaw clenched. "You know that's not what I meant."

Ailin shrugged. "I'm heading to my partner's office to check up on the rest of Brinnswick's stations since every one of them, including this one, seems to be incompetent." *He actually called me his partner. Wow. But then he was kind of an ass. Wow.*

Chief Gillman's nostrils flared and I could tell he was about to explode. "My office. Now." He looked at me. "You too." He turned on his heel and strode into his office.

Well, shit.

Ailin grabbed my arm, and I gasped as his fingers grazed my skin, and I felt the heat of his hand. It felt... tingly and electrified like there was a current between us. Ailin froze and looked at me with wide eyes. He felt it too, he had to have. That was the only reason he made that weird face at me. *What the hell is that?*

We stared at each other, and for a moment, the entire world disappeared. His green eyes looked... like they were swirling and changing before my very eyes even though he wasn't moving at all. I felt like I was caught in his gaze—his beautiful, handsome, sexy, amazing gaze, and I couldn't look away, I didn't want to. I felt myself step closer to him, but it was like my feet moved of their own accord. Ailin moved too, but he didn't look away or remove his hand from my arm. I wanted him to move even closer. I couldn't explain it, but he was suddenly a beacon that was pulling me in. I wanted to know what it'd feel like to have that current running through my entire body. I wanted to know what it'd feel like to have his smaller body pressed against me, what it'd feel like to surround him completely.

"Fitz! Ellwood! Get in here now!"

We both startled at the sound of Chief Gillman's voice.

Ailin's eyes widened a little, and he looked around the room, then back at me before letting go of my arm and stepping away from me as if I'd shocked him. He cleared his throat and brushed his shirt off even though there was nothing there, then cleared his throat again. "Right. Uh... we better get in there. And, uh, don't worry. He's only going to yell at me. He knows you have nothing to do with the... animal thing." He stared at the ground and headed toward the chief's office without looking at me.

I cleared my own throat and shook myself out. What in the fucking hell was that? Why did I feel... drawn to him all of a sudden? We'd been together for days, why would I suddenly feel this weird... connection with him? *Maybe because that's the first time he's touched your skin.* I cringed at the thought, then brushed nothing off my own shirt, shifted Sera on my shoulder and followed in Ailin's trail.

As soon as I shut the door, Chief Gillman yelled, "What the fuck, Ailin?"

I heard Ailin mutter, "Fucking full moon."

I didn't think Chief heard him because he kept yelling, "Don't you *ever* disrespect me in front of my detectives like that *ever again*, Ailin."

"Don't treat me like one of your minions you can boss around, and we won't have a problem." Ailin and Chief Gillman glared at each other.

"You can't bring animals into the station, Ailin. We've had this discussion a thousand times before. Take them home."

"Why is it such a big deal? I really don't understand you humans! First Seb with his 'no animals in the car' rule, and now this! Why do humans care so much about it? It's not like they're going to hurt anyone." *Why does he keep saying 'you humans' as if he* isn't *one?* Ailin shot me a glance, but refocused on the chief.

"Ailin. We've been over this. Animals aren't allowed in the building."

"Then all of you humans should leave, too, since you're a fucking type of animal, too!"

Chief Gillman sighed and pinched the bridge of his nose.

Ailin waved his arms around. "Al, they aren't going to hurt anything, and quite frankly, standing in here discussing it is a waste of time. Do you want me to go to your boss and get special permission or something equally ridiculous? I'm sure I could convince any one of them that it's not a big deal." He shot me a glance. "And anyway, we'll keep them in Seb's office, isn't that right, Seb?"

My eyebrows shot up. That hadn't been part of the deal, but since he'd finally called me his partner, I wanted to back him up. "Y-yes, that's right. My office only."

Ailin grinned and nodded at me before looking at Chief Gillman. "See? We're all good here."

My chief sighed after a minute and waved at the seats across from his desk. "Fine. But they're gone if they cause any problems, you hear me?" At Ailin's nod, he sat in his own chair and we followed suit. "Have a seat and catch me up." He eyed me. "I see that Sera is a fan."

"She hasn't left his side since we left for Almahast County," Ailin replied.

Chief Gillman frowned at me. "I've known her for a long time and she still hates me. She hisses anytime I try to get close."

Ailin chuckled. "Well, we both know there's a reason for that, and she likes Seb more than me, too, so you're in good company."

I turned my head a little to look at Sera. She licked my cheek, then rubbed against it.

Ailin and I told him everything we'd discovered, which admittedly wasn't much. Once we were done, Ailin and I walked to my office, he shut the door and leaned against it. "Thanks for backing me up even though I know you hate having them in here."

"I don't hate having them in here." I glanced at George. "Okay, maybe I'm a little uncomfortable with

George, but he's... fine, and I like Sera. I just don't like breaking the rules."

Ailin smirked. "I might have to change your mind on that."

I snorted. "Great. You going to turn me to your criminal ways?"

He chuckled. "I might just have to."

I laughed and sat in my seat. "You ready to go through an endless amount of files?"

He sighed and pushed off the door, then sat across from me. "Not really, but I suppose we don't have a choice."

I nodded and started up my computer after plugging it in.

Chapter Five

After spending three days searching every case, we found sixteen cases that fit our perp's MO. The crazy thing was that the cases were spread out so there was one murder per month, almost exactly a month apart. So according to this pattern, the perp was due to kill again in the next two weeks.

Unfortunately, we were being called away from our case to help out with a missing police officer. There was a call of suspicious activity in an old, unused factory late last night that a local officer went to investigate. The officer had gone missing shortly after reporting that he was going inside the warehouse. That was where we came in. The Brinnswick Central Agency had gotten the call an hour ago, so we were already on scene.

Ailin and I both suited up in heavy gear, so we were in bulletproof vests and had helmets on with earpieces to communicate with our whole team. Nearly everyone in my office reported to the scene because we weren't sure what we'd find. The officer had been armed when he went in, and since he'd been taken down—we assumed—we figured that the perp or perps were armed as well.

Ailin insisted on taking the lead on this one, and since he was my partner, I insisted on being up front with him even though he'd tried to fight me on it, wanting me to stay back and watch from a distance. Asshat.

I followed him to the side door. We had the place surrounded and one of the officers at the front door yelled, "This is the Brinnswick Central Agency! We have the place surrounded! Come out with your hands up!"

After waiting for a minute without hearing a response, Ailin said into his mic, "Okay, we're going in. Alpha Team only. Everyone else stay where you are and stop anyone from exiting the building."

He looked at me and nodded. I nodded back, and he silently counted to three, then opened the door. I followed behind him, watching his back and checking every corner with him. Detectives Darren Thompal and Anita Long were right behind us. Thompal had reluctantly agreed to work with Ailin again, just for this one mission. But he'd been getting little jabs into Ailin every time I turned around, and it was really pissing me off. I'd told him to keep his mouth shut, but of course, he'd ignored me. On Ailin's part, he'd just been letting the insults roll off his shoulders, and barely even acknowledged Thompal's existence. Surprisingly, he'd been the bigger man with this. I hadn't thought it was possible for Ailin to keep his mouth shut, but he'd proved me wrong. Although, he hadn't been able to hide his smile from me when I'd told the asshat to lay off him.

Everyone followed Ailin deeper into the warehouse, and I wasn't sure what the hell we were seeing. The farther we got into the building, the stranger our surroundings became.

The first hallway was white, but when we turned the corner, a smell hit me so strong I almost gagged. The walls were covered in... slime or something. It looked slimy, and with every step, the smell grew and grew.

By the time we turned the third corner, I was fighting back vomit. I was pretty sure that the walls had blood on them, too. Slime and blood. And it smelled like death. Like rotting bodies. It was appalling and nearly impossible not to gag.

We finally made it to an open area, and the sight before me made me want to puke. The police officer we'd been looking for was tied up to a pentagram made from branches. No, he wasn't tied to it, the branches were going straight through his body, that was what was holding him up. He had so many branches coming out of his body that there was no way to count them; he was covered in scratches, bruises, and blood. He'd only been missing for a couple hours, and he looked like that already. I took a step closer to him and realized that the scratches were actually symbols *carved* into his skin. *Uhhh, god, so gross.*

A deep fear hit me quickly, and I looked around the room, but everywhere I turned, there were more and more symbols, more and more strange twigs hanging from the ceiling. *Oh god, oh god, oh god.* I was in a witch doctor's shrine again. He was going to kill me, he was going to kill Ailin.

Zane's broken body flashed through my mind, and suddenly, I was back in Gauhala again. I was back there fighting to get through the barrier, fighting to get to Zane. I needed to save him. I needed to stop that crazy asshole from cutting him apart. I needed to get through the barrier. Zane's eye stared back at me as he went lifeless before me.

A quiet sob escaped my lips.

"Sebastian?" I heard Ailin's voice, but I didn't see him. "Seb, you're safe. You're in Brinnswick." A hand landed on my neck, and I jumped, then leaned into the touch a little. "You're safe, Sebastian."

I blinked a few times until Ailin came into focus. His expression was concerned, but also… gentle, and nothing like him, which caught my attention.

"Hey," he whispered and squeezed my neck. "It's okay. You're safe. We're safe."

I stared into his green eyes for several seconds as I willed my heartbeat to go back to normal. Ailin was patient and held me there with his hand on my neck, grounding me to the here and now.

"Ailin," I whispered.

He smiled at me. "We're safe, Seb." I nodded, and he asked, "Do you know where you are?"

I blew out a breath. "Yeah, in the warehouse with the missing officer."

He nodded. "Good. Do you think… you're okay now?"

I sucked air into my lungs. My chest still felt tight, but I wasn't panicking anymore. "Yeah, I'll be fine."

He nodded and squeezed my neck again before letting go. I had half a mind to ask him to keep his hand there, but I wasn't that pathetic. It was bad enough I just had a fucking flashback in front of all of my coworkers. I didn't need them thinking I was weaker than they already thought.

"No one's paying attention to us. I sent them away as soon as I realized what was happening. Don't worry about them, okay? You have nothing to be ashamed of, anyway. Having a flashback doesn't make you weak, not at all."

I nodded.

"You good to keep going?"

"Yeah... I'll be fine."

He eyed me for a long moment before nodding and continuing to move forward. I kept half my focus on Ailin in front of me so I wouldn't freak out again. Somehow, he kept me grounded.

We checked the perimeter of the room, and Ailin called the rest of the teams in to clear the building. We were pretty sure that the perp had left before we'd arrived on scene.

Once everything was cleared, I walked closer to the officer's body to examine the symbols. Some of them looked like the same symbols as our murdered girls. When the memories tried to force their way out again, I pushed them down and glanced at Ailin. *I'm okay. We're okay.* Taking a deep breath, I concentrated on the officer again.

I jumped out of my skin when the officer suddenly took a deep breath. *Holy shit balls! He's alive.* "He's alive! Jesus Christ, he's alive!"

Ailin ran over and checked the guy's pulse. "He's alive, but he won't be for long. Get the medical team in here stat!" He looked at me and frowned. "You okay?"

"Yeah, I'm just... how can he be alive? He must be in so much pain."

Ailin nodded. "Our perp likes to torture his victims before draining and killing them. I think we just got here before he could finish the job."

I nodded and moved out of the way as the medical team pushed through to the officer. Ailin and I put on gloves and began examining everything in the room. There were sticks hooked together with twine in weird shapes. Some were hanging from the ceiling, some were on the floor or on the tables. Everything was rusty and painted in red. At first, I'd thought it was just red paint and rust, but the closer I looked, the more convinced I was that he'd actually painted with blood, and what I thought was rust, was actually dried blood. *This place is fucking disgusting.*

There were animal bones and rotting dead animals all over the place. I frowned as I watched Ailin examine the body of a dead wolf, then look at a dead rabbit. There were cats, too, and I couldn't help but shiver at the thought of this sociopath getting ahold of Sera. How could someone hurt so many living things?

I moved on to another table that seemed to have a bunch of different ingredients in jars. I picked up a few. Some of them were herbs, others were... eyeballs and fingers and frog legs and... I stopped looking after that. This place was sure to give me nightmares.

When I moved on to the next table, I was surprised to find it clean of any blood and slime—not that I had any idea what the hell the slime was. This table had gems and stones spread out on it. The jewels were laid out in a circle with a huge red crystal in the middle. I'd never seen anything so bright and shiny. It was the most beautiful thing I'd ever seen, and it was calling to me. Something about it made me move closer. The longer I stared, the more I wanted—no, *had* to touch it. I just had to hold it and examine it up close. I wanted to take it home with me. What kind of jewel was it? Where did it come from? I wanted to keep the beauty forever. I reached out my gloved hand to pick it up and see what the hell it was. It looked like a giant red diamond or a huge ruby or something.

"Wait!" I heard Ailin yell, but I was too distracted by how shiny the jewel was. "Don't touch that, Seb!"

I snatched the crystal up and gasped as it shocked me so hard I felt it reverberate through my entire body. I tried to drop it, but it was stuck to me as searing pain shot through my hand and up my arm. After about thirty painful seconds, I was able to let go, and the thing fell back on the table as I winced and gasped and shook out my hand. "What the fuck?" The stupid thing must've been covered in some weird chemical.

"Shit, shit, shit." Ailin was at my side in an instant. He grabbed my hand and pulled my glove off. I stared in horror at the burn mark on my skin. It was in the shape of a pentagram. "Motherfucker!" Ailin's yell made me jump. "I told you not to touch it! Why the fuck couldn't you listen to me just this once? You have no idea what you just did, Sebastian, no fucking idea." He looked at me with those storming green eyes that looked like smoke was moving through them.

"I didn't... I don't know what happened. I-I heard you, but I couldn't... I couldn't stop myself from..."

Ailin's eyes softened and he ran his gloved finger over the pulse point on my wrist. "I'm sorry. It wasn't your fault. I'll fix this, don't worry. I'll take care of it."

It sorta was my fault since I was the idiot who touched it, but I didn't argue. "It's just a burn, Ailin. There's nothing to fix. I'll just get the medical team to bandage it."

He opened his mouth to respond, then snapped it shut and nodded. "Okay. Go get this taken care of." He smiled a little, but it looked forced. He couldn't hide the worry on his face.

I got bandaged up and we finished examining the room as the forensics team took pictures of everything and packed it up. We were there for hours and hours, and every time Ailin looked at me, I could see the concern written on his face.

But it was just a little burn. A weird burn, yes, but a burn nonetheless. He had nothing to worry about. I mean, right? I didn't need to worry, there was nothing weird about a pentagram being burned on my hand.

Maybe if I said it enough, I'd actually start to believe it.

***

"Hey, so my house is under a little construction today, so I was wondering if I could crash on your couch tonight?" Ailin said a little before midnight. We'd been there all night going through the pictures of everything from the warehouse this morning.

I furrowed my brow. "You didn't say anything earlier. What's going on at your house?"

He sighed and pushed the hair behind his ear—the none braided side. "My little brother sort of caught the bathroom on fire."

My eyebrows rose. His little brother crashed his bike the other day and set the bathroom on fire? *Troublemaker* must run in the family. I wonder if he'd been arrested as much as Ailin claimed to have been. "Do I even want to know how that happened?"

He snorted out a laugh. "Probably not. But he... has a room to stay in, so I was wondering if you would mind if I crashed on your couch?" I didn't miss the way his eyes examined my bandaged hand.

"Uh, sure. Of course, you can."

He shot me a smile. "Thanks, Seb."

I waved him off and yawned. "No worries. Are you about ready to head out? We missed dinner and I'm starving."

"Yeah, let's pick up a pizza on the way to your place."

We packed up what we could, and I grabbed Sera off the floor as we headed out the door. She'd stayed in my office while we were at the warehouse and seemed a little mad when we got back. She hadn't even climbed on my lap all night. I kissed her head as I followed Ailin out of the station, and I whispered to her, "I'm sorry you couldn't come with us earlier. I didn't want you getting hurt. And trust me, that place was no place for such a sweet little kitten, anyway. Don't be mad, I just wanted to keep you safe."

Ailin snorted in front of me—*the jerk, like he didn't talk to Sera like this all the time, too!*—and Sera meowed and rubbed my neck. I was pretty sure that meant she forgave me.

I smiled when she stayed on my lap for the drive back to my apartment. Once I parked and we got out, I saw Ailin staring at the building like he'd never seen an apartment complex before.

I cleared my throat. "Uh, I'm on the third floor. Come on." I carried Sera and my laptop bag, and Ailin carried the pizzas we'd picked up. When I opened up my apartment door, I waved him in and made sure to lock both locks behind him. "We can eat on the couch or at the table. It's up to you."

"Let's relax on the couch. My ass could use a break from sitting on an uncomfortable chair." He walked in front of me, and at the mention of his ass, I couldn't help but examine it. It looked pretty damn nice to me.

I blew out a breath and sat beside Ailin, grateful that he hadn't caught me perving on his ass. Ailin smirked at me, and I suddenly felt like maybe he somehow knew I'd been checking him out. *Dammit!* I ignored him—and his scent that was a mix of rosemary and weed, surprise, surprise—and grabbed a slice of pizza and the remote. After I took a bite, I said, "Oh, shit. Let me grab us drinks. Do you want water or beer? That's all I have, sorry."

"Water is fine."

I nodded and jumped up to grab glasses of water from the kitchen. I came back into the room with the glasses and some plates. Ailin took his, so I settled in and turned on the television as we ate.

"Today was really crazy. This guy is... a sociopath."

Ailin nodded in agreement. "He is."

We fell silent and finished off an entire pizza. When I finished eating, I was going to get up and go to bed, but Sera climbed on my lap, and I decided to wait until I finished my glass of water, so I settled back into the couch with Ailin only a foot away from me. I glanced at him as he watched the news, and I couldn't help but stare. He really was a gorgeous guy. Again, I wondered what he looked like under all those clothes. I'd only gotten a glimpse of his torso, really. All those tattoos, all that creamy skin. I'd like to examine those tattoos with my tongue. And those muscles. Thinking about licking him made my cock stir in my pants. Shit. Not cool. Not cool at all. *This guy is your partner, Sebastian, you can't keep fantasizing about him!* His lips curled up, and I knew he'd caught me staring, so I jerked my head forward and pretended I didn't do anything wrong.

I took a deep breath, then set Sera on the couch cushion and got up. "I'm going to bed. See you in the morning."

"Sleep tight, Seb."

I walked as fast as I could into my bedroom and shut the door behind me before Ailin noticed how interested my body really was in him.

***

"Do you still think this is some kind of weird religious ritual? I mean, it has to be, right? But we haven't found anything in your books about it yet." I leaned back in my chair and propped my feet up on my desk. After being around Ailin all the time, I'd taken up the habit. It was a lot more comfortable to put my feet up while sitting on my ass for hours on end. Not to mention it was easier to have Sera in my lap that way—yes, Ailin brought her back to the station, and told me he planned to every single day. Luckily, he'd been leaving George at home, though. He said that George was having fun chasing mice around his yard, but that he'd been sleeping in his living room... so weird.

"Yes, it's definitely a ritual. I know it's a kuma mali demon ritual; I just can't find the book with the details on it. I remember reading about it when I was a kid, so I know it's gotta be here somewhere."

He'd said the whole kuma mali demon thing a couple times already, so even though I didn't know what it was, I was at least familiar with the term. "Do you have a photographic memory or something?"

"No. I wish because we wouldn't need the damn book if I did. I just have a... basic knowledge of all the... religions."

The way he kept pausing and thinking about his words so hard made me believe that he was hiding something. I wasn't sure how I felt about it. I knew he had a higher clearance level than me, so I wasn't sure if that was why he was sometimes so secretive about stuff like that, or if he didn't trust me. I'd told him that I trusted him because I did, but I never asked if he trusted me. I frowned at the thought.

"I trust you, Sebastian." Ailin's voice was soft.

I looked over at him.

He sent me a small smile. "I trust you. But there are things you don't know about... yet, so I'm unsure of what to say at times."

"Is it because I don't have the clearance?"

He nodded his head back and forth as if he were thinking about it. "Uh... yes, in a sense."

"I have no idea what that's supposed to mean."

"I know. I'm sorry." He sighed and dropped his feet to the ground to sit up straight. "I promise that I'll tell you everything you need to know in order to stay safe and be helpful with the case."

I stared at him for several seconds. He was being truthful, I could tell. "Fair enough."

He nodded and went back to reading one of his books, so I did the same. His books were... really crazy. They talked about demons and beasts and all kinds of weird things like spells, potions, and magic. And they talked about these things as if they were real. It was very... strange. I'd been wondering why Ailin had all of these things in the first place. I understood that if someone was performing these rituals or spells or whatever, they obviously believed them to be true. But if Ailin had all of these books, did he have them for research purposes only, or did he, too, believe these crazy things, this... magic, was in fact real?

"Ailin?"

He looked up with an eyebrow lifted in question.

I almost chickened out, but I needed to know. "Do you... do you believe in this stuff?"

He hesitated for a few seconds, then blew out a breath. "I believe there are things in this world that many people do not understand."

That wasn't an answer. "I..." I didn't know what to say to that.

"I can't answer your question, Sebastian. I'm sorry."

I blinked at him. What the actual fuck? *Why can't he answer me?*

He blew out a breath, then pinched the bridge of his nose. "If I tell you that I believe in this stuff, you're either going to think I'm insane or you're going to be scared of me, or both. If I tell you I don't believe in it, you're not going to believe me. So either way, you look at me differently. I don't want that to happen."

I opened my mouth to argue, then snapped it shut when I realized he was right. I huffed out a breath, then went back to reading, snapping the page as hard as I could to let out a little of my anger. Why couldn't he just be honest with me for once?

After several minutes, Ailin asked, "Do you want to go grab something to eat?"

I nodded. "Fine."

"You're mad."

"What gave you that impression?" I slammed the book on the desk and stood up, making sure to scoop Sera up so she didn't fall. I angrily packed up my laptop and put the strap on the shoulder Sera wasn't sitting on.

He blew out a breath and stood, grabbed his jacket off the back of his chair, then shrugged it on and grabbed his bag. "Come on. Let me buy you lunch to make it up to you."

"Buying me food doesn't make up for you lying to me."

"I'm not... I'm not lying."

"Omitting the truth is a form of lying."

He sighed, and I followed him out of the building.

Once we were in the car and driving to a restaurant with outdoor seating—they didn't mind Sera being out there—on the other side of town, I said, "If you want this partnership to work, you have to be honest with me."

"I know. But it isn't that simple."

I huffed out another annoyed breath and parked the car at the restaurant. The entire time we were there, I ignored Ailin every time he tried to talk to me. I was pissed. I didn't really know why this, specifically, was pissing me off more than anything else he'd said—or *not* said—but it was. Why couldn't he just be honest with me for once? He knew something that I didn't know, and it was really shitty that he wasn't cluing me in.

After eating, we drove back to the station in silence.

"Look, Seb, I'm sorry. Why don't we just... take a break from the case for the night. We've barely left your office all week, and I know we're both exhausted."

I stared at him, shrugged, then took Sera from my lap and handed her to Ailin. "Fine. I'll go home." I waved for him to get out of my car.

"That's not what I meant. Let's both just get out of here. We can go back to my place and—"

"Get out of my car, Ailin."

Ailin stared at me for several seconds. "Can I just come with you?"

"What? No. Just... I need to be alone, okay?"

He sighed and got out. "Please be careful." As soon as he shut the door, I took off. I probably should've told Chief Gillman I was taking off for the day, but I didn't have the energy. I was sick of being left in the dark.

***

I studied some more files on my laptop before I decided to go to sleep. Ailin had been right, I was exhausted and I found myself going to bed before the sun was completely down.

I jerked awake at the sound of crashing glass. I blinked and looked around, squinting in the dark. I glanced at the clock on my nightstand; it was after midnight. What had woken me up? I heard crunching coming from my living room, like maybe someone was walking on broken glass.

Shit. Shit, shit, shit. Someone broke into my apartment.

I quietly opened my nightstand drawer and unlocked my gun safe, then pulled out my gun and checked that it was loaded. I slowly got out of bed and walked over to my bedroom door. It was only cracked, so I managed to peek out. I couldn't see anything except a shadow moving closer to my bedroom. I quietly closed the door and held my gun at the ready with one hand while pulling out my phone. For whatever reason, I dialed Ailin instead of the precinct or even just nine-one-one.

He picked up on the second ring. "What's wrong?"

"Someone's in my apartment. They broke a window to get in," I whispered.

"Shit. I'll be right there." I could hear rustling coming from the other end of the phone, so I assumed he was getting ready.

"Okay, I'm going to make my way out there and see if I can cuff the guy."

"Sebastian, do *not* go near the intruder. Do you hear me?" I'd never heard him more serious.

"I'm pretty sure I know what I'm doing, Ailin. I've been doing this for over fifteen years."

"Seb, I know you think I'm being crazy, but there's a chance this is our perp, and I'm telling you, he's not going to go down easily. Remember what that officer looked like when we found him? That could be you. This guy is strong and will use... chemicals and bullets. He drugged that officer with a... tranquilizer gun; he could shoot you with a dart!"

I pictured the guy we found in the warehouse and I cringed. Maybe Ailin was right, I didn't want to end up in some crazy sacrificial ceremony.

Ailin was breathing heavily into the phone. "Please just wait for me. You need backup before trying to catch him."

"Fine, but you better hurry."

"We're on our way. Just... can you barricade yourself in your bedroom or somewhere else?" *We?*

"Yeah. I locked the door."

"That's not enough, Seb. You need to move something in front of the door. Or better yet, can you escape out the window?"

"Uh... maybe." I looked over at my window. "I'm three floors up."

"Don't you have a fire escape?"

"Yeah, but... it's sorta broken on this side of the apartment."

"Son of a bitch." There were a bunch of mumbled voices for several seconds. "We'll be there in three minutes. Stay where you are. Barricade yourself." He clicked off the phone, and I took a deep breath as I put my cell in my pocket.

I looked around my room for something to put in front of the door. The only real thing I had was my dresser, so I pushed it over. It made noise, but I didn't think it mattered. If the guy was here to kill me, he already knew I was here; if it was just a robber, the noise would likely scare him off, or at least I hoped it would.

Once the dresser was in place, I yelled, "I'm a BCA Agent and I'm armed. The police are on their way, so I suggest you take off unless you want to be arrested or shot."

There was a weird cackling sound on the other side of my door. It almost didn't sound human. *What in the hell is that?*

"I have a gun, and I *will* shoot you if you come any closer!"

The cackling got louder and closer to my door. "Silly, human, your bullets can't harm me," the voice hissed at me, and I had a sudden jolt of déjà vu. I recognized the strange hissing voice, but I couldn't place it. It was like the memory was just out of my grasp, or maybe it was just from a strange dream when I was a kid.

"What do you want?" Maybe if I kept him talking, he wouldn't make a move before Ailin got here with backup.

The sound of nails scratching wood reached my ears, and I realized he was scratching my door. If his goal was to freak me out, he was already doing it. "Sebastian Cooper Fitz, thirty-five, orphaned at four-years-old, grew up at Eastbrook Youth Academy, joined Special Forces at eighteen." *What the fuck? How does he know me?* A cold chill ran down my spine. This was personal. "Faced a witch doctor in Gauhala, came back to Brinnswick at thirty, joined Strimville police, slowly moved up the ranks, came to the lovely city of Arronston to join the Central force where you partnered with *Ailin Talamh Ellwood*." I shivered at the amount of hatred in his voice when he spoke Ailin's name.

"What do y—"

Suddenly the door exploded, sending me flying through the air. Pieces of wood shot in every direction, and I barely had enough time to scream out before I landed, hitting my head on the corner of my nightstand. There was smoke and fire everywhere and everything looked blurry. I blinked as pain filled my entire being. It felt like I'd been shot by a hundred bullets. I looked down and saw a huge piece of wood sticking out of my chest. I was covered in scrapes and bruises and blood. *What the fuck is happening?* I sucked in a deep breath, but I couldn't get enough air in my lungs. I reached behind my head and felt something wet. A lot of liquid... a lot of blood.

The cackling sound moved closer, and I saw a reddish shadow move toward me. It was surrounded in a red haze as it hissed, "You're *mine*, Sebastian Cooper Fitz." The shadow moved closer to me, right in my face. *Wait, it's not a shadow, it's solid. How is a shadow solid?* Its hot breath brushed over my skin as it spoke. "You will make a lovely sacrifice." It opened its mouth and red fog poured over my face, burning my skin and blurring my vision further.

I gasped in pain and tried to block my face with my arms, but only one arm moved on my command. My ribs were screaming in agony. Everything hurt. I couldn't breathe; it burned.

"Demon!" a familiar voice yelled, but I couldn't place it.

The shadow moved away from me and hissed, "I thought you'd never show up, Sage."

A loud growl startled me, so I dropped my arm and blinked a few times, but everything was still fuzzy. Wait, where'd the shadow go? Another growl made me blink, then I squinted. *Is there a leopard on my bed? No, wait, that's a dragon. Or is that the shadow again?*

Oh god, I was hallucinating.

A green light filled the room, so I slammed my eyes shut and coughed. It was getting harder and harder to breathe. I opened my eyes and saw Ailin standing in front of me. Or at least, I thought it was him. I hoped it was him. Maybe he could capture the shadow. I hoped the shadow didn't hurt him, too. Everything started to fade again, but I saw red and green smoke circling everywhere. I closed my eyes as the room brightened in red and green lights.

"Sebastian?"

I heard my name, but it sounded far away.

"I know, Basil. I need you three to follow it. It's injured, there should be a trail." I recognized that voice.

"I'll call you if we catch up to it." *Who's that?*

"Sebastian?" I blinked a few times. That voice sounded warm; I wanted to crawl into that voice and live there. "Seb, open your eyes for me." Why did that voice sound like home? I felt warm hands cup my cheeks. The warmth of his hands spread through me, and I was suddenly able to suck in a bigger breath. "Sebastian, come on, honey, wake up."

I coughed a few times. "I thought Honey was your cousin," I mumbled almost unintelligently.

"Oh, thank the Mother." I felt the sweet voice move closer and suddenly my body was being lifted, then placed on something soft. "You've lost a lot of blood, Seb. Just rest. I'll take care of you."

"Ailin?" I muttered.

"Yes?" the warm voice said.

"Was there a leopard on my bed?"

A surprised laugh came out of his mouth, and I finally opened my eyes. Ailin was staring down at me, and his eyes looked glossy. He ran his hand through my hair. "You have a concussion."

"I know."

"Rest, Seb. I'll fix you up." He smiled and ran his hand through my hair again. Every time he did that, I felt a little better. That made no sense, but I'd take it since everything on my body hurt. "I know everything hurts. I promise you'll be okay." He leaned closer to me and blew his breath across my face. "Sleep, Seb. I'll take care of you."

Everything went black.

Chapter Six

I groaned when I woke; I had a splitting headache.

"Shh, shh, shh," Ailin whispered from somewhere on my right. "Your body just needs to adjust to the... medicine. The headache will pass in a minute."

I squeezed my eyes shut against the pain and settled down under the blanket I could feel over my body. "Wh-where are we?"

"In my back yard."

I didn't even have the energy to ask what the fuck we were doing in his back yard. I'd thought I'd be in the hospital.

"Nature will help you heal."

I groaned. Him and his weirdo nature-is-the-best-for-everything bullshit. I was probably bleeding out in the middle of his back yard. "If I die back here, you're going to be charged with murder."

He chuckled. "If you die back here, they'd never find the body."

I groaned. "That's not funny."

He chuckled a little and moved around beside me, but I didn't bother to open my eyes to see what he was doing. I felt him brush my hair off my forehead, and despite the fact that my head hurt, I got chills from the contact. When he did it again, my headache faded even further. He moved closer and when he spoke, I could feel his breath brushing across my neck. "I know you think I'm a crazy freak, but I promise you that being out here with me is the best thing for you right now."

"I never called you a freak."

"Maybe not out loud, but you thought it. More than once."

I opened my eyes and noticed it was still dark out. I frowned at him as I turned my head. "I don't think you're a freak."

He lifted a brow but didn't say anything.

I sighed and looked down at my body. "What the fuck, Ailin?"

"It's helping you heal."

"You covered me in grass. I don't think that's an actual medical procedure." I moved a little, trying to get the grass off me, but I was stuck. It felt like I was in a fucking grass cocoon.

He sighed and put his hand on my chest, stilling me. "Will you please just trust me on this. I promise I'll explain."

"Are you going to explain why a-a-a *shadow* attacked me?"

"Yes."

I blinked at him. I'd expected him to correct me and tell me that it wasn't a shadow, that it was a man, but I'd hit my head too hard to see correctly. "What about the green light?"

"Yes."

"And why you didn't take me to the hospital?"

"Yes. I'll explain everything. I promise."

"Okay, well... get to explaining, then."

He rolled onto his back and looked up at the sky, so I looked up, too. I wasn't sure how far from the inner city we were, but there were more stars in the sky here than at my apartment. We lay there in companionable silence for a long time, so long I didn't think he was going to tell me anything.

When he finally spoke, his voice was quiet and soft. "There are things that the normal human population doesn't know about—"

"Why do you keep referring to me and other people as humans like you're not one of us?"

He huffed out an annoyed breath. "Are you going to let me talk or not?"

"Sorry, but I want to know why."

"Sebastian, I told you I'd explain everything, didn't I? So let me talk."

"Fine, but I expect to hear *everything*."

"Ugh." He put his hands in his hair and tugged. "You're incredibly frustrating."

"Me? You're the one that never gives a straight answer."

"For the love of the Mother, would you just shut the fuck up?"

I looked at him with a frown. "Fine. Continue on."

He sighed and dropped his hands again. "I call you and the others 'humans' because that's what you are and I'm... not." I opened my mouth to argue, but he held up a hand to cut me off. "No questions until the end. I'll explain." I nodded and bit on my lips so I wouldn't interrupt again.

"I'm not human. I look like I am, but I'm… a little different." He turned sharply and glared. "And I'm not an alien, you asshat."

"I didn't say anything."

"You didn't have to. Anyway, I'm a witch."

My eyes widened and I felt icy fear fill my veins. He was a witch? Like that guy that kidnapped Zane was a witch doctor. *Oh my god, Ailin has me trapped in his back yard. He's going to do some weird ritual and kill me. Oh god, he's a witch doctor.*

Ailin turned on his side and leaned over me on his elbow, looking at me with wide eyes. "I'm not a witch doctor, Seb. Witch doctors are usually humans that dabble in the dark arts. I'm a witch. I was born a witch, just like you were born a human. I'm not into black magic, I swear."

I eyed him warily. "Witches and witch doctors aren't the same?"

"Not even close. They're evil, and witches, well, *most* witches aren't evil. At least not in my coven. We try to help humans, not harm them. You know how I feel about harming animals." He lifted a shoulder. "Humans are animals, too."

I opened my mouth, then closed it. I was pretty sure he just insulted my entire species, but I was more concerned that he might want to hurt me.

"I'm not going to hurt you. I would never hurt you, Seb, you know that."

His green eyes were bright in the moonlight, and once again, I found myself stuck in his gaze as my worries began to wash away. "Y-you won't?"

"Of course not, Sebastian."

Staring at his face and thinking about everything he'd done since I'd known him, I really couldn't argue with the fact that he wasn't malicious. He was an asshat, not evil—big difference.

"I'm not evil. In fact, I'm trying to help rid our world of evil beings. Like the one that broke into your apartment."

As I stared at him, I could see the truth written on his face. "So... magic is real?"

He nodded. "Yes."

I took a deep breath. I'd known from the first time I'd seen him that he was different. And after all the little things I'd seen, that I'd brushed off as coincidence, maybe magic really was real.

Ailin lifted his hand over my chest with his palm facing the sky, and a green smoky ball suddenly grew over his hand. My eyes widened and I wished I wasn't stuck under the grass so I could move away. "I'm not going to hurt you. I'm just showing you that it's real." He threw the ball of smoke into the air and mumbled under his breath. As the ball started to fall, it transformed into a hundred little dragonflies, and all I could do was blink.

"Wow."

"Yeah."

I took a few moments to absorb the information. It just didn't seem like it could be real.

"There's a whole world of magic that you don't know of. All the stories you've heard growing up, the ones people say are fantasy and fake? They're all based in fact. Vampires, werewolves, faeries, mermaids, all of them, they're real."

"So that shadow tonight was…?"

"A demon."

"Holy fucking shit."

"He's… powerful, but rare. It's not like you're going to find demons everywhere you go now or anything."

"Have I met other… what? Supernaturals?"

"It's very likely, yes. Well, actually, your old captain is a hunter."

"A hunter?"

"Uh, yeah. They're like humans, only stronger, more powerful; some have special abilities, and they can sense other supes, which is what makes it easier for them to hunt the bad ones down. And they…" he trailed off when he noticed me staring at him with wide eyes. "I think maybe we should hold off the lessons before your brain explodes. Why don't you sleep on everything I told you, and I'll answer your questions later."

"Uh… yeah." This was a lot of information to absorb, but for whatever reason, I found myself believing Ailin again. I didn't know why, but he had a way of convincing me of the most ridiculous and crazy things.

"I may be a witch, Seb, but I'm not a liar. I don't lie to you."

"Except for the whole keeping a huge secret thing. You know, the whole you're not a fucking human and we've been chasing a fucking demon this whole time, and you knew it."

He sighed. "Except for that."

"So... humans really don't know?"

Ailin shook his head. "No. Only certain government officials know so we can work together, but the general population thinks we're just fairy tales. One of the biggest rules of my world is that you can't tell humans of our existence because it will upset the balance. There are only a handful of exceptions to the rule, but I trust you, so I know it's safe to share my secret."

"You said you trusted me before. Why didn't you tell me sooner?"

He tilted his head and examined my face. "I've trusted you for a long time, but I didn't tell you because... well, you've never been," he waved at the grass blanket, "tied up or held down before. I knew you'd make a run for it if I told you any other time."

I snorted. "Fair enough."

H grinned at me, then frowned a little. "I should've told you before I let you go home by yourself. That was my mistake, and for that, I'm truly sorry."

"It wasn't your fault."

He took a deep breath. "Are you freaking out right now?"

"Only a little."

He smiled a little. "How are you feeling?"

"Sore, but not terrible."

He nodded and laid back down. "We'll stay out here tonight. I think it's best if you stay under there for a few more hours to heal your body."

"Why does grass help?"

He put his hands behind his head and turned it to face me. "Oh, right, I left that part out. My affinity is nature."

I just blinked at him.

"I get my power from nature, from all the living things around us and the elements that surround us. I use it for spells and hexes and everything."

"Hexes?"

"A hex is kind of like a spell, I guess, and can be literally anything as long as you have the right words. A spell is a lot more complicated and used for more complex situations. It usually requires more specific... ingredients, like gems and plants or whatever."

That was... too much for me to take in. "So you really were speaking snake?"

He barked out a laugh. "Not exactly. Animals don't communicate in the same way we do, but I can sense their intentions, and they can understand me. Sometimes they know human words if they've been around humans enough, so I pick up a stray thought of a word."

That sounded fucking insane. "That's how you knew his name was George?"

"Yep."

Oh shit. George likes to hunt in Ailin's back yard. He'd told me a million times.

Ailin laughed a little. "Don't worry, George knows to stay away until you're fully healed."

"So I'm not going to wake up with him in my face or on top of me or something?"

"No, I promise. You need your rest for healing, I won't let George interrupt that."

"Good." I yawned and felt sleep trying to pull me under even though I had so many questions for him, so many things I wanted to ask, wanted to know.

"Go to sleep, detective. Rest. I'll keep you safe, and you can ask me whatever you want in the morning."

I closed my eyes and settled into the surprisingly comfortable grass. Right before I nodded off, I jerked myself awake and looked at Ailin. "You'll be here when I wake up, right?"

He smiled. "I won't leave your side all night, I promise. I'll be right here."

I nodded and closed my eyes, settling back in.

"Goodnight, Sebastian."

"Goodnight, Ailin." I found myself falling asleep with contentment in my heart. Knowing Ailin would stay by my side made me feel safer and less lonely than I'd ever felt in my whole life.

***

As soon as I woke up, I turned my head to make sure that Ailin had kept his promise. Sure enough, he was lying there with his hands behind his head and a smirk on his face as he stared at the sky.

I looked down to find Sera stretching herself awake on my chest. She licked my chin, then jumped off my chest and trotted up to the house—no, not a house, a fucking mansion. How the hell did I miss that huge-ass place last night? I watched her for a few seconds, then looked up and squinted at the bright sun.

"She kept watch of you all night," Ailin said.

"She's sweet."

"She is. Feel any better?"

I took inventory of my body. My legs and arms felt okay, my stomach was fine, and my lungs were able to fill completely again. I moved my head back and forth, and it felt... okay. I felt completely healed. "I'm... good."

He rolled on his side and smiled at me. "Good." He brushed the hair off my forehead, and I closed my eyes as a warm sensation brushed my skin everywhere his fingers touched.

"Are you planning on letting me out of this... grass blanket?"

He chuckled. "I'm not sure. I kinda like you in this position."

My body flushed with sudden lust at such a simple statement. I felt my cheeks heating again. God, when did I start blushing this much? I cleared my throat. "Can you please release me?"

He smirked. "I don't know if I want to."

"Ailin."

"Sebastian." He said my name in the same tone as me and moved his face a little closer, mocking me.

"Come on, man. Let me go."

He laughed. "Fine, but just know that you're no fun."

I huffed and rolled my eyes.

Ailin put his hand on my chest and muttered under his breath. A second later, the grass blanket opened up, and I was finally able to move my limbs. Once it released me completely, I sat up and shook out my arms, brushing the grass off my body.

"Still feel okay? You're not woozy or anything, are you?"

"Yeah, I'm fine." I looked down at myself. I was shirtless, but still in my pants from the night before and they were completely ruined. They were ripped up and bloody, and I had dried blood caked on my chest. I rubbed my fingertips over the skin where the large chunk of wood had punctured my lung. There wasn't even a scar, my skin looked unmarked. I looked at my hand where the pentagram symbol had been, but it was gone, too.

"My shirt's gone." Of all the things I could've said, that was what my mouth went with.

"Sorry I couldn't save your shirt. I was more worried about your ability to breathe."

I turned to look at him. "Sorry, I didn't mean it that way, I'm just... I dunno, this is a lot to take in. You're really a witch. You healed me. You can't even tell I was stabbed."

He sat up and bent his knees, resting his elbows on them. He looked at me cautiously, and I suddenly felt guilty.

"Hey, I appreciate what you did for me."

He nodded, but didn't otherwise respond.

I didn't know what to do about that, so I stood up to stretch my arms and legs out, and I took a good look at my surroundings. There was a dirt road off to the right that was surrounded by a lush forest. Actually, we—and the house—were completely surrounded by a huge forest; we were simply in a break in the trees; a clearing. I took a closer look at the mansion, and all I could do was stare. The entire gigantic house was made up of trees. Not like wood, but *trees*. As in, trees and branches twisted every which way to form something that looked like it should be in a fairytale. A house of trees, he lived in a freaking house of trees. There were doorways and so many windows, I couldn't count them. At first, I thought that maybe it was a trick, but the closer I looked, the more it seemed that the trees were real and alive. *Ailin lives in a fucking tree-house. How is this even possible?*

I shook my head and turned away from it before I flipped out. I needed to stretch, so I walked back and forth in front of Ailin, circling my arms and shaking out my muscles. After a few minutes, I felt like my blood was pumping, so I asked, "Can we get something to eat?"

He eyed me for several seconds. "You're not afraid of me?"

My brow furrowed. "Why would I be afraid of you?"

He blew out a breath and picked up a loose piece of grass, playing with it in his fingers. "The last human I told flipped out and thought I was trying to kill him."

"I thought you weren't allowed to tell humans."

He glanced at me for a moment before focusing on the blade of grass. "One of those exceptions is if you find your... mate or if you take a lover, and you expect to be with them for a long time." *Mate? Is that just a weird supernatural name for a boyfriend or girlfriend?*

"You told your... girlfriend? Boyfriend? And they flipped out."

"That time it was a boyfriend. And yeah, he flipped out."

I sat down in front of him and ignored the flare of... *something*—hope?—at his admission that he'd dated a guy before—he was gay or bi, but that meant that... *no, stop that thought right there, Sebastian! You have zero chance with him! Like it's a good idea to date your partner, anyway.* "What did you do?"

He shrugged. "Broke up with him and stayed away, at his request."

"I'm sorry, Ailin."

He sent me a sad smile. "That's why I vowed to never date a human again."

And just like that, that little spark of hope was stamped out. But why did I even care? I'd never date him, he was too much of an ass.

We fell silent for a while, lost in our own thoughts, but Ailin looked at me and asked, "You're really not scared?"

I took a breath and decided to go with brutal honesty. "I was at first, but after I thought about everything that's happened over the past few weeks, I remembered that I could trust you, that you're a good person, and you'd never hurt me."

"I wouldn't. But you're not... freaked out?"

I shrugged. "Maybe a little, but I'm mostly overwhelmed and amazed. I want to learn more about your world."

We fell silent again, but after a long time, he whispered, "Thank you, Seb."

I sent him a smile. "You want to grab some food? I'm starving."

He smiled back. "A healing usually makes you hungry, and sometimes you need extra rest, so don't be surprised if all you want to do today is nap and eat."

"We have to work."

"Let's get some food and I'll drive to work. You can nap at the office if you need to."

He led me inside his house, and I was overwhelmed by it. Once inside, I realized that the entire house really was made of trees and other plants. There were vines covering some of the windows like curtains, and flowers decorating the rooms. There were chairs and couches that looked like they were made of moss, and light seemed to glow from some yellow flowers in every room we passed. I reached out and touched a couple leaves just to make sure they were real. They felt real, but I still couldn't believe it. Living plants were made into a functioning home. *How in the hell did he do all of this?*

"This place is amazing."

"Thanks. You can grab a shower while I make some breakfast. I already laid clothes out for you."

"When did you do that?" He hadn't left my side the entire time.

He grinned at me. "Magic, remember?"

My eyebrows lifted, but I nodded and headed to the bathroom he'd pointed out. Before I walked out of the kitchen, I asked, "Will your clothes even fit me?"

"Magic, Sebastian, magic."

With that, I headed to the bathroom. The awesome bathroom formed by a freaking huge-ass tree. When I stepped into the shower area, the water poured out of one of its branches without me turning anything on, and it just ran down through the floor. I didn't even see a drain. There was a big leaf holding a bar of soap and another holding a bottle of what I was guessing was shampoo. I washed and when I was finished and ready to get out, the shower turned off by itself. "So cool."

I dried off with a towel made out of soft fur or feathers or something. After getting dressed, I headed downstairs and found Ailin finishing up breakfast. Seraphina padded over to me and rubbed against my legs, so I picked her up and kissed her head, holding her to my chest. He smiled at me and gestured to a chair, so I sat on the wooden chair at the wooden table, and Sera climbed up on my shoulder, purring and rubbing against my neck.

He placed a plate in front of me with fruits and some weird looking mush stuff that I wasn't sure I could eat. But I was starving, so I picked up the fork and scooped some into my mouth. I was surprised by how flavorful it was, I'd been expecting it to taste like cardboard. I scooped in another bite. "What is this?"

Ailin smirked. "It's a secret family recipe made with sweet potatoes, but I can't tell you anything else."

"So I guess I can't get the recipe from you, huh?"

"Never. My mom made me swear an oath."

I narrowed my eyes at him, then chuckled. "Liar."

He grinned. "I just threw some stuff together that my sister left in the fridge." He ate a bite of his own.

"It's good."

Once we finished eating, I felt like I was going to pass out, so Ailin suggested that he drive us to the office so I could nap in the car. When I agreed, I hadn't known he'd driven my car without permission last night to get me here—not that it mattered since he'd saved my life, but just to be a pain in his ass, I grumbled when I climbed into the passenger seat with Sera on my lap.

I fell asleep before he'd even started the car.

"Seb, we're here."

I groaned at the sound of Ailin's voice.

"I've let you sleep as long as I could, but we need to head inside."

I groaned and rubbed my face. "Ugh. I want a bed."

He chuckled. "Come on, I'll help you get inside. You can sleep in your office once we get there, but Alec needs to know what's going on."

"There's nowhere to sleep in there."

"There is now. I put a futon in your office."

I glanced at him. "When the hell did you do that?"

"Actually, I had my brother do it last night. I knew you'd be tired today, and I didn't want to leave when you were still healing, so Basil did it." He laughed a little. "He was excited to break into the station, too."

I huffed out a laugh. "You're a bad influence."

"Probably."

I shook my head and got out of the car with a sigh and Sera on my shoulder. "Where's George? I expected to see him this morning."

"He didn't want to upset you, so he stayed away."

I shrugged and went straight to my office, then spread out on the futon. I was asleep before Ailin pulled the door shut.

Chapter Seven

The whole day was pretty much a bust. Well, except that I'd slept so much, I was feeling energized now. Right before we'd given up hope of finding anything, Ailin's phone rang.

"What's up?" he said into his phone. There was a long pause. "Shit. Okay, give me the coordinates." Another pause. "We'll be there as soon as we can. Keep it secure until I call you." He waited a beat before hanging up and looking at me. "My brother found another dead girl drained of blood out in the Kokulm Woods. He picked up a strange energy coming from there earlier, so he went to check it out. We have to go check it out. It's a fresh kill, so the demon could still be close by."

I nodded. "Alright, let's go." I stood and grabbed my gun, putting on the holster and securing it before picking up Sera and putting her on my shoulder. The cute kitten hadn't left my side since we'd arrived this morning.

"I have something for you." Ailin pulled out a box and passed it over. "Your bullets won't harm the demon, but these have light energy mixed with iron. They'll be able to slow him down. It isn't likely that you'll be able to kill him with these, but at least it'll serve as some protection."

I examined the box of bullets, then unloaded my regular bullets from the clip and replaced them with the demon ones. I was trusting Ailin with this completely. "If these won't kill it, what will?"

"Demons are nearly impossible to kill. The most we can hope for is sending it back to hell where it belongs. I'll have to use a spell for that. If you manage to injure it, I might be able to capture it and send it home."

"Are you saying that hell is real?" I felt like my eyes were gonna bug out of my head.

"Yes, but not in the way you're thinking. There are... different realms that some supes have access to. One of the realms is the demon realm. It's dark and on fire in many places. That's where humans came up with the whole hell thing. If demons didn't come here to kill innocents, they'd be welcome to stay, but unfortunately, every demon I've ever come across has only had one thing in mind; kill innocents and become more powerful."

There were no words for that.

Ailin stared at me for a few seconds. "It's not like people's souls go to the demon realm when they die. Or at least, I don't think they do."

I absorbed what he was saying, then shook my head. I felt like I'd never be able to grasp just how big this... paranormal world really was. "Does that mean angels are based off of a... heaven realm?"

"If there are angels out there, I've never met one, but it's possible."

I nodded, completely overwhelmed. I didn't even know where to start with this shit.

"If you're uncomfortable with this, you don't have to come with me."

My brow furrowed. "Of course, I'm coming with you. I'm not letting you face this thing alone, A." Apparently, I'd given him a nickname. Whatever. It worked.

He smiled, just a little. "I'll drive. You can rest until we get there."

"I've been resting all damn day."

"Trust me. Your body still needs the rest. You were... almost dead when I got to you."

I cringed a little and nodded. "Fine." I threw him my keys, and he grinned at me before walking out of the office with me trailing behind him.

We drove for an hour to Kokulm Woods, and when he pulled the car off the road, parking it along the tree line, he pulled out his phone and made a call. "Yeah, we're here, you're good to go. I'll see you later."

"Who was that?" I asked as I grabbed Sera off my lap. "Should Sera stay in the car?"

"That was my brother. He's going to head out to see if he can pick up the demon's trail again. And no, don't leave her in the car."

I nodded and got out, then followed Ailin into the woods—again. "Is there a reason this... demon has been killing the girls in different places? Sometimes he does it in a house and other times in the woods."

"I think he might be making a large pentagram, but I'm not sure. We'll have to get a map and mark all the places the bodies were found."

"Aren't there way too many bodies for that to make sense?"

He grimaced a little. "Not if it's been using the blood of its victims to fill in all the open spaces as well as the points and intersections. You know how you see a pentagram with the star in the middle and a circle around it?" I nodded. "Well, depending on its end game, it may be using the girls in the open spaces and the points. A few of the symbols we found at the crime scenes were a little different from each other. I'll have to draw it out and see if I recognize what spell it's working."

I didn't like the sound of that.

"Whatever it is, it's nothing good."

I nodded and looked around, a little uneasy. What if this demon was still in the area?

"I'll feel him approaching before he can reach you, Seb. You have nothing to worry about. I don't feel his slimy energy here."

"O-okay." I continued to look around before something caught my eye. I blinked a few times as I saw a giant black creature fly out of the trees up ahead, then right over the top of us. I actually ducked when it flew over us. *What in the hell was that?* "Did you see that? What was that thing?" I'd never seen a bird that big before.

"It was just a heron or something, probably."

I narrowed my eyes at him because I had the feeling he was lying. "What was that thing?"

He huffed. "Nothing you need to concern yourself with. It's not evil and has zero intention to cause you or anyone else any harm."

"And how the hell do you know that?"

"I'm a witch, Sebastian. I know things."

I narrowed my eyes again. "You're not going to be able to use that to win every argument."

He laughed. "Trust me, I know."

I shook my head at him with a reluctant smile, but we both sobered when we reached the poor girl's body. It was exactly the same as the rest with symbols under her body and carved into her skin, and I assumed the poor girl had been drained of blood, too. This demon was a sick bastard.

Ailin did his weird voodoo shit by putting his hands on the girl's head and chanting, so I walked around the scene to see if there was anything else that could help us. Although, I really didn't have a clue what to look for at this point. What did one look for when it was a demon murdering people?

I walked over and knelt beside a tree where a few stones were sitting at the bottom. Were they a part of this ritual or were they there before the demon got there?

"I picked up part of his essence still on the body. He drank most of her blood, but harvested some for later use."

I wrinkled my nose. "That has to be the most disgusting sentence to come out of your mouth."

He shrugged. "It has four more bodies it needs to collect before its ritual is complete."

"You picked all that up from the dead girl?"

"Yeah, but I couldn't tell what ritual it's performing or why, but I have a feeling that there's a bigger plan in place that we're not seeing yet. Did you find anything?"

I pointed to the stones. "I'm not sure if these mean anything to you or not, but this is the only unusual thing I found." I reached down to pick one up as Sera hissed loudly in my ear.

"Wait, don't touch that!"

I heard Ailin's warning—again—but it was too late.

The stone zapped my hand, but this time I was able to let go before it burned me and the stupid stone fell to the ground.

"What is with you picking shit up? Didn't you learn anything last time?" Ailin knelt beside me and grabbed my hand. "I shot out some energy to knock it out of your hand before it could take hold of you." He brushed his fingers over my hand where the pentagram had been before he healed me, and luckily, there were no new marks. "It looks like I got it in time." He looked me straight in the eyes. "I know that the pull can be strong, but you need to fight it when you feel an object pulling you to touch it."

I nodded. "I don't know what's wrong with me. I know better than to touch shit at a crime scene."

"It's not your fault. That jewel the other day had a strong curse on it, and these stones do, too. They lure you in so they can mark you. I just need you to try to be more careful."

"What does that mean?"

He cringed. "The jewel marked you, so the demon will be able to find you wherever you go."

"I... I'm gonna be chased by a demon my whole life?"

"No, Seb. We're going to send it back to hell where it belongs. Once it leaves our realm, the curse will be broken."

My chest heaved. *Oh my god.* "Are you saying that the stupid red gem is the reason it came after me?"

"Yes. You're on its radar now."

That statement sent a chill of fear through my body. Having a demon hunt me was completely terrifying.

"I won't let him get to you again, Seb."

The intensity of Ailin's stare made me uncomfortable, so I nodded and stood, putting some space between us. Ailin made a weird face, then pulled a little pouch out of his pocket. "Take this and keep it in your pocket. It should help fight against the pull." He shoved it in my hand. "Worrying won't do you any good, and you have me on your side. You'll be okay. I promise."

"Thank you, Ailin." I took the pouch and held it up to my nose for a second, surprised that it smelled minty, then I shoved it in my back pocket.

"Give me a minute to wipe the stones free of all spells so other humans aren't compelled to touch them. We don't need this demon breaking into anyone else's apartment and trying to kill them." He knelt down again and examined the stones. I watched as he chanted away, but then he cut himself off and looked up sharply.

He slowly stood and turned away from the tree. "Brace yourself, Seb. It found us. Stay right behind me."

I drew my weapon and looked everywhere, but couldn't see anything. When Ailin took a few steps forward, I followed right behind him. I wasn't sure how close he wanted me to stay, but I figured he'd tell me to back up if I needed to.

The ground rumbled under our feet, shaking like something huge was coming at us. I saw a red light in the distance through the trees, but it was getting closer and closer until it finally stopped fifteen feet away from us. It was like a red gas swirling around. It had no solidity, but it carried such a strong evil energy, I could feel it from where I stood, and my hands began to shake a little as I aimed my gun. But what good would a gun do against gas?

The red gas spoke, "We meet again, Sebastian." Hearing it say my name made a shiver rack my whole body. *Why the hell is it talking to me?* "Seems we have some unfinished business left."

The gas suddenly solidified, forming into an eight-foot tall red creature with huge black horns and eyes that were endless pools of black—creepy as fuck. It had black talons on the ends of its red fingers. It moved one of its huge muscular red arms through the air, and a force of energy hit me like a ton of bricks, sending me flying backward until I hit a tree. I coughed and wheezed, trying to pull air into my lungs. Sera had flown off my shoulder, but I could hardly see anything that was going on. *Sera?* Luckily, I hadn't let go of my gun, so I aimed it in the direction I thought the demon stood even though I could hardly see. *Is Sera okay? Ailin?*

"Your fight is with me, demon," Ailin yelled, gaining the petrifying creature's attention.

"Sera?" I rasped out and heard a little meow close to my feet in response. She shook out her head and sneezed, but otherwise looked unharmed, thank god.

"Don't move, Seb!" Ailin yelled before muttering something I didn't understand and throwing his arm out in my direction. Suddenly, a green haze surrounded Sera and me, like we were stuck inside a translucent green bubble. I squinted through the bubble and saw Ailin surrounded by a green energy that looked like it was radiating off his skin. "Stay inside the protection shield," Ailin shouted to me, sounding out of breath. "Sera, protect him."

The kitten hissed and walked to the front of the bubble, watching her owner and the red demon fighting. What Ailin thought a small kitten could do, I didn't know, but maybe he just wanted to acknowledge her since he'd locked her in with me.

I tried to keep up with the fight, but it was hard to see what was going on with the green and red sparks shooting in every direction. The ground was rumbling as Ailin shot energy balls at the demon. At least, that was what they looked like. Unfortunately, they kept bouncing off the demon's hide. The demon was shooting its own red energy balls at Ailin, but Ailin evaded them or shot them with his energy or somehow made them dissipate before they reached him. The trees around us were getting burnt, and when the demon sent a huge ball at Ailin, and Ailin redirected it, one of the trees split in half. Thank god Ailin had been able to push it out of the way. I didn't even want to think about what would've happened if it had hit him.

I lifted my gun and aimed for the demon, but Ailin was in the way, and I wasn't sure what would happen to this weird bubble if I shot a bullet at it.

The demon suddenly flew at me. I put my hands up in front of my face and prepared to take a hit, but the demon crashed into Ailin's bubble. It banged and punched, but it couldn't get through. The demon turned back into its weird gassy substance and surrounded the entire bubble. I turned my head back and forth, trying to figure out what to do, but the red gas was everywhere I looked. Sera was hissing at my feet as the demon shook the bubble rigorously, and I was afraid that the gas was going to find a way inside the bubble, but suddenly, there was a flash of blinding light and a loud roar. I closed my eyes and hunched over Sera, tucking my head down to protect us both from the assault, expecting the bubble to burst. I heard a loud hiss and Ailin's voice in the background, but everything was so loud, I couldn't pick out individual words.

I opened my eyes at the sound of another loud hiss. The demon's red gas was swirling around the bubble, but through it, I could see Ailin surrounded by his green energy with his palms out and green light shooting from them. The demon hissed again, then suddenly flew through the air. Before it flew from my sight, I heard its voice in my head whispering, *"I will have you Sebastian Cooper Fitz, your Sage cannot protect you forever."*

I shivered at the strange feeling of having that thing's voice in my head, and chills popped out on my skin as I began to shake with fear. I couldn't get enough air in my lungs. *Get out of my head!*

"*You belong to me now, Sebastian. I will have your blood. I will have your soul.*"

I couldn't breathe. It was going to take me, kill me. That thing's voice was the creepiest thing I'd ever heard. When it was finally out of sight, I blew out a breath and sagged down until I was kneeling on the ground, and I could pull Sera into my arms. The cat meowed at me and snuggled into my neck.

Ailin ran over and placed his hand on the bubble. After a few seconds, the bubble disappeared into a light mist that drifted away on the wind. Ailin walked closer and knelt in front of me. He gently cupped my cheeks so I'd look him in the eyes, and he searched my face as his hands generated a warmth on my skin that tingled from his palms over my face and scalp, then over my entire body. He was healing my scrapes and bruises from being thrown against the tree.

When I closed my eyes and savored the feeling, Ailin whispered, "What am I going to do with you, fragile human?" Then he pulled my shaky body toward him and pushed me to rest my forehead on his shoulder. He rubbed my back. "Shh, it's okay. He's gone now. I injured it enough that it will need time to regenerate. I won't let anything happen to you."

I nodded and Sera jumped off me as Ailin pulled me even closer, and I wrapped my arms around his waist. I wasn't happy that he'd had to protect me, but I couldn't deny the fact that I wasn't equipped to take out a fucking demon. So I had to set aside my pride and appreciate the fact that Ailin cared enough to make sure I was okay.

He hugged me for way longer than was strictly necessary, but we'd already moved past what was normal, so I didn't pull away. The longer we stayed like that, the more something settled in my chest until finally, I felt okay enough to deal with everything.

Ailin and I parted, and I stood up right away, not really wanting to look him in the eyes after that.

Ailin got up a little slower and picked Sera up, whispering to her before he said to me, "I'll call in the body to the local station. There'll be less questions if I do it."

I nodded and busied myself with checking my gun and promising myself that I'd get at least one shot in the next time the stupid demon found us. I heard Ailin making the phone call as Sera trotted over to me, so I scooped her up again and walked to a tree to lean against it and wait.

When he hung up the phone, he said, "Don't say anything about the demon, obviously. Just tell them our serial killer led us to this place, and we found the body when we arrived. They'll pack up the body and the rest of the evidence and send it down to us, so we can take a closer look once our coroner sees her."

I nodded. Of course, he'd be able to pull strings and have the body sent to our coroner.

Ailin and I were silent for the entire twenty minutes it took the locals to find us, and once they were there, I was able to avoid talking to him since we were both busy being interviewed. Unfortunately, it took us a few hours to get everything under wraps, and I was so not looking forward to the drive home.

While Ailin and I walked to our car with Sera riding on my shoulder, Ailin said, "Let's get a hotel for the night. It's dark and we're both worn out and need to replenish our energies."

"We're not that far away from home. You don't need to baby me, Ailin."

"I'm not. I'm wiped out, too, so I'd rather drive the three minutes to the hotel than the sixty back home. It's dark, I'm tired, you're tired, and there's a hotel three miles down the road."

I eyed him for a minute and realized that he really did look tired, so with a sigh I agreed, "Fine."

We walked the rest of the way in silence, and when we got to the car, I didn't argue when he wanted to drive again. Arguing with him took way too much energy, and I didn't want to talk to him, anyway. We checked in, then made our way up to our room. I was so tired, I didn't even think twice about stripping off my jeans, putting my holster and gun on the nightstand, and climbing into bed as soon as we walked in. Sera jumped on my bed and settled on my pillow as I pulled the blanket up. Ailin eyed me for a few seconds before taking off his pants—he even had tattoos on his legs!—taking off his arm bracers, and climbing into his own bed. He flicked his fingers and the lights went out.

After lying in the dark for several minutes, I whispered, "Ailin?"

"Yeah?" His voice sounded a little hoarse.

"Thank you for saving my life... again."

"Anytime." He shifted on his bed. "Get some sleep, detective."

"G'night."

***

"Sebastian."

I looked around the dark room, but didn't see anyone.

"Sebastian."

I sat up. "Who's there?"

An eerie laugh filled the room and my heart raced. I looked at Ailin's bed, but he wasn't there. *Where the hell did he go?* I looked for Sera, but she was missing also.

"Wh-what do you want?" My voice was barely a whisper. The laugh got louder, so I reached for my gun and aimed it toward the door. I didn't see anyone or any*thing* in my room, but I knew it was coming. I got out of bed and walked to the door. "I will kill you, demon."

The demon's voice tsked at me. "You can't harm me, Sebastian Cooper Fitz."

"What do you want?" My voice was a little stronger even though I was growing more and more terrified. Where the hell was Ailin? "What did you do to Ailin?" I put my hand on the doorknob and quickly opened it, hoping to take it by surprise, but no one was there. I looked up and down the hallway, but couldn't see anything, so I walked down the hall toward the voice. "Where is he?"

It laughed again, and I felt a breeze brush across my face. "You would so easily give up your life for a witch? After what his people did to yours?" It tsked again. "I thought your kind learned their lesson long ago, but they say old habits die hard."

"Give him back to me."

"I didn't take your precious witch. He left you, like all of the others."

"I won't fall for your mind games, demon. Give him back, and maybe I'll make your death swift."

It laughed. "Big words for such a terrified man." There was a huge gust of wind and a red light so bright I had to squint. The light rushed at me, and a red face with black endless eyes and black horns popped up in front of me. "Boo."

I shot my gun six times, but the demon only laughed and laughed, and when my gun ran out of bullets, it opened its mouth revealing an endless depth of black coming straight at me like it wanted to swallow me whole. I looked around for something to block myself with, but I was only surrounded by a long hallway, there was nothing there to help.

The demon rushed forward and grabbed ahold of my arms, making my skin burn like it was pouring lava on me. I screamed out, and suddenly, my arms erupted into huge flames. I screamed and screamed as the flames spread over my body, engulfing me whole as the demon held me, and its endless depths began to surround me. I was going to die, it was going to take my soul.

"There's nowhere you can hide that will keep you safe from me, Sebastian."

"Sebastian."

I heard another voice, but the pain was so severe I couldn't grasp on to it.

"Sebastian!"

I snapped my eyes open and gasped in a much-needed breath.

"You're okay, Seb."

I blinked, taking in the dark room. I looked down at myself and saw that I wasn't on fire; I was twisted in my sheets. I looked over and saw Ailin kneeling beside my bed with a worried expression. The demon hadn't gotten him. Thank god he was safe. I gasped in a few more breaths and put my hands over my eyes as I rolled onto my back. It was a dream. *It was just a fucked-up nightmare.*

"You're safe, Seb. He's not here."

I nodded, but didn't uncover my face. I couldn't even remember the last time a nightmare had gotten me so worked up. "It was just a nightmare."

"I know."

"Sorry I woke you, A."

"It's okay."

I felt the bed dip beside me, so I dropped my hands and looked at Ailin with wide eyes. He'd crawled into my bed and was lying beside me. "It's okay," he whispered as he slowly put his palm in the center of my chest. A tingly feeling spread under his palm and slowly fizzled out to the rest of my body. Ailin smiled at me and laid his head on the edge of my pillow so his face was close to mine. Sera tucked herself on my chest between Ailin's hand and my neck, nuzzling against me. Ailin scooted a little until his chest was against my arm. "Go back to sleep."

I was so shocked by his actions, that I simply nodded and closed my eyes.

It was a long time before I fell back asleep. It was weird having him so close, but I couldn't deny how nice it felt. No one had ever comforted me after having a nightmare. I'd had them—a lot—growing up. Usually when I'd wake up screaming, one of the wardens would punish me as if I'd given myself the nightmares on purpose. I spent a lot of time in solitary at the Academy. It wasn't a good place to be when you were a terrified five-year-old kid.

Ailin scooted close enough that his entire body and legs were pressed against my side. After a long time I settled into him, and I finally fell asleep.

Chapter Eight

Ailin was already showered and dressed by the time I woke up, and I couldn't help but wonder if he'd stayed in my bed all night or if he'd gotten up and moved back to his own bed. For some reason, I kinda liked the idea of him staying close to me all night. He'd even ordered breakfast and surprised me by bringing me a plate filled with food—even meat—as soon as I woke up; he'd brought me breakfast in bed. That was maybe the nicest thing anyone had ever done for me.

As soon as I had the thought, Ailin froze and frowned at me, but luckily, he didn't say anything about whatever was bothering him.

"I've been thinking about a spell I might be able to use to track the demon." Ailin was on his own bed, eating his food, not looking at me.

"Uh, okay."

"We've dealt with demons countless times, but a kuma mali is a lot stronger than your everyday, average demon. The fact that he's been here for so long and already made so many sacrifices means that he's probably the strongest demon I've ever seen myself. Normally, I can take one out without assistance, but I might need to gather some stones and possibly ask my sister if she can come vanquish it with me."

"And what am I supposed to do?"

"If I had it my way, I'd leave you on my property where I know you'll be safe since our lands are well warded and guarded by our Bonded Ones, but I know you won't stay there."

"There were so many parts of that sentence I didn't understand, but... it's way too early for me to comprehend any of that, and I got the general gist. No, I won't stay there while you're out there fighting a demon. Is there anything I can do to make it harder for it to knock me over? Some kind of shield or something?" *God, what am I even saying right now?*

"Actually, that's a good idea. I cou—" He was cut off by his phone ringing. "It's Alec. Let me see what he wants real quick."

I nodded as he took the call from my chief, and I ate a few bites of my food while I listened to Ailin's side of the conversation.

"Whoa, whoa, whoa. Slow down, Al." Ailin looked at me with a furrowed brow. "Sebastian is right here with me." He tilted his head. "Yes, I'm looking at him right now. He slept with me last night." Ailin waggled his eyebrows at me, and I choked on a slice of bacon. *Oh my god! The chief is going to think I slept with my partner—with his brother-in-law!*

Ailin smirked at me, but as he listened to the chief on the other end, his smirk turned into a frown, then turned into a look of concern aimed right at me. I mouthed *what?* But he just kept looking at me until he said, "Don't touch anything else. Get your people out of there right now. Your DNA test will have to wait until after I examine the body and the scene. We'll get on the road just as soon as Seb has time to eat and shower. We're an hour away, but I can make the trip faster if I use a siren. Just... keep it locked down. No one else in or out, Al. I mean it."

Ailin hung up the phone and stared at me with wide eyes. "The demon... broke into your apartment again last night, and it murdered a man that matches your description. Same hair, skin, height, weight. But the demon... mutilated his face, so everyone thought it was you. The victim was found naked in your bed, clearly tortured, possibly raped." Ailin stared at me with very intense eyes. "It seems the demon caught your scent, Seb, and it's not going to stop until it finds you."

I shivered at the implication. "Let me jump in the shower so we can go."

"You need to finish eating first."

There was no way in hell I could finish eating now. "I'm full."

Ailin frowned, but didn't stop me from rushing into the bathroom. After showering, I found my clothes I'd just taken off folded neatly on the counter, looking clean and smelling fresh. I shook my head in amazement at Ailin's magic and got dressed, and when I came out, we checked out, then got in my car. Ailin drove again. I was officially annoyed, but I only grumbled a little at him. His excuse was that I had to be healed two days in a row, so my body needed the extra rest. Not that I was able to sleep with the damn siren blaring the whole time.

When we got to my apartment, I wasn't surprised to see so many of my coworkers there, but I was surprised by how many back slaps and hugs I received. It was almost like they'd really been worried about me.

My bedroom was a disaster. There were still wood chips and shit from the other night, only now, everything was covered in blood. I cringed when I looked at my bed. The body was... just so mangled and torn up, and it was really easy to see why everyone had thought it was me. This demon had gone out of its way to find someone that could easily pass for me, and he'd tortured him. This poor, innocent man was tortured, likely raped, and murdered because of me.

I felt bile rise to the surface as I thought about what this man's last moments had been like, and the fact that it was my fault. I tried to hold it back, but it came anyway. I pushed past Ailin and ran into my bathroom to empty the contents of my stomach into the toilet. Ailin followed me inside and shut the door. I wanted to yell at him to leave, but I was too busy hanging over the toilet.

Ailin surprised me by rubbing my back while I took deep breaths and tried to settle my stomach. His warm touch helped. I couldn't tell if he was using magic to calm me, or if it was the simple, kind touch, but my stomach settled down. He walked to the sink and grabbed a little cup I had sitting there, filled it with water, and handed it back to me.

"Thanks." I took a couple small sips. "That guy in there is dead because of me."

"No, Seb, not because of you. He died because a demon killed him. That isn't your fault."

I glanced at him, then away. "He died because the demon is after me. He died because I wasn't here, and he was. He died because of me."

Ailin stepped closer to me, grabbed the cup out of my hand to set it on the counter, then he placed both hands on my neck with his thumbs on my jaw, forcing me to look at him. "That isn't your fault, detective. You can't control what anyone else does. You can't control a damn demon." His green eyes flashed, and I suddenly realized he was having trouble keeping his energy in control.

I didn't exactly agree with him, but I didn't want him upset, so I nodded. "You okay?"

He took a deep breath. "I'm not sure. I'm… concerned with the level of obsession this demon has for you. I don't want anything to happen to you. I'm… not leaving you alone until this threat is contained." He squeezed my neck before letting go. "Go ahead and brush your teeth so we can examine the body before we get going."

I nodded, but frowned a little at the loss of his warmth when he backed away.

We finally finished up at the crime scene, so Ailin and I headed back to the station to see if the coroner had any new information on the body we'd discovered last night. The body count for this case was rising every time we turned around. Of course, she hadn't had time to examine the body yet, but Ailin was able to convince her to push our victim to the front of the line, so hopefully, we'd hear from her soon. Not that we expected much to go on, but we'd take anything we could get. We needed to figure out where this creature's home base was.

***

"I know you hate this, but you *have* to go and make nice with these people, Ailin. You've made me do it the last three times. I can't do it this time," Chief Gillman said as he paced my office. "You know how these people get. And they found out about the demon, they're threatening to contact the Supreme Assembly themselves. I need y—"

"They're what?" Ailin's tone was chilling.

My boss cringed. "They think we're hiding something. That officer from the other day? He's the son of one of the Lords of Brinnswick. He wants blood, A, and he's willing to go over your head to get it. You know he's scared of you and your power. He'll use this to his advantage if he can."

I frowned. The Lords of Brinnswick were made up of members of the founding families, and they ran the entire country.

Ailin's jaw ticked. "Which lord is it?"

Chief Gillman winced. "Uh, Lord Damian Schurlz."

"I *hate* that guy," Ailin muttered, then glanced at me. "Want to be my date to some stupid-ass dinner party?"

My eyebrows rose on my forehead. He didn't really mean he wanted me as a date, right? It was just a figure of speech. "Sure."

He smirked at me and waggled his eyebrows. "You know what usually happens *after* a date, don't you?"

My eyes widened, and my cheeks flamed, but Chief Gillman shook his head and looked at Ailin. "You're a pain in the ass, you know that?" Ailin grinned at him, and the chief looked at me. "I don't know how you deal with him for such long periods of time. He's been making me crazy for years. I can only handle him in small doses."

Ailin snickered, and I shrugged. "You're the one that assigned him to me."

Chief Gillman chuckled. "Only to get him out of my hair."

"Asshole," Ailin said with a laugh.

I snorted.

The chief sobered. "Okay, you don't have to stay for long, but I need you to convince them not to bring the Supreme Assembly into this. You know the others have been trying to knock you out of your position since you took it."

I was so confused. "Wait, what position?"

Ailin looked at me and sighed. "The Supreme Assembly takes care of all supernatural crimes around the world. They try to protect humans from evil beings and from finding out our secrets. I'm the Representative of Brinnswick. Nearly everyone else is a douche."

"So you're like... a government official?"

"Yeah, I guess. It's not like I want to be, but it's better than having someone that doesn't care whether or not humans live or die." He shrugged like it wasn't a big deal, but it very clearly was. There was so much more to him than meets the eye. "If I call the other members to come help, there's going to be a lot of political issues that we don't want to deal with. Most of the others aren't very happy that I'm working with the human government." He glanced at Alec with a tiny smile. "They don't appreciate everything that Alec and I have built here over the years. Plus, most of them want to kill me."

"Why?"

"Everyone wants to kill him," Chief muttered.

"Very helpful, Al. They don't take kindly to having some kid more powerful than they are save their asses from a fucking invasion."

"Invasion? Invasion of what?"

He waved me away. "Not important. What time are they meeting, Alec?"

"Six."

"Okay, I'll keep working on this tracking spell, and Seb can figure out where our next victim will be killed until then."

***

While I was reading over one of Ailin's books, I came across some weird information on warlocks I didn't understand, so I'd spent at least ten minutes asking Ailin about it, and every time I asked him a question, he was getting more and more pissed. So I kept asking. "Why is your spell book talking about warlocks like they're bad?"

"Because they're evil bastards that deserve to die."

I wrinkled my nose at him. "But... what do you mean they're evil?"

Ailin looked unreasonably angry. "They're a bunch of assholes, Seb. Just drop it."

"Why are you freaking out about warlocks? You're a warlock."

"I'm a witch, Seb. Get that through your fucking head."

Wow. Asshole, much? "I thought witches were girls and warlocks were guys?" *Why the hell is he so worked up over this?*

"Mother, help me, fuck. Why do humans always think that? Most warlocks are evil, demented, old bastards that turn green from letting demons and spirits pass through their bodies and out into the world. Do I look green and demented to you?" he shouted at me.

Wow. Just wow. "Well, you don't look green, but you don't want me to answer the demented part." I smirked at him.

Ailin narrowed his eyes and started mumbling in another language. When he stopped, he shot me that stupid cocky smile of his.

I stared at him for a second before gasping. "Did you just hex me?"

The cocky smile remained. "Yes, yes I did."

"Are you fucking serious?" I asked, exasperated. "What did you do?"

His smile turned into a grin. "For the next twenty-four hours everything you eat will taste like sour apples."

"Are you fucking kidding me? We're going to that dinner tonight! Chief said they're gonna have lobster!"

"I know." The stupid bastard sent me a cocky smirk.

I narrowed my eyes, trying to figure out how to take him by surprise.

Ailin tilted his head. "Don't even try it or I'll make it forty-eight hours."

"I hate you."

He winked at me. "No, you don't. I gotta grab a drink." Then he turned and walked out the door.

I grabbed my pen cup and chucked it at him, but he moved out of the way even though his back was to me. As my door started shutting by itself, I shouted, "I'll get you back, dickhead!"

"Uh huh, I'm sure you will," he said lazily just as the door shut behind him.

Fucking bastard.

I plopped in my seat and opened up my top desk drawer, pulling out a chocolate bar. I unwrapped it with a deep breath and took a bite. As soon as it hit my tongue, I started gagging and spit it out into my trashcan. I shuddered at the disgusting taste of sour apples. I took a sip of my water, silently thankful for it tasting normal. After I gurgled and spit a few times, I yelled, knowing he'd hear me no matter where he was in the building, "I'm going to fucking kill you, Ellwood!"

I could hear him chuckling somewhere outside my office. He was a dead man.

He walked back into the office with some papers and a smirk.

I pointed at him. "You're a huge asshole. I'm going to be pissed at you for eternity if you don't fix this."

One side of his mouth lifted. "I wouldn't want that, now would I?" He muttered under his breath, and I felt a weird little rush over my body.

"Is it gone?"

"Yes, detective, you're fine. But you're no fun."

"Don't hex me anymore."

He waved me off as he sat down.

I rolled my eyes and hesitantly took a bite of my chocolate bar. When it hit my tongue, I cringed, but realized it tasted normal, so I sighed and chewed it. I grabbed another chocolate bar. "Want one?"

He grinned at me. "I'm good, Seb."

I shrugged and threw it back in my drawer.

Shouts came from out on the floor, and Ailin and I exchanged a look, then jumped to our feet. I drew my weapon that was now infused with earth magic bullets, and Ailin had a green ball of energy at his fingertips as he threw open our office door.

I took in the scene before us. Everyone was on their feet, and Darren Thompal was shouting and running, looking at the floor, then Anita Long screeched and jumped on her desk. The others were taking the high ground, too, jumping on their chairs and desks and keeping their feet off the floor.

Ailin dropped his hand and the green ball dissipated—no one saw since they were too busy scrambling—so I lowered my weapon and whispered, "Are they screaming because of a... rat?"

Ailin nodded and walked out the door toward the commotion.

Anita yelled, "It ran right over the rat trap, and the stupid thing didn't go off. Someone kill it!"

Ailin shouted, "No one harm the animal."

I wrinkled my nose. *Not again.* "A, it's vermin. They're gross and can make you sick."

Ailin looked at me. "She's not sick; she's just a lost rat searching for food."

I followed him over. Anita, Darren Thompal, and Walter Madler each had something heavy in their hands as they cornered it. The rat was trying to find a way out, but was pressed up against the wall, blocked off completely. Ailin pushed through the detectives and squatted down in front of the vermin.

He calmly said, "You three hurt her, and I'll hurt you." His voice was calm and quiet, but something about it was cold. It made me shiver, and if I'd been in their shoes, I would've been afraid he'd go through with that threat. As it were, I knew he was full of shit. Although, I knew he'd protect that damn rat from them.

The three of them all lowered their weapons and took a small step back.

Ailin held his hand out and whispered to the rat, "You're okay. You're safe."

The rat took a small step toward him.

"Ailin," I said in a quiet voice. "Do not pick up the rat."

"She needs protection."

I sighed and shook my head. "No one will hurt her. Just let her go back to wherever she came from."

Ailin looked at me over his shoulder. "She's lonely."

"Seriously? *Again*?"

"She's all alone, Seb, what do you want me to do?"

"Don't touch the rat, Ailin."

He shrugged and whispered under his breath. A second later the rat scurried over and crawled onto Ailin's hand. Everyone around me—including me—groaned in disgust. How could he touch that thing? It was so gross. It probably came out of the trash.

Ailin stood and held the rat close to his face. "You're a cutie."

"Don't kiss the rat, Ailin. For the love of god, do not put your mouth on that rat!"

Ailin grinned at me with that gleam of mischief in his eyes, then puckered his lips and kissed the rat on her head. Everyone groaned in disgust again.

"You're so fucking gross, man."

Ailin shrugged at me and headed back to our office with the rat in hand. I sighed, shook my head, lifted a shoulder at the others, and followed behind him. Once I shut the door, I asked, "Does your new pet have a name?"

"Matilda."

I nodded. "Okay, then. Keep it off my desk and off of my things. It's gross."

Ailin lifted a brow at me, but didn't comment.

"I won't even bother to remind you that animals aren't allowed in my car because I know you'll just bring her in anyway or convince me somehow or… wait. Do you spell me to agree with you?"

"What?"

"Do you cast spells or whatever on me to make me agree with you or change my mind or something? Is that why I let you bring Sera and George in my car?"

He sighed and kissed the rat on the nose before letting it crawl up his arm to his shoulder. "I don't spell your mind, Sebastian. I'm not that much of a jerkface."

I narrowed my eyes at him. "I don't know if I believe you."

His eyes hardened. "I would never do that to you."

I think I believe him. Whether it was because he did weird voodoo on me or he was just really convincing, I wasn't sure. But I knew deep down that I trusted him.

"I trust you, too, Seb. Are you ready to go to the dinner?"

"Only if you leave the rat here."

"Not a chance."

"You really are a buttface."

He grinned. "Matilda needs a friend, so here I am."

"Whatever you say, witchface."

He tilted his head and eyed me. "Did you just call me 'witchface'?"

I grinned. "It just came out."

He snorted and shook his head. "Let's go see if we can convince these people not to call the assembly. Maybe our job will be easy tonight, and we'll even get to enjoy some free food."

"With our track record? I very much doubt it."

He set the rat on my desk and shrugged at me with a smirk—jerkface—then grabbed his jacket and threw it on. He held his arm out, and the damn rat crawled right up it. Blech.

"Ready to be my plus one?"

"As I'll ever be."

We headed out the door. I let Ailin drive this time because I didn't know where I was going since it was some weird secret banquet hall place, and only the *it* crowd knew about it. Ailin told me, obviously, but I'd never been there, so this was easier. I still couldn't believe I was this okay with someone else driving my baby. Never in my life did I think I'd be okay with that.

He parked the car in the middle of downtown. We were surrounded by tall buildings, so I had no clue which one we were here for. When we got out, he put Matilda on his shoulder and pulled me over into a dark alleyway.

"Wh-what are you doing?"

"We need to dress properly."

I looked down at my jeans and t-shirt and frowned. "We should've stopped to get suits or whatever."

"No need." He winked, then put his hands on my shoulders. The usual warmth I felt when he touched me made me take a deep, calming breath. After a few seconds, I felt the warmth travel over my skin. It sorta tickled and made me squirm. I looked down and was surprised to find myself in a suit instead of my regular clothes. I touched the fabric, and sure enough, it felt real.

"It's real. I just... reconfigured what you were already wearing."

I shook my head a little, then followed him out of the alley. He had Matilda on his shoulder, and he kept giving her kisses. On. Her. Mouth. It was so fucking gross. I shuddered every time I saw him do it. But as I looked at the people we were passing, not even one of them was giving Ailin a second look. It was really weird.

"What's going on?"

"What do you mean?"

"Don't people notice Matilda? I mean, it isn't every day that someone walks around with a fucking disgusting rat on their shoulder. Why aren't people freaking out and backing away from you?"

Ailin shrugged, making the rat move up and down on his shoulder as he said, "I can spell her to either be invisible or look like another animal to humans, depending on the situation."

I furrowed my brow. "Then why can I see her?"

Ailin stopped in his tracks and turned to look me in the eye. "Not gonna tell you."

I felt my nostrils flare. "Sometimes you're a fucking prick."

"So you've said."

I clenched my jaw to keep myself under control. He'd been pushing my buttons all damn day. I swear he wasn't this annoying yesterday. Maybe a nice punch to the nose would knock him down a few pegs.

"You'd never make the hit. You're slow as hell, and I'm too fast," he said in that careless manner of his. How did he know what I was thinking?

"Motherfucker," I huffed out before sticking my foot out in front of the bastard.

I must've managed to somehow take him by surprise because he tripped and almost faceplanted, though he caught himself at the last second and stumbled to a standing position again, holding the stupid rat so she didn't fall. When he turned around to look at me, I expected him to throw a punch or something, but all he did was look me up and down before saying, "Nice one." Then he turned on his heel again and kept on walking down the sidewalk.

Hmm. "I wonder why he didn't fight back?" I muttered to myself.

"Because it wouldn't be a fair fight," he shouted back to me.

"Fucking asshole!" I shouted back.

A woman was walking in the opposite direction on the sidewalk with her daughter, so I nodded at her, but she pulled her daughter as far away from me as possible as they passed. I sighed out loud as I followed after the most aggravating man I'd ever met.

We finally made it to the dinner, and as soon as we walked in, I wanted to leave, but Ailin grabbed my hand and leaned in to whisper in my ear, "Sorry for being a dick. I'm stressed because I hate this shit, and these people are the worst. I didn't mean to take it out on you, so please don't leave me stranded here by myself."

My eyebrows rose on my forehead. I couldn't believe he'd just said that, and one look at his face proved that he was being sincere. "I won't abandon you."

He squeezed my hand. "Thank you."

I studied him for a moment as he pulled me through a hallway—still holding my hand. His face was resting in his usual *I-don't-give-a-fuck* expression, but if I looked closely enough, I could see the tension in the corner of his eyes and the set of his jaw. He really was stressed.

I squeezed his hand. "Just tell me if you need me to do anything."

He sent me a small smile before we walked into a big banquet hall. I didn't know what I was expecting, but it certainly wasn't this. The hall was absolutely huge, and it was filled to the brim with people. I thought we were going to a dinner, not to a huge-ass party.

From all the disgusted looks we were getting, I was sure that Ailin hadn't spelled Matilda on his shoulder. The thought of these humans being scared and disgusted of Ailin made me want to chuckle.

Ailin kept ahold of my hand as he dragged me around to meet a bunch of people I'd never remember, and when we finally got to Lord Damian Schurlz, he leaned in and whispered something to the man. The lord's face turned red with anger, but all he said was, "Fine. Keep us posted."

Ailin nodded at the guy, then pulled my hand toward the buffet.

"What did you say to him?"

He shrugged. "I just reminded him that I helped the city get rid of a pack of quoala a few years ago, and I maybe told a little white lie and said I kept one alive and would release it on his family if he called the assembly."

I wasn't surprised at all that he'd threatened the guy. "What the hell is a qu-oh-la or whatever you said?"

"These little evil beasts that derive from the demon realm and like to snack on human eyes and brains." He pointed at the table. "Eat up, detective. I want to get out of here and head home."

I wrinkled my nose. "Not sure I want to eat after picturing brains and eyeballs."

Ailin smirked at me. "Eat up, you'll need your energy for tonight."

"What's tonight?"

Ailin smirked. "You're spending the night with me."

I tripped over my own foot. "Wh-what?"

He chuckled. "I need to find a stargem bloom for this tracking spell, so we're going to have to camp out tonight to get it. They bloom at midnight, and the flower only remains open for one minute. If we miss it tonight, we'll have to wait until tomorrow night."

"You're serious."

"Don't worry, we'll be on my property, so we'll be well within the wards. There's no way the demon can crossover onto my land."

I blinked at him. "My life got incredibly complicated and weird when you showed up."

He chuckled.

***

Ailin and I found one of the plants he was looking for, so we laid out some sleeping bags near it and waited.

"You didn't need me here with you," I said as I lay on my back looking up at the stars.

"Maybe I just wanted some company."

I snorted. *Yeah, right. He wanted my company. Ha!*

I saw him shift on his sleeping bag so he was facing me. "I like spending time with you, Seb."

I didn't know what to say to that, so I didn't say anything at all.

We stayed quiet for the rest of the wait, and after he got his bloom or whatever, we went to sleep. Sera slept on my chest, and Matilda slept on Ailin's.

Chapter Nine

Ailin and I couldn't find any new information on the kuma mali demon, so he decided that we needed to go to some underground bar place to find this guy that might have some info on it. Well, actually, he was arguing that he had to go by himself, but that wasn't happening. He'd already let it slip that this thing was stronger than anything he'd ever fought before.

There was no way in hell he was going to some crazy supe bar place by himself.

Ailin groaned and gripped his hair. "Ugh. I never should've told you how strong it is."

"I'm coming with you."

"You're a human."

"So what? Why does that matter?"

"Humans are too fragile for my world. You'll get hurt."

"I've already been hurt. Would you rather I go back to my apartment by myself again?" I was playing dirty and I knew it. For whatever reason, Ailin seemed like he wanted to protect me. He'd shown me a weakness, and I wasn't afraid to use it.

He sighed and pinched the bridge of his nose. "You could get hurt, Seb. This is serious."

"I know, that's why you're not going by yourself."

"I could just strap you to your chair so you can't leave. Basil said he'd sit with you while I'm gone."

"But you won't because you know I'll be pissed at you forever, and on top of that, you know it's a bad idea to go to this place by yourself." I crossed my arms over my chest.

He stared at me for a long time, mirroring my position. I swear I could feel wind rustling my hair. Even a few pieces of paper blew off my desk. Was Ailin so angry he was about to create a wind storm in my office?

"Yes, I'm that angry, but I'm not doing it on purpose. You... piss me off a lot." His eyes looked smoky again.

I frowned at him. "I don't want you to get hurt, A. Just like you don't want me to get hurt, I feel the same. I want to protect my... partner, my friend."

He huffed out a breath, and a little of the wind died down.

Before he could say anything, a thought occurred to me. "How did you know what I was thinking? Can you read my mind?"

His eyes flashed. "You think too loudly sometimes."

I blinked at him. "Does that... have you been reading my thoughts? My *private* thoughts, Ailin?"

He cringed a little. "I'm not doing it on purpose."

"Those are private! You need to stop invading my privacy!"

"Then stop thinking so loudly!" He turned on his heel and stomped to the other side of the room.

"You're the one that's doing it, not me." Now I sounded like a two-year-old arguing. "What the hell? How are you doing that? Did you cast a spell on me to get into my head?" I felt the blood drain from my face as another thought occurred to me. "Oh god, are you *in* my head? Are you controlling me or something? Oh god, what if—"

"I'm not controlling you, Sebastian. I'd never do that to you or anyone else, for that matter. I swear." He looked completely earnest. And once again, I believed him, for whatever reason.

"Then what's going on?"

He sighed and paced the other side of the room. "Honestly, I don't typically have this issue. Usually I have to actively go looking for a person's thoughts, but with you, it's like your thoughts are bleeding through to me. I don't know why."

"That's comforting." *What the hell am I going to do?*

"I doubt there's anything you *can* do. I only know how to teach witches how to keep mind-benders out. I have no idea how to help a human. Plus, I'm not even a mind-bender by nature, so I don't even know if that would apply to this."

What the fuck is he talking about? Mind-bender? "Will you please stop reading my mind? It's rude." *Asshole.*

"I heard that, you know? It's not like I'm doing it on purpose."

"How is that even true? I don't believe you. You need to turn off your mind reading spell or whatever it is!"

"It's not a mind reading spell, it's just... you're thinking really loudly, and I can't block you out. I've never had this happen before."

"In your entire life, you've never had this happen? I find that hard to believe." I huffed at him.

"I'm not lying to you, Seb, but you're welcome to think whatever the hell you want. You've already been cussing me out constantly since the first day we met."

"Yeah. In. My. Head! It's not my fault you're reading my thoughts!"

His nostrils flared. "Why the hell would I even want to listen to your head, anyway? You're a fucking human. I don't associate with humans unless absolutely necessary."

"Wow, you're the biggest egotistical dickhead I've ever met. You just insulted my entire species. So sorry we're not all big bad witches. So sorry we're not all great and powerful like the mighty Ailin Talamh Ellwood." My voice was dripping with sarcasm.

Ailin clenched his jaw and took a few deep breaths before picking up one of his spell books again and reading it. *Fucking dickhead.* I heard him sigh and smiled at the fact that I could sit here and call him every single name under the sun. Or maybe I'd just repeat the same word over and over again to drive him crazy. Yeah, that would be way more annoying. Serves him right for all the embarrassing things he'd pulled out of my head without me knowing it.

Asshole.

Asshole.

Asshole.

Asshole, asshole—

"Okay!" Ailin suddenly screamed. "I get it! I'm sorry! Holy Mother of All, I swear if you don't shut the fuck up, I'm going to strangle you!" He yelped and grabbed his chest, rubbing it like it was suddenly hurting him. "Fuck! Fucking fuckity fuck!"

"Are you okay?"

"Yeah, that was... weird." He looked over at me as he continued to rub his chest. "Please for the love of all things stop saying 'asshole.'"

I blinked innocently at him. "But Ailin, I'm not *saying* anything at all."

His eyes narrowed. "Watch it or I will hex you."

I couldn't help but chuckle a little. "You sure you're okay? Did you injure your chest?"

He lifted a shoulder, but winced in pain a little.

"Let me take a look." I moved closer to him and tentatively grabbed the hem of his shirt, then looked him in the eyes as I lifted it so I could get a better look. He pulled it over his head with a slight wince, and I found my eyes drawn to his inked skin. He was covered in tattoos, and it was sexy as hell. *Dammit! He probably heard that!*

He chuckled, so I shot him a glare before refocusing on his chest. "Where does it hurt?"

He placed his palm right over his heart and circled it around a little. I moved his hand away, then moved my face closer to examine his left pec area. His skin looked unmarked other than the tats, so I gently brushed my fingertips over his skin to see if I could feel anything. I watched in fascination as little goosebumps formed over his skin following the path of my fingers. I still didn't see or feel anything wrong, but I had the sudden urge to press myself against him, feel his skin against my own. His skin was soft; I bet it'd feel amazing rubbing against me. Naked against me. Ailin suddenly sucked in a gasp, and I had no doubt that he'd heard my thoughts. *Dammit! So embarrassing.*

"Don't be embarrassed. If you knew what I thought about doing to you, *then* you could be embarrassed."

I looked up to find him staring at me with those intense green eyes. I stood abruptly, dropping my hand and moving back to put some distance between us. I cleared my throat. "Uh, I don't see anything wrong."

He shrugged a shoulder. "It stopped hurting as soon as you touched me, so I guess you healed me." He grinned.

I could only blink at him. I didn't even know what to do with that, or with what he'd said about doing things to me... what things? Sex things? Because I could totally be about that. *Shit. He probably heard that, too!*

He blew out a breath, then grabbed his shirt and shrugged it back on. "I've been researching what the problem is with the mind reading thing, but nothing explains it. I've never had this issue before."

I groaned and flopped onto the futon, covering my face with my hands, and wishing I could take back every thought I'd had since I'd met him. It was so fucking embarrassing. Every single thing I'd thought about since he'd known me, he'd heard.

"Not *every* single thing."

"Not helping, asshole."

He sighed.

Oh god, I'd been picturing him naked, like *a lot,* and thinking about his body, his tattoos, about *licking* his tattoos! Oh, holy shit, I'd even thought about what he'd look like if I was fucking him, and he was writhing under me. *And. Oh. My. God. He can probably hear me now.* I groaned and pushed my face farther into my hands as if that would help block my thoughts from him. Of course, because I didn't want to think about picturing Ailin naked, that was exactly where my mind went, and now that it was there, the picture wouldn't go away. *Fucking hell.*

I heard Ailin chuckle, so I dropped my hands and glared at him. "You're such an asshole. Get out of my head."

"But it's so fun in there. And you might think I'm an asshole, but you also think I'm sexy."

"I hate you."

He chuckled, then sobered and cleared his throat. "If you come with me to Sting, you have to promise me that you'll follow my lead, and that you won't... touch anyone."

I cringed. "Why the hell would I be touching people?"

He sighed and dropped into his chair, rubbing his hands over his face. "This is what I'm talking about. You know nothing of my world. It's not safe." When I opened my mouth to argue, he lifted a hand to stop me. "I'm not trying to stop you, I understand why you want to come, but I need you to understand that it isn't safe. Supes can be... manipulative, more so than any human could ever want to be. Some will use their... powers to persuade you, so I need you to promise not to leave my side. I don't want someone getting their hands on you and trying to claim you."

"Claim me?"

"Yes. Most supes are, uh, possessive creatures. It's a part of our nature. Try to understand that I'm only protecting you."

"Okay, I'll stick to you like glue."

He snorted.

***

When we were in the car, Ailin said, "Drive to Sting. You know where that is?"

I rolled my eyes, grunted at him, then stifled a sigh as I put the car in gear. Apparently, he was back to Mr. Grouchy Asshat tonight.

Sting was a bar in Arronston, so it was a short drive over. It had several floors; the ground floor was just a normal bar, but the other three floors were the home of some fucked up fetishes. Not my kind of place, but I'd been to the normal bar with some of the other agents after work before.

The parking lot at *Sting* was pretty packed for a random weeknight, but I found a spot easily. I parked and started to get out, but Ailin grabbed my forearm, stopping me before I could open my door. His grip was light, but the heat from his hand was almost burning me, even through my jacket. I looked at him in question.

"I need you to do something for me," he said after an awkward pause.

"Ookay," I drew out the word.

He released my arm, taking away his heat, but turned his body to face me. He puffed out his cheeks before saying, "Look, this is gonna sound like a weird request, but I need you to listen." I didn't say anything, I just waited, intrigued. He pulled his leather cord necklaces out from under his shirt and started pulling one apart from the others and over his head. Then he held it out to me. "I need you to wear this while we're in there."

I blinked at him, trying to gauge whether he was messing with me or not, but he looked completely serious. Finally, I said, "You're right, that is a weird request." Why would I wear his necklace? He was being so odd today— odder than usual. I put my hand on the door handle and tried to push it open, but the damn thing wouldn't budge. Great. Now my door was stuck. *Fuck this day.*

While I was trying to unstick my door, the little butt threw his stupid necklace over my head. I jumped and reached for it to rip it off, but he grabbed the back of my neck, making me look at him again as his hot hand warmed my skin.

"I know you don't understand, but I need you to trust me. There's a special quality about this necklace that you may need when we're inside."

"It's magic?"

He looked into my eyes. "Uh, yeah... please just do me this favor and keep the damn necklace on."

"If you would've told me what it was right away, I would've agreed. Stop trying to boss me around and just talk to me like a normal person. It's not like I'm unreasonable."

"Fine." He looked irritated, but I had the feeling he was irritated about something other than me right now, he was just taking it out on me—again. *Lucky me.*

I closed my eyes and breathed in deeply, praying for a little patience. "Fine."

He still didn't release me. He actually tightened his grip on my neck. "Promise me you won't take it off. No matter what you see or hear in there."

Fuck. This was really strange. I didn't even know what this necklace did, but I guess there was no harm in going along with him. I sighed. "What does it do?"

"It will protect you from injury, and in the case that someone takes you from me, I'll be able to track you."

I frowned. "Is that really necessary? Do you really think someone will... try to kidnap me?"

"No, I don't, but I like to have contingency plans in place. Please leave it on until we exit the building and *I* tell you it's okay to remove it."

"Fine."

"Promise you won't take it off inside, even if I ask you to."

I squinted at the strangeness, but said, "Fine. Can we go in now?"

"Say the words, Sebastian." When I didn't follow his orders, he softly added, "Please."

I rolled my eyes at that. "Fine. I promise I won't take the damn thing off while we're inside no matter what, and even if I leave the fucking building, I'll wait till you say it's okay. There, is that enough for you?"

He blew out what sounded like a relieved breath, and at the same time, I felt a sharp sting on the back of my neck where his hand was. I jumped. "Ow. Fuck. Did you just stab me with something?" I pushed his hand off the back of my neck.

He grinned at me with what could only be a mischievous smile. "No. Sorry for the pinch."

"Did you just... *spell* me?"

"Maybe."

"Ailin! You told me you wouldn't do that to me anymore!"

"No, I told you I wouldn't put an influence hex on you, or make you change your mind by using magic. I never said I wouldn't put a promise hex on you. If you try to take that necklace off before we exit the building, you'll feel a lot more than a simple pinch."

"What the actual fuck, A?"

"It's stuck to you until your promise is fulfilled. Which means that no one else can take it off you, either."

"You could've explained the stupid promise spell to me *before* you did it."

"But this was so much more fun." He grinned, winked, then tucked his stupid necklace I was now wearing into my shirt, mumbling something under his breath. He turned to get out of the car before I could ask what other spells he was putting on me.

Fucker.

This time when I pulled on the door handle, my door opened immediately. *Just add that to the weirdness of the fucking week.* I started heading toward the front door, but soon noticed that Ailin was walking toward the side of the building. I stifled a sigh before following him to the employee entrance. He rang a doorbell, and a huge guy that I swore was close to seven feet tall and at least twice as wide as me answered.

Ailin told him, "Esslamal." *What in the fuck does that mean?*

Beefy looked Ailin up and down, gave a nod, then assessed me. Instead of nodding at me, he looked back at Ailin.

Ailin waved a hand over his shoulder at me. "He's with me."

Beefy nodded again and moved over so we could pass him. His reaction made me wonder if Ailin came here often. I pushed the thought aside since I really didn't want to know what the hell he got into in order to need the side entrance and some secret password or whatever that was. *Is he into kinky sex?* Shit, he probably heard that.

Ailin's chuckle confirmed that he had heard it. "Wouldn't you like to know."

I closed my eyes and took a deep breath, willing my cheeks not to flush.

I followed Ailin through a long, dark hallway, passing several closed doors. Beefy stayed behind to man the side door. When we got to the end of the hallway, Ailin turned to face me. When he reached his hand out, I sidestepped, unsure of what he was doing, and I bumped into the hard, black-painted wall. I glanced down at Ailin's hand as he rested it on my upper arm.

He had a sweet smile on his face that I didn't understand, and when he spoke, his voice was almost gentle and soft. "You ready to check this place out, baby?"

All I could do was blink at him for an elongated moment before I realized what he was doing. Would've been nice for him to let me in on his little plan ahead of time. I offered what I hoped was a sincere smile. "Sure thing, sweetie." Apparently, we were a couple for this strange mission. *God, do I even want to know what he's gonna make me do as his 'boyfriend'?*

His smile grew and somehow seemed more genuine. "Follow me."

Then he released my arm and stepped up next to me. A second later, he walked through a fucking wall.

Seriously. He fucking walked through the wall right next to me. I reached out a tentative hand to touch the wall—there had to be some kind of trap door or something—but before I could touch it, a hand reached back through the wall, grabbed my forearm, and yanked me forward.

I closed my eyes, expecting to hit my head on the hard barrier, but I suddenly felt like I was walking through jello. Almost as soon as the strange sensation started, it disappeared. I opened my eyes only to find myself at the top of a dark stairwell with Ailin next to me, holding onto my arm. I glanced over my shoulder to see the trap door, but it just looked like a black-painted wall behind me. Some kind of crazy elaborate trick, I guess. Or no, it had to be magic, right? I wanted to ask Ailin, but this wasn't the time nor the place for that discussion. I had a feeling that before the night was through, I'd have hundreds and hundreds of questions to ask him. I should've brought a notebook to keep track.

Ailin chuckled, probably picking up on my random thought, so I elbowed him. *Stop reading my mind!* He laughed a little louder, then slid his hand down my arm to my hand where he slipped his fingers into mine. In a voice gentler than he usually used, he said, "Come on, baby, you're in for a real treat." He tugged me to follow him down the stairs.

I wasn't so sure I liked the sound of that.

I hadn't even known there was a basement in this building, but apparently, there was. The walls and floor all the way down the stairs were painted black with a black door right at the bottom. Ailin put his free hand on the doorknob, glanced at me with an unreadable expression, then pushed it open, making a small gust of wind come out, along with a very loud baseline.

He pulled me through the door, and I automatically stopped in my tracks. The lighting was dark with a blue tint that made me squint my eyes to adjust to it. There was a packed dance floor, a stage, four giant cages hanging from the ceiling with people in various stages of dress inside, tables and couches packed with people around the perimeter of the huge room, and a bar that ran the whole length of one wall. For about two seconds I thought it was just a crazy bar, but then I got a closer look at what everyone was doing as Ailin dragged me through the crowd toward the bar.

At first, I thought the people sitting at a table we passed were just making out, kissing and licking one another, but it was impossible not to notice that they were actually drinking and licking blood off each other. I cringed at the sight. *Are those vampires?*

Ailin looked over his shoulder. "Yes."

"Would you stop," I whisper-yelled. He should *not* be in my head.

Ailin stopped and looked at me. "Sorry, I thought you really wanted to know."

I mean, I had, but still.

Ailin shrugged and pulled me along again.

The next table we passed had cups, shot glasses, and plates floating up about a foot from the tabletop, swirling around in circles. I watched in amazement as one of the guys plucked a shot glass out of the air and tossed its contents down his throat. I didn't know how they were making everything float, but it was pretty damn cool to watch.

There were only two people sitting at the next table, and they were arguing loudly in a language I didn't recognize. The woman looked like she had actual steam rising off her skin in waves, and the guy was surrounded by sparks.

It's like I've landed in the land of the bizarre.

I heard a deep breath right behind my ear, so I turned around, halting my and Ailin's movements. My eyes widened at the very tall, very handsome man staring at me. The stranger moved closer to me and leaned in so quickly, I didn't have time to stop him or even back up a step. He grabbed my waist and pulled me against him, taking another deep breath near my neck. "Such enticing fresh meat." His tongue came out and licked a stripe up my neck and I shivered involuntarily.

My eyes widened, but before I could do anything, the man was being yanked off me and pushed back. Ailin stepped in front of me with two green balls floating over his upturned palms. Since he was shorter than me, I could see over the top of his head as the stranger grinned at Ailin, his sharp teeth and red eyes on display—they hadn't been there a moment ago. I gasped at the sight. *What the hell is that guy?*

Ailin spoke through clenched teeth, "Hands off, incubus."

The stranger—er, incubus—took a step closer and looked Ailin up and down. "I claimed the human."

I shivered in disgust; I could still feel his saliva on my neck.

Ailin growled low and dangerous and not human-like at all, and suddenly there was a green flickering haze surrounding his body, like a second skin. *Shit, he's pissed.* Ailin stepped closer to the incubus and his green energy sparked. I was pretty sure if anyone touched him right now, they'd be burned to a crisp. "You just found yourself at the top of my shit list, incubus. That's not a place you want to be. You better watch your back."

If I hadn't been watching so closely, I would've missed the moment when the incubus's eyes widened and fear flashed across his face, but it was gone in an instant. "You're no match for my brothers and me." I glanced behind the guy and saw three other red-eyed, sharp-teethed incubi.

Ailin stepped even closer and his body sparked further. "Touch my human again, and your brothers will have nothing left of you to bury. I am *Sage.*"

At the word *Sage*, the incubus turned pale and took a step away from Ailin. "I-I didn't know."

"I suggest you run. *Now.*" Ailin's voice was so cold, it sent a tendril of fear down my spine even though it wasn't directed at me.

The incubus ran off, and once he and his brothers were out of sight, Ailin turned back to me. His body was thrumming with untamed energy; he looked pissed, like he wanted to rip someone's head off. Ailin looked into my eyes and took a few calming breaths.

"So I'm your human now, huh?" Okay, so provoking a pissed off witch probably wasn't my smartest move, but I couldn't take the intensity of his eyes any longer.

I expected a smart-ass answer or for him to blow it off, but he simply said, "Yes, you're my human."

That blatant statement did weird things to my chest. I was sorta offended, but also maybe a little touched at the same time. Maybe he'd only said that because there were others around us that he probably didn't want to overhear otherwise, but I didn't think that was the case. I should've corrected him and told him that I was his partner, not his human, but I didn't, all I did was stare. But maybe if I was his human, then he was my witch. Maybe that was all he'd meant since we *were* partners; witch and human working together. He didn't mean any more than that.

He grabbed my hand and pulled me through the bar again. As soon as he touched my hand, his anger and the magic that'd been dancing along his skin dissipated. He looked calm and collected again, as if nothing had even happened. But from the wary looks we were getting, and the way everyone was backing away from us, I was pretty sure no one else was going to forget what happened so soon, and that they'd likely stay away from me. Just how powerful was Ailin? I'd thought he'd just been being cocky before, but maybe he'd only been stating facts, maybe he was really powerful among the supernatural community. I'd have to ask him. Add that to the list.

Maybe this was that possessive supe shit he was talking about. Maybe he was just as possessive as the ones he warned me about.

Ailin stopped suddenly, and I almost ran into him. I hadn't realized we'd already reached the bar. *Whoops.*

The barman was at the other end, but slowly started making his way down. When the guy turned to approach us, I swore it looked like he was glowing. There was a soft blue light emanating from his skin, and I gasped at the stunning sight. This guy was the most beautiful creature I had ever laid eyes on, and when he made eye contact with me, he took my breath away. He had the bluest eyes I'd ever seen, and they seemed to sparkle like a bright gem. His sky-blue hair was brushed off his elegant, perfect little face. He was toned, though very lean, and with his tank top on I could see that he had perfect pale skin that looked as soft as a cloud.

I felt Ailin's finger under my chin—his small touch made my stomach flutter. He pushed my mouth closed, but I couldn't look away from the beautiful man. Ailin's amused voice broke through my one-track mind, "I think you're drooling, baby."

I took a deep breath and with much difficulty, turned away from the beautiful man to look at Ailin.

Ailin addressed Blue over my shoulder, "Tone it down a bit, Nikolai. This is his first time."

I turned back to Beautiful Blue—Nikolai, apparently—who pouted at him. "You're no fun, Sage." Then the gorgeous man turned his attention to me and leaned over the bar to drag a slow finger down my cheek. "You sure are a handsome one." My eyes widened as he dragged his finger across my lips—it felt nice, and I had no intention of moving away.

Ailin's hand snapped out, grabbing Nikolai's wrist, and he growled, "Hands. Off."

Nikolai looked Ailin over for a second before chuckling. "You claim this one, then?"

Ailin spoke through clenched teeth, "Yes."

My eyebrows shot up. *Claim.* Hadn't that been what Ailin warned me about? Shit, he really was as possessive as the other supes. Should I be worried? A part of me was almost thrilled at Ailin's answer, but I ignored it because I didn't want to analyze what that meant.

Nikolai chuckled even harder as he backed away from me. "That's a first. However, I don't see his *mark.*" The way he said *mark* sounded like he was mocking Ailin.

Ailin grabbed my chin between two fingers and turned my head to him, holding me there. He looked over my shoulder and glared at Nikolai. I heard the blue man quietly say, "Yeah, okay, okay."

Ailin's eyes softened a little when he looked back at me, and he suddenly leaned up and brushed his lips against my forehead, letting them linger there for a moment. I felt a strange tingly burn under his lips, but it only lasted a moment before he leaned back to look into my eyes again. Without releasing my chin, he ran two fingers of his other hand across my forehead, making me gasp and blink a few times. Then he put his palm over my heart and started mumbling under his breath, but I couldn't understand what he was saying.

He rested his forehead against mine and closed his eyes as I stared at him in confusion. I had no fucking clue what he was doing, but for some unknown reason, I felt compelled to stay there—no, I *wanted* to stay there. That strange tingling sensation ran through my body, then settled in my chest where Ailin had his hand. He slowly moved his hand up my pec, over my shoulder, then up to the side of my neck, the sensation following his hand as he went. It didn't hurt, in fact, it was almost pleasant.

He used his other hand to pull my hand up, resting it on his neck, and I felt my hand generate the same warm feeling into his neck. *What is this?* We held each other like that for what felt like a long time, but could've been only seconds. He slowly moved his hand, ending with it in my hair before he leaned up and kissed my forehead again. When he pulled back, my hand dropped, and Ailin searched my eyes for something, then seemed to find it because he released me and turned back to the bar.

What the fucking fuck was that?

I stared at the strange man—witch—for a moment before following his line of sight to the bar. Nikolai was still standing there. But this time when I looked at him, I didn't see the most gorgeous man alive. I mean, he was gorgeous alright, but honestly, not really my type. I rubbed my forehead, trying to figure out what in the hell that had been about, then looked back at Nikolai, who looked like he was laughing at me. I glared at him which made a loud laugh bubble out of him.

I looked at Ailin to ask him what he'd done, but he shook his head, so I knew I'd have to add that to my list of questions for later.

"Nikolai," Ailin hissed from his stool next to me. "I need to speak to him."

The smile fell from Nikolai's face as he looked at Ailin with a serious expression. "No." Nikolai handed me a bottle of beer that I gratefully took.

"No, baby, don't drink that." Ailin casually took the bottle out of my hand without even looking at me and gave it back to Nikolai, who Ailin glared at. Ailin spoke to Nikolai, "I wasn't asking. Either you let him know I'm on my way or I'll just head back right now." I almost protested that I did want that beer, but something told me that I really wouldn't want that particular kind. *What the hell did I walk into? Is there drugs or magic or something in the alcohol?*

"I said no, Sage," Nikolai growled. *Sage?* What the hell did Sage mean? *Why does everyone keep calling him that?*

"You know as well as I, that this was just a courtesy. I could easily walk back there with my eyes closed and my hands tied behind my back. He's had six months to get over it."

"You blew up half the building!" Nikolai yelled.

"I didn't have a choice! You know as well as I do that this whole place would be gone if I hadn't taken care of your little problem." Ailin's jaw clenched, but he wasn't shooting green sparks yet, so that was a plus. "*Now,* Nikolai."

Nikolai did not look happy at that demand. He looked Ailin up and down. "Dammit, Sage. He's not going to like this."

"You know I wouldn't be here unless it was important."

Nikolai rolled his eyes, closed them for a second, then looked back at Ailin. "Fair warning; he's pissed."
Wait, what? Who's pissed? When did he talk to someone else? I had a lot to learn about this magic shit. A notebook really would've come in handy.

Ailin stood up, tapping his knuckles on the bar. "Knew he would be. Thanks Nik." Then he grabbed my hand and pulled me along the bar.

Nikolai shouted after us, "The best part of you showing up is watching you walk away."

I frowned at that. Nikolai shouldn't be looking at my witch's ass. *You have no right to be mad, Sebastian. And you* know *he's listening to you right now!* There was no missing Ailin's grin as he walked through the small space at the end of the bar and disappeared through another fucking black wall. I felt the thick jello sensation as he pulled me with him, then we popped back out on the other side of the wall into a room that was completely filled with plants, trees, and flowers of every color imaginable. The bright light was harsh after being in such a dark room, and the sudden silence was almost deafening. I couldn't hear the bass from the bar at all. Ailin continued holding my hand as he led me through the random greenhouse in the basement of some random-ass warehouse. *Where in the fuck am I?*

A very loud and angry booming voice echoed through the large room that could probably fit my entire apartment in it. It was so loud, I jumped and resisted the urge to cover my ears. "This better be good, Ailin."

"Well, *good* isn't the word I'd use to describe the situation, Talon," Ailin said at a normal volume.

"If you blow up my bar again, no one will find your body," the booming voice growled out.

"If I hadn't vanquished it, you and your brother would've died months ago. Give me a break." Ailin looked bored with this conversation, although I knew him well enough at this point to recognize the tension underneath. To anyone that didn't know him, he appeared calm, like he didn't have a care in the world.

"What do you want, Sage?"

"Information. I need something from Faela so I can access the demon energy."

"Why do you need me for that?"

Ailin mumbled so quietly I almost couldn't hear him, "My brother stole my ring." *His brother's starting to sound like a little shit.*

The booming laughter hurt my eardrums. "Remind me to give your brother drinks on the house next time he's here."

"Don't be a dick," Ailin mumbled.

There were a few more chuckles before the voice sighed. "Why do I get the feeling that you just brought a shit-ton of work to my doorstep?"

Ailin glanced at me. "Kuma mali demon."

I jumped back and nearly yelped when a man suddenly popped out of nowhere right in front of me saying, "You can't be serious."

Ailin pulled my hand slightly so I was forced to step closer to him, then he patted the back of my hand with his other hand. "It's okay, baby." To the magically appearing man, he said, "Have you heard anything?"

I examined the newcomer and decided that he looked exactly like Nikolai, only everything on him was green, including his eyes and hair, and he had beautiful dark brown skin. He sort of matched all the greenery we were surrounded by as if he were a part of nature itself or something. I couldn't decide which of the brothers was more gorgeous.

He scrubbed his hand over his face, looked back and forth between me and Ailin, then sighed. "Come to my office." Then he just vanished from the spot.

I stepped back again, shaking my head. "What the fuck?"

Ailin still had ahold of my hand, so I didn't get far. He tugged me closer to him again and made me look into his eyes as he whispered, "Just be patient for a little while longer." He leaned in closer so his mouth was right up against my ear. "I know you're overwhelmed, but I'll explain everything when we leave." His hot breath sent chills down my spine. I nodded to him, and he pulled me along down a path of shrubbery until we came to a small clearing.

There were trees and branches wrapped all around, almost forming walls and a ceiling, and right in the middle of the clearing, there were branches wrapped around each other to form a desk and several chairs. Apparently, Ailin wasn't the only one with the talent of making living plants into furniture. The disappearing guy— Talon, I guess—was sitting behind the desk. Ailin dragged me into the room, and we each took a seat on the chairs made of vines.

Talon nodded at me, but was looking at Ailin. "Who's the human?"

I stifled a sigh. I may have been a human, but he didn't have to speak about me as if I wasn't in the room. *Are all supes this rude?*

"This is my partner, Sebastian." I guess that could be taken either way; his partner on the job or his partner in life, and I had a feeling he wanted it to be taken as the latter.

Talon turned an assessing eye on me. "I'm Talon. I'd offer you a drink, but I don't think you could handle it."

I furrowed my brow at that, but I chose not to comment. I was surrounded by assholes today.

Talon looked back at Ailin. "Tell me what's going on."

Ailin sighed. "Eighteen human bodies; sixteen of them over sixteen months, same symbol, drained of blood, plus a man drained of blood that managed to live. The demon came after Seb a few nights ago, but we lost its trail. I need to know if there's any chatter or if you're able to pick up on its energy so I can narrow the area down. I can't find its home base, and it must have figured out a way to block my normal tracking spells."

Talon nodded as he reached behind his desk and pulled out a silver mirror. It was a large circle, far bigger than an average dinner plate. I could see carvings in the silver, but I didn't get a good look since Talon set the mirror flat on his desk. He pulled out a small vial and poured clear liquid onto the mirror. The liquid started swirling around in circles over the mirror even though no one was moving it.

I couldn't decide if I should be terrified or excited by all of the magic everywhere in this place. Maybe I was a little bit of both.

Talon and Ailin leaned over the mirror to look at it. When I scooted closer, Ailin reached his arm out blocking me from getting a good look. I pushed the jerk's arm out of the way to scoot up, anyway, but he shot me a look that I somehow interpreted as *'you don't want to get any closer. Just trust me.'* And for reasons unclear, I listened and stayed back, stifling another sigh. He put his hand flat on my chest and held me back even though I was no longer trying to move forward. I tried to ignore the way the heat traveled into my chest from his palm, and instead, I glared at him. Damn crazy person next to me. I hated being in the dark about this shit.

What a jerkface.

They both stared into the mirror for a few tense minutes, but nothing happened. Eventually, Talon sighed and leaned back. "There's nothing. It's quiet, almost too quiet."

Ailin nodded and sat back, but still hadn't removed his hand from my chest. I was pretty sure he didn't even realize it was still there. He looked at the green man across from us. "You know what this means, don't you?"

Talon nodded with a grim expression. "It's being cloaked."

"And if it's hidden from you, it can only mean one thing."

Talon's expression turned even more worrisome. "You can't mean...? But that's not possible."

"I'm sorry, old friend, but one of your brethren are involved. Someone has turned to the dark."

Talon looked completely shell-shocked. "I... I... I don't know what to do."

"Just lie low for now. Do not speak to any of the others, not until we have an idea of who it is. Keep your brother and yourself safe. That's all you have to worry about. I'll call on you when the time comes."

Talon nodded, but it didn't look like his mind was with us anymore. He almost looked like he was grieving, but I didn't understand exactly what was going on.

Ailin used a quiet voice when he spoke again, "Keep Nikolai informed, but make sure he doesn't crossover by himself."

Talon nodded, but was still lost in thought.

"Talon, I need to know you're hearing me."

Talon finally looked at Ailin, his face ashen. "I hear you, Sage. I'll do as you ask, but be careful. If it has turned one of my own, it must be very strong. You know what you have to do, don't you?"

Ailin blew out a breath. "I'll give him a call if I need to."

"Good." Talon nodded, then stood abruptly. "Be on your way. I need to check my wards."

Ailin nodded and went to stand, but turned to me with wide eyes. He looked at his hand on my chest with a slightly confused expression before looking into my eyes. He blinked a few times before snatching his hand away as if I'd burned him. I frowned at him as I stood, and he stood up without looking at me. *What the hell?*

I grabbed his forearm and forced him to look at me. "You okay?"

Ailin's gaze shifted off to the side, and without looking, I knew he was glancing at the green man, but he looked back at me, and his gaze softened just a tad. "Yeah, baby, I'm fine." His voice was hoarse, but the way he was looking at me made me think the *baby* was just as much for my benefit as it was for Talon's, although I didn't really understand why. He looked at Talon. "You know how to reach me if anything comes up. If you find anymore information or if it shows up here, call me immediately. This thing is too strong for you to handle by yourself. And please try to convince Nik not to do anything stupid."

"I'll call you. But just so we're clear, if you blow up my home again, you'll be banned for life."

Ailin narrowed his eyes. "You know I saved your life. You should show a little appreciation."

"Everywhere you go, destruction follows."

Ailin sighed. "Not *everywhere* I go."

Talon actually grinned at that. "Go before you catch something on fire."

Ailin rolled his eyes with a small grin and grabbed my hand, pulling me along. I could feel his energy thrumming under his skin, and for some reason, it felt almost pleasant. He pulled me through the greenhouse, back through the bar where he nodded to Nikolai, then up those steps and through the first wall we'd passed to get in. We walked down the long hallway to the same door we'd come in through, and Ailin nodded at the doorman on our way out. He held my hand all the way to my car where he stuffed me into the driver's seat, shut my door, then jumped in the passenger seat.

"Don't say anything yet," he muttered under his breath.

I nodded, turned the car on, and drove out of the parking lot as Ailin rolled down the window and hung out it to smoke a joint. I rolled my eyes at him, but whatever. Maybe he'd be less of an asshole after he chilled out a little.

Chapter Ten

After five minutes, he got rid of the joint, sat back down, and said, "We should be far enough away now."

I blew out a breath. "What's a Sage?" I was surprised that this was the first question out of my mouth, but I just went with it.

"Witches have a hierarchy based on the amount of power you possess. Sage is one of them."

"I'm guessing it's pretty good? That incubus, or whatever you called it, was scared of you after you mentioned it."

He snorted out a laugh. "You could say that."

"What's that supposed to mean?"

He sighed and put his feet up on the dash—I no longer bothered to yell at him, I'd forever have boot marks on it. "Sage is high, yes."

"So you're really powerful?"

I saw him shrug out of the corner of my eye. "If you call being the most powerful witch in the world powerful, then yes, I am."

My eyes widened. Was he just messing with me? "Are you serious?"

"Yeah, I'm up in the top spot, have been since I was sixteen. I'm the youngest to reach Sage level in history." He shrugged again, and I could tell that he didn't really care about this Sage stuff which was surprising considering how self-centered he was all the time. He shot me a sharp glance and I cringed, figuring he'd heard my thought.

"Sorry," I muttered.

He waved me off. "Whatever. I know what you think of me."

Wow. He was even pissier than usual. That joint didn't help at all. "Stop reading my mind and you won't have that problem."

He actually snorted out a laugh, which made me smile a little.

"So the youngest witch to become a Sage, huh?"

"Just 'Sage' not 'a Sage,' but yes. Witches tend to get stronger with age, so it was not received well by many of the elders."

Wow. So basically, no one would be able to surpass him... ever.

"Actually, if anyone could, it'd be Basil. He's younger than me and very powerful, probably the second most powerful in the world, although we've kept this a secret after the many assassination attempts on me and my family. We don't need another bullseye painted on our backs."

"Assassination attempts?"

He waved me off. "I'd rather not get into the bullshit of witch politics right now. This day has been stressful enough as it is."

"Okay, understandable. Can you explain what you were talking about back there? With the cloaking thing or whatever?"

"Demons give off a certain energy, and the stronger they are, the easier it is to track them, but I haven't been having any luck tracking our kuma mali demon on my own, so I thought a little fae magic was in order. Demons are basically the anti-fae, the dark to their light. Without one, you cannot have the other; they balance each other. They're two ends of the same string, which means that they're connected, and therefore, they have an easy time picking up the energy of their opposites. The fae try to keep the demons in check because they know if left to themselves, they'd destroy our world and nothing would be left."

"That's why Talon helps me when I ask, and I help him; we both strive to keep the universe in balance. Plus, if anyone's heard any chatter about it, Talon and Nikolai are the ones that would've heard it. But they haven't heard anything, and when Talon tried to track the demon, there was nothing to track. Zero energy. Which makes no sense, unless the demon has a fae helping him by cloaking and hiding his energy from us."

He blew out a breath. "And there should've been other demons, there's always demons in our realm. Usually smaller ones, but still, Talon should've picked up some demon energy to track, even if it wasn't our demon. So something is off, and the only explanation that makes any sense is that a fae is involved with our demon. It could be why I haven't picked up on the energy imbalance this whole time, too. It makes a lot of sense now that I think about it. I just never in a million years thought a fae would be involved. It's just so... strange."

He sighed and started pulling on the bracer on his forearm. "It also means that this mission is far more dangerous than I'd first suspected."

I cringed a little at that, but before I could question him further, a black blob appeared on the dashboard with a loud-ass hiss. I screamed out and hit the brakes, stopping the car as fast as I could, and was out the door with my gun drawn by the time Ailin put his feet back on the floor.

I squinted at the black blob and took a closer step as I realized what it was. I lowered my weapon, then tucked it back in its holster. "Did Seraphina just magically appear on my dashboard?"

Ailin nodded at me, then looked at Sera. "Way to make an entrance, Sera." He looked back at me. "Uh, you can get back in."

I glared at him, but slid into my seat. "What the fuck, Ailin? A little warning would've been nice, especially when I'm driving."

"Uh, I didn't know she was coming."

I narrowed my eyes at him. "What do you mean? Cats don't just magically appear places."

He sighed and pinched the bridge of his nose. "I know that, Jesus. I keep forgetting how little you know about everything. I've been trying not to overwhelm you with information, but I guess that's not going very well." He dropped his hand and looked at me. "Seraphina is my Bonded One. All witches have one."

"I have no idea what that means."

"Witches form a special bond with an animal, usually when we're teenagers. She and I are connected in a way that's hard to explain to a human. We can read each other's thoughts, feel one another's emotions, and even see through the other's eyes if we want. We're linked in a way that's deeper than friendship, deeper than family. Does that answer your question?"

"Uh... no. Not really. How did she get in my car?"

"She can appear wherever I am because of our bond. I can do the same with her."

I just blinked at him. Of all the things I'd heard in the past week, that had to be one of the strangest ones.

He shrugged.

"I thought you said she was a baby? How is that possible if you've had her since you were a teenager?"

"Many supes age differently, and Sera is Bonded to me, so her aging is closer to a witch's."

I opened my mouth, then snapped it shut and put the car back in gear to pull out on the road. After a few minutes, Ailin asked, "You're not even going to ask me anything about it?"

I blew out a breath. "Honestly, I think I've reached my limit for the day. Just keep all of your witchy shit to yourself until my brain can process it."

He didn't say anything for a long time, but I didn't miss the way Sera climbed onto his lap and started licking his chin and nuzzling him. When I glanced at him and saw him staring out the front windshield with a sad expression, I thought about what I'd said to him and realized how that sounded, especially given his history.

I cleared my throat. "I'm sorry, I didn't mean that the way it sounded. I—"

"Forget it, Sebastian." His voice was cold, and I knew without a shadow of a doubt that I'd hurt him deeply, even if he was too proud to ever admit it.

"Ailin?"

"What?"

"That came out the wrong way. I just meant that I'm having trouble with all of the new information coming my way, and I need to wrap my head around it before I can think of things to ask you."

"Whatever, Sebastian. I get it. Humans are afraid of me and my *witchy shit*."

Fuck. Fucking fuck. Fuck! "Would you just shut up and listen to me? I'm not afraid of you. I'm just overwhelmed. Today has been a lot, this week has been fucking insane. Everything I thought to be true about my world is false. Can you for one minute, just put yourself in my shoes, please? I'm not afraid, I just need some time to understand."

"Whatever."

"You stubborn little... witch!"

He snorted out a laugh, but I could tell it was a reluctant one, but I'd take it. "Nice come back."

"I thought it was brilliant."

"You're a dorky little *human*, aren't you?"

"Yep. But apparently I'm *your* human." *Whoops. Didn't mean to say that out loud.*

He snorted again. "Well, apparently I'm *your* witch, or so you thought back at the club. More than once."

"Stay out of my head, Ailin Ellwood. But yes, that sentiment still remains."

"Good."

"Can I take this necklace off now?"

He sighed. "Yeah, you can take it off."

I pulled it over my head and handed it to him.

After a few minutes, he sat up a little straighter and looked around. "Where are you going?"

"Uh, back to the station. Or actually, maybe I should drop you off at your house, then head home."

I saw him slowly turn to look at me. "Your apartment is still messed up. Why don't you stay with me again tonight?"

I frowned. Shit. I forgot about the state my apartment was in. I didn't really want to go back there after that poor guy was tortured in my fucking bed. Dammit, I really wanted to sleep in my bed tonight instead of the fucking ground again. "Do I have to sleep on the grass again?"

He blew out a relieved breath, then chuckled a little. "No, you can use a bed. I only made you sleep in the grass because I wanted the extra boost of earth magic to help you heal fully after everything your body's been through this week."

I nodded and Sera climbed from his lap to mine, so I gave her a few pats. "I don't know if I said this enough yet, Ailin, but thank you for saving me, and for healing me. I appreciate it."

"You're my partner, Seb. I'll always do whatever I can to help you."

I ran those words over in my head. He just meant he'd do whatever he could to help me while we were working together, right? Because the way he'd said it, and with the amount of conviction in his voice, I almost felt like he meant forever.

Before I could question him about it, his phone rang. I didn't look at him, but I heard him sigh in annoyance before answering, "What?" *Geez, what's his problem now? Rude much?*

He glanced at me with a little glare, but I shrugged. He shouldn't be reading my thoughts if he didn't want to hear me call him out. There was a long pause before he asked, "What the hell were you thinking? Why didn't you call me sooner? You know, *before* you did something so stupid?"

Seraphina started wiggling around a little, like she was getting restless, but she didn't get off my lap.

"Fine," Ailin said into the phone. "Ten minutes." He shoved his phone in his pocket and barked out, "Change of plans. We're going to Riverland."

"Excuse me?" I asked. *Jerk.* "I thought we were past this bossing me around bullshit."

He sighed. "Can you please take me to Riverland?"

"Sure, if you explain what's going on. I'm not walking into a situation where I don't know what to expect. And if you plan on acting like I'm your boyfriend or whatever again, I'd appreciate a heads up so I'm not just flailing around in the dark again. I like to plan ahead, and I hate when you do shit that makes me look like an idiot."

"I don't do that on purpose, you do that enough on your own."

I flipped him off. "Not true. So... what's going on?"

He didn't answer right away, and when I glanced at him, I could tell he was trying to calm his anger—anger at whatever this situation was, not at me—before answering. He had some serious anger issues sometimes. It wasn't like I was asking a whole hell of a lot. I should know what to expect before entering a possible dangerous situation. But I gave him the time he needed. He'd been better about the whole partner thing lately, but I knew it was still very much a work in progress. Especially when it came to this supe shit.

When he finally answered, he sounded more annoyed than angry. "My baby brother is an idiot and tried to perform a hex-removal he'd never done before without me. He is currently fighting off a werewolf because the idiot took the wrong spell with him, so now the man that was a wolf has turned into a man-wolf instead of a man and is currently trying to kill my brother because of it."

I shook my head. "I have no idea what that means, but okay." I reached over and hit the lights and siren on my car and pressed the gas pedal harder. "I'll get you there in five."

I didn't even get a thanks from him. He just shifted his booted feet around on my dash, leaving more footprints, and continued playing with his bracer. Sera slid off my lap and climbed over to him, eventually settling around his neck.

When we were approaching Riverland I asked, "What part of the river is he at?"

"The curve," he answered. I knew what he was talking about since everyone called the huge twist in the river *the curve*. He added, "Your car will be okay to drive on the field, right?"

"Sure."

When I got close to the area, I drove through the tall grass for a minute, but slowed down when I saw a teenager running from a huge monster. As I pulled to a stop, I noticed that the teenager had a huge stick in his hand. It sorta looked like a staff. There was no possible way a stick would do any good against the huge fucking *thing* running after him, but I guess he was limited to his options out here.

Ailin was out of the car before it was in park. I opened my door and Sera jumped out, padding after Ailin. I jumped out, too, drawing my gun and running closer to the scene. As I aimed my gun at the giant monster, the *werewolf* was suddenly thrown through the air with greenish wind, landing about twenty feet farther away from the teenager. I glanced at the teenage boy; he was surrounded by a green wind tunnel. When I looked back at the werewolf, Ailin was already bent over it somehow. I had no clue how he got there so fast.

As I continued walking, I watched the werewolf thrashing around on the ground. Ailin bent down, and I was about to yell at him to stop so he wouldn't get clawed or bitten, but then I walked closer and realized that the werewolf was stuck to the ground with vines wrapped around its arms, body, and legs. Suddenly, the area around Ailin and the werewolf started glowing green.

"Backup, human," Ailin yelled at me.

I took a step back and said, "Dick."

"Don't shoot him. He's not really a monster," Ailin yelled at me again.

I rolled my eyes. "He looks like a fucking monster to me."

Ailin ignored me and started mumbling in his witch language or whatever it was. The werewolf started howling and thrashing all over the place, but it couldn't break free of the vines. The green glow intensified, making me squint, but I watched in amazement as the werewolf slowly transformed into a human teenage boy. He was human. Ailin's words from the car replayed in my head, and I finally understood that the werewolf had been in some kind of *magical trouble* or something. *Maybe it got stuck in its werewolf form and couldn't change back.* I looked away since the poor guy didn't have any clothes on, and I shrugged out of my shirt, throwing it behind me in Ailin and the kid's direction. The other teenager was still in the middle of a windstorm with his arms crossed over his chest and his stick—or branch or staff—in one hand. He looked pissed.

"You okay?" I heard Ailin ask the kid.

"Yeah." The kid cleared his throat. "Thanks, Ailin."

Ailin didn't answer, but the two of them walked past me a minute later, the kid in my shirt that was hanging down to his knees. The kid looked at me and nodded. "Thanks."

I nodded back, then followed them as Ailin stalked toward the windstorm kid. About ten feet from the storm, the werewolf kid, put his hand in front of my chest to stop me. I glanced at him and decided to wait there to see what

Ailin was going to do next. I was surprised when Seraphina started rubbing on my legs. I hadn't seen where she'd gone after she'd jumped from the car when we'd first gotten here. I bent over to scoop her up, and she climbed on my shoulder, then wrapped around my neck and hummed at me. I smiled, knowing she was content there.

The werewolf kid grinned at me, and I was taken aback by his yellow eyes. I'd never seen eyes that color before. The kid said, "Even Sera doesn't want to be caught in the middle of that." He nodded his head toward Ailin and the other kid. *God, when will this day stop getting more and more weird?* The werewolf kid reached up and scratched Sera's neck, but then my attention was drawn toward my witch partner.

The windstorm stopped swiftly, and all the little pieces of debris fell to the ground.

"What the hell, Ailin?" the windstorm kid yelled.

"What were you thinking, Basil? You could have been killed or killed Thayer," Ailin yelled, pointing back at the kid next to me—Thayer, I guess his name was. "Do I need to take that away from you?" Ailin pointed at the stick thing the kid was holding.

"Don't be a dick. We were just practicing," the kid—Basil—yelled. I guess this was the troublemaker brother Ailin had mentioned so many times.

"Yeah, practicing how to be an idiot," Ailin yelled back.

The kid scoffed. "Yeah, of course, because everything I do is stupid, right, Ailin?"

"I didn't say that, Basil, but you need to be more careful."

"Maybe if you were around to teach me, I would know how to hex right."

"I've been working, you ungrateful little shit." Even from where I stood, I could see the anger radiating off Ailin.

"You're never here, even when you're not working. In the past month, you've only been home a handful of nights, and some of them, you banned me from our back yard and told me to give you and your *human pet* some peace." Basil's voice broke and he looked away from Ailin.

"Do not disrespect Sebastian that way." Ailin's voice was steely and terrifying, like it'd been when he'd protected me from that incubus.

Basil looked unaffected, though. The kid rolled his eyes dramatically and shrugged a shoulder. "I'll do whatever I damn well please."

Ailin moved into Basil's face quicker than I thought possible and even though he whispered, I could still hear him because it was like everything around us went silent, like everything was holding its breath. "Sebastian is *mine*, Basil, and brother or not, if you disrespect him, you'll regret it for the rest of your existence."

What. The. Actual. Fuck.

Did he seriously just say that? Does that asshole suddenly think he owns me? I took a step forward to put my foot down about this whole fucking weird claiming thing or whatever the fuck Ailin had warned me about, then turned around and did himself, but the werewolf kid put his hand on my chest to stop me.

"Don't get in the middle of them. They're both too powerful and sometimes don't know their own strengths. You might not come back with all your limbs intact."

I huffed out a pissed-off breath and crossed my arms over my chest, glaring at Ailin even though he wasn't looking at me.

Ailin stood there, his chest heaving, but after a long moment, he stepped forward and pulled Basil into a hug. Basil resisted at first, but then he shut his eyes tight and grabbed onto Ailin firmly. After a long embrace, the two let go, but Ailin kept his arm over Basil's shoulders, and they walked away from us, talking quietly to one another.

"By the way, I'm Thayer." The kid next to me drew my attention, so I shook his outstretched hand. I'd have to deal with Ailin later, when I could yell at him in private.

"Sebastian." After we let go, I asked, "So you're a werewolf?" *Is it rude to ask someone what supernatural— what species?—they are? I'll have to add that to my mental list, too. Sigh.*

Thayer laughed loudly at that. "No, I'm not a werewolf." He kept chuckling at me. "I'm a witch, just like Ailin and Basil."

I blinked at him. "Oh. But... you were just a werewolf." This shit was confusing as fuck.

Thayer stopped laughing and sighed. "Yeah that was a hex gone wrong."

"That was just a hex?"

Thayer eyed me for a moment, then looked at Sera on my shoulder before nodding at her. When he looked back at me, he had a serious look on his freckled face. "Ailin hasn't told you much, has he?"

"Actually, I think it's that he's told me so much that my brain can't wrap itself around anything else."

The kid chuckled.

"Actually, I was wondering about the whole... what did he call it? Affinity...?"

"What about it?"

"Um, do all witches have the same nature affinity or whatever it's called?"

He shook his head and scratched his ear before telling me, "My affinity is light, as in natural light *or* artificial light. I tap into my light energy, then speak the correct words to transform the energy and ta-da, magic. I can do the same things as other witches, but my power comes from light energy, does that make sense?"

I nodded. "I think so."

"Ailin's affinity is nature; Basil's is shadow."

"Well, what makes Ailin so powerful, then?"

He scratched his ear again. "So I pull the energy into myself and release it in the way I want, right?" I nodded, so he continued, "But I have a limit of how much power I can pull into myself, all witches have a limit, and when we release our energy, it wears us down after a while or if we expel too much. But, Ailin, he doesn't really have a limit, at least, not that I know of. He still gets tired if he expels too much energy, but he can keep tapping into his nature energy. I've never seen anyone else do that except for maybe Basil."

I glanced over at the brothers, who were deep in conversation. If they were both that powerful, no wonder Thayer had kept me back from them. That Basil kid seemed like a handful even on a good day. "Okay, I think I get it."

Thayer grinned at me, his yellow eyes lighting up. They were kind of cool looking, but also intimidating. "I imagine it's hard to understand if you didn't grow up with magic."

I huffed out a laugh. "That's an understatement. Okay, so if you can do whatever you want, what happened with this werewolf thing just now?"

"Apparently, Basil had the words to turn me into a wolf, but not the right ones to turn me back, so I became a werewolf, kinda caught mid-shift, and I lost control of myself. Luckily, I didn't hurt anyone. Basil and I practice on each other all the time, and we're usually not this... disastrous."

I closed my eyes for a moment to take everything in. So much. This was all so much. *Did I actually get knocked out the other night when the perp broke into my apartment, and maybe I'm in a coma dreaming up all this shit?* "Wait a minute." I opened my eyes. "Your affinity is light? Does that mean you can't do spells at night?"

He grinned. "No, there's moonlight, and if I'm inside or in the city, there are lights on or even candles lit. Plus, I have a gem that Ailin gave me a long time ago that has light energy stored up in case of an emergency." He pulled out a necklace and showed me a large yellow stone. "I would've killed Basil if this had gotten lost when he changed me."

"You can store energy in stones?"

"Stones, gems, even staffs, and things like that." He pointed at Basil, who was still holding a staff.

"This is a lot to wrap my head around."

Thayer patted me on the shoulder.

After a few minutes, I asked, "You can do anything? Anything at all?"

He shrugged. "I mean, yeah, pretty much. You can't, like, bring someone back from the dead or stop someone from dying if it's their time or anything like that, but yeah, anything else."

"Their time?"

He waved me away. "Don't worry about that. Here, see that frog over there?" He pointed at a little green frog hopping a few feet away toward the lake. I nodded, so he continued, "I can make him freeze." He pointed at the frog and muttered a word I didn't understand as bright light shined from his hands, and the frog stopped moving; completely frozen in place.

All I could do was stare for a moment. "Uh, can you unfreeze him?"

"Yeah, of course," he answered, pointing and muttering under his breath. The little frog immediately started hopping again, although it quickly turned and sped away in the other direction.

"Wow," was all I could muster.

"Alright, Seb, time to take these brats home," Ailin shouted from next to my car before getting in.

I rolled my eyes at his lack of manners, but still walked over with Thayer beside me. I popped open the trunk and pulled out an extra shirt I had back there—I'd learned a long time ago to keep a change of clothes in the car because you never knew what you'd come across on the job. Before we got in, I said, "Thanks for answering my questions, Thayer."

He smiled at me and pet Sera's neck again. "Anytime."

Then the two of us joined Ailin and Basil in the car.

Chapter Eleven

When I started the engine, Sera jumped in my lap and settled down. I looked in my rearview mirror at Basil, who looked like a younger version of Ailin. Pale skin, black hair braided on the left with beads in it. He was even wearing all-black and an angry scowl like his older brother. When the kid made eye contact in the mirror, I had to stifle a gasp. His eyes were black. Like darker than any eyes I'd ever seen, and even though it was getting dark out, I could see everyone else's eyes fine. Basil had black eyes. Oh my god, was he some kind of demon or something? *He's evil. Basil is evil.*

Ailin snorted beside me, then placed a gentle hand on my thigh, making me look at him. "While I don't disagree with that sentiment on most days—he's a little shit—Basil's affinity is shadow, Seb. Mine is nature." He pointed at his green eyes. "Thayer's is light." He nodded back at Thayer, who grinned at me with those weird yellow eyes.

"Y-your eyes match your affinity?"

Ailin nodded and released me with a small grin before looking in the back seat and glaring at Basil. When Ailin settled in the seat, he crossed his arms over his chest, looking pissed-off again as he propped his feet up. *This is going to be such a fun car ride.*

I looked over at Thayer and noticed for the first time that he, too, had his red hair braided on the left side

with beads in. *Must be a witch thing, like a freaking cult.*
Ailin snorted out a laugh, clearly hearing my stray thought.
"Get out of my head."

"I like it in there."

Mocking little asshole twatwaffle, I thought as loud
as possible as I put the car in gear and made a wide turn to
get back on the road. Ailin snorted again, so I glared at
him.

He smirked and lifted a shoulder.

"Can every one of you hear my thoughts?"

Ailin turned and glared at the teens in the back
seat, but they both said, "Nope," at the same time.

Be thankful for small miracles.

When I realized I hadn't introduced myself, I looked
in the mirror at Basil and said, "Hey, I'm Sebastian, by the
way."

The kid didn't say anything, but Ailin cleared his
throat, and I almost laughed when I saw Basil roll his eyes.
But the kid said, "Basil," then he leaned forward and held
his hand over my shoulder so I could shake it. I let go of
the steering wheel with one hand, and as soon as I shook
it, Basil gasped and yanked my hand back toward him.
What the hell.

"Basil," Ailin hissed and the kid let go immediately,
but he didn't move away, in fact, he moved his face right
next to mine.

"What the hell are you doing? You're going to
make me get into an accident."

The kid ignored me and stared at my neck for several beats before sitting back in his seat and turning to Ailin. "What did you do?"

"Nothing," Ailin said immediately, making me suspicious.

I put my hand on my neck, but didn't feel anything weird there. I wanted to look in the mirror, but I'd have to wait until I stopped the car.

"I'd recognize your mark anywhere, Ailin. What did you do?" Basil sounded pissed.

"None of your damn business," Ailin said.

"Wait. What's he talking about? What did you do to me? What's this about a mark again? Is that what you did when Ni—"

Ailin slapped his hand over my mouth and moved closer to whisper into my ear, "I'll explain when we're alone. Please don't say anything further."

I nodded, then pushed his hand off me. "Would you quit it? You guys are gonna make me get into an accident. Assholes."

"Sorry," both Ailin and Basil said together.

I huffed, but didn't say anything else.

"You know how to get to our house from here, right?" Thayer asked.

"Yeah, I'm good. Wait. Our? You live with them?" I asked.

"Yep," Thayer said cheerily. He was the only person in the car that didn't have a bad attitude at the moment.

Everyone fell quiet after that, but luckily, the drive to the bridge that led into their property wasn't very long.

When we were about halfway across the bridge, I felt a weird little tingle fall over my body. Sera nosed my cheek and the strange sensation went away as if it'd never been there—maybe it hadn't. I looked over at Ailin and in the mirror at the boys in the backseat, but none of them seemed to notice anything.

I pulled in front of the large tree-house and parked where Ailin pointed, and everyone got out. When I shut my door, I said, "Shit, we should've stopped by my place for some clothes. I don't have anymore clothes in my car."

Ailin glanced at me. "No worries, I have plenty of clothes here."

"Are you sure? I could run over there really quick."

"It's fine, Seb. Let's go inside. I'll cook some dinner." He looked at his brother. "You really can't hear him?" *Huh?*

Basil glanced at me. "Nope."

"Try," Ailin said.

Try what?

Basil looked me in the eyes and squinted at me. His black eyes clouded over with black smoke, and I took an involuntary step back.

"He's not going to hurt you, detective."

Basil's face tensed further, and I felt a small prickle in my head, like he was tickling my fucking brain or something. But then the prickle turned sharp, and I yelped at the same time that Basil yelled and bent over, grabbing his head and groaning in pain.

I rubbed my temples. "What the hell was that?"

Basil groaned again. "I couldn't hear anything, A. It's like he's impenetrable."

"Nothing at all?" Ailin asked him.

"Not a single thing."

Ailin frowned at me, so I asked, "What the hell are you two talking about? What did he do?"

"He tried to read your thoughts, but apparently, he couldn't."

I narrowed my eyes at both of them. "You read my thoughts all the time."

"Yeah, I know. I just needed him to try so I can figure out what's different about you."

I didn't know what to do about that.

"Don't worry about it." Ailin looked at the teens. "Go on, then."

The two teenagers walked to the front door, so I sighed and followed Ailin inside. Even though I'd been inside before, I was still amazed at how they'd managed to make a group of living trees form into a house, and a huge one at that. Ailin walked straight to the kitchen, stopping in the doorway, and I was surprised to see a young woman, four teenagers, and two preteens in there already. A few gave me curious looks, but didn't say anything other than hello to Ailin. Then the young woman that looked just like Ailin and probably about the same age—mid-twenties—turned around from the stove, looking pretty angry as she walked over to us. She was glaring at Ailin with her yellow eyes as she walked over to him and smacked his arm before pulling him into a hug.

When they pulled apart she said, "You going to be home for a few days like you said?"

Ailin took a deep breath before answering, "No, Opal, I'm sorry, but the kuma mali demon is still out there. I have to find it. The amount of blood magic happening in the past year is astounding. Something big is happening, but I'm not sure what yet."

The girl—Opal—sighed. "I figured as much." Ailin whispered to her for a second, then she looked at Basil and Thayer. "You two better start helping with dinner or you'll be grounded for a week for what you did."

Basil opened his mouth like he was about to argue, but Opal held up her hand and snapped, "Save it."

I was surprised Basil actually listened to her, but he did. He and Thayer stalked off to the counter where two of the teens were cutting up vegetables. Thayer gave me a little salute along the way. Opal looked me up and down, then glanced at Ailin with a raised eyebrow. Ailin sent her a little shrug, then Opal walked over to me and grabbed my hand.

"Hi, Sebastian. I'm Opal, Ailin's sister," she said to me, then she looked at Ailin. "At least he's handsome. Good pick." And with that, she let go and walked back to the stove, leaving me alone with Ailin. *Good pick? What the actual fuck?*

After a long awkward pause, I asked, "Do you want to tell me what's going on?"

He sighed. "Not here."

I crossed my arms over my chest. "Then where? You can't keep avoiding this. What the hell did you do to me?" I grabbed the side of my neck. I still hadn't looked in a mirror. I'd totally forgotten when I'd parked the car because I'd been so distracted about not having clothes.

"After dinner. I'll take you somewhere where young ears won't be able to hear us."

I looked around and noticed that while none of the kids were looking at us, they were very obviously listening to our conversation. I blew out a frustrated breath. "Fine. Who are all these kids, anyway?"

Ailin grinned. "Part of my coven."

I blinked at him.

He snorted out a laugh. "You should see your face." He chuckled, then pointed at each kid. "I'm sure you remember Honey, that's her sister, Sugar. Their older siblings aren't in this house any longer, but they live on my property about half a mile west. Then there's Willow, Clover, Delaro, Tiordan, and Jorah." Each of the kids sent me a little wave when their name was called. Honey and her twin were the oldest, maybe eighteen, and the youngest was about twelve.

I nodded, a little overwhelmed by the names that I'd probably never remember.

"Some of them are my cousins, and the youngest over there, Jorah, is Thayer's little brother. They're not actually related by blood, but they're all members of my coven, so they're all my family."

I looked around at all the teens and frowned. "Where are their parents?"

He stared at me for several seconds before answering, "Their parents were killed along with my parents when I was sixteen." He turned and walked into the kitchen where he kissed the little boy—Jorah—on the temple before helping him make a salad. Clearly talking about *that* was off the table. Killed as in, they were murdered? Or there was an accident? Some kind of magical accident, maybe?

I stayed where I was for several seconds and took in the scene as I thought over everything he'd just told me. I wasn't sure exactly where to start. I had so many, many questions. Ailin had already told me that he was the oldest of his siblings, and if he was twenty-six, and all of their parents died ten years ago, did that mean that Ailin had been raising these kids this whole time? Since he himself was still a child? Ailin laughed loudly at something Jorah said, and I couldn't help but stare at him. He looked so free and comfortable, like he wasn't afraid to drop his macho act and just be himself. I'd never seen this side of him before. He was smiling and talking among the kids, and I swear that I'd never seen him look happier. He was beautiful like this.

From the bits and pieces of his life that he'd let slip out, I wasn't surprised that he always wore a tough exterior for the rest of the world. It was his armor, and I couldn't blame him. His life had been—and still was—so different from my own. His life was loud and full and surrounded by a family that obviously loved him. Mine was quiet and lonely; I had no one else, no family, not even any real friends. Sure, I'd gone out with my coworkers a few times, but I didn't really know them, and they didn't know me at all. I frowned as I realized just how lonely I'd been in the past few years. At least when I'd lived at the Academy and in the military, I'd been surrounded by other people in the same boat as me—well, minus the solitary confinement time. Now, though, I was always alone when I wasn't working.

I cleared my throat and walked over to Opal. "Do you need any help?"

Opal smiled at me with her yellow eyes. "Don't be silly, you're our guest. Just relax."

I frowned because I'd feel better if I was doing something, but I didn't respond because I didn't want to be impolite.

Ailin walked over and placed his hand on my upper arm, making his warmth seep through. "Do you want to come help me set the table?" When I looked at him, I had a feeling he knew I was feeling weird and uncomfortable, and I was grateful for him saving me without pointing out my discomfort in front of everyone.

"Sure."

He shot me a small smile and tugged my arm before dropping his hand away. I couldn't keep the small frown from my face when he took his heat with him. Why did I suddenly want to pull Ailin into my arms to see what he'd feel like up against me?

Ailin sent me a smile before walking out of the kitchen with me trailing behind. He pulled a bunch of plates and silverware out of a big cabinet, and I suddenly realized that their plates and silverware looked like regular dishes and not things made out of wood. I hadn't even realized it when I ate breakfast here the other day. There was just so much to look at and take in, it'd probably take another twenty times in the house before I truly saw everything. *I wonder if they just buy silverware like everyone else or if they make them?*

"They're actually made out of natural elements we've found in the forest, like rocks and things," Ailin said as he passed me the plates.

"It's really freaky when you do that." I started setting a plate at each seat.

"Do what?"

"Talk to me about what I'm thinking about."

Ailin hesitated for a second, then blew out a breath. "I'm sorry. Sometimes I don't realize I'm doing it. Your thoughts come in so clear that every now and then I think you're speaking out loud."

"Really?"

He nodded as he walked behind me, placing the silverware next to the plates. "Yeah. Which is also weird because thoughts don't usually come in so clearly. Usually they're almost staticky or jumbled, but yours aren't."

"And you have no idea why that is?"

He grinned. "I have a few theories."

"Care to share with the class?"

"No thanks."

"Ailin."

"Sebastian."

I huffed out a breath and tried to push my frustrations down so I wouldn't murder him.

He chuckled. "Look, I promise that as soon as I know for sure, I'll tell you, okay?"

I stared at him for several seconds and figured that was as good as I was going to get. "Fine." I set down the last plate.

"Would you like something to drink? We have water and juice."

"I'll just have whatever you're having."

He nodded and headed back into the kitchen, so I walked over to the cabinet he'd left open and decided to be nosey. There were more plates and silverware inside along with some glasses and cloth napkins, and what I figured were a few tablecloths. On the bottom shelf, there were a bunch of candles and a very old book. I was tempted to pick up the book and open it up, but I wasn't that much of an impolite guest, so I left it where it was with a longing glance. I couldn't put my finger on it, but I sorta felt compelled to pick it up. What was with some of this magic shit wanting me to grab it? So annoying.

"You okay, Seb?"

I looked over my shoulder to find Ailin standing behind me with a small frown on his face. "Yeah, I'm fine. Thanks." I grabbed the glass and took a small sip of the juice he'd brought me. *This is delicious.*

"Opal made it. She mixes a bunch of the fruits we grow, so she's always coming up with new ones. I'm not even sure what's in this one."

I took another sip. "It's really good."

"Thank you," Opal said as she walked out with a large tray of something that smelled so good my stomach started grumbling.

The kids all followed behind her, each of them carrying a different tray. They set them in the center of the table, and I was surprised by all of the colors on the platters. Everything looked and smelled delicious. Ailin grabbed my arm again, and I gasped, unable to hold it in. We both froze and stared at each other with wide eyes. I swore it felt like there was electricity zinging between us, and I was pretty sure that Ailin felt it, too.

Ailin flicked his tongue out to lick his lips, and my eyes caught the movement. *I wonder what he tastes like, or what it'd feel like to have his tongue licking my lips... or my skin.* One corner of Ailin's mouth quirked up, no doubt hearing my idiotic thoughts.

A throat clearing on the other side of the room jolted us out of our weird stare-off, but Ailin didn't release my arm. Opal was staring at us with a confused, but amused expression. "Sit down so we can eat."

Ailin cleared his throat and gently pulled me to a chair, and we both sat down with Ailin on my left. When he let go of me, I managed to keep the groan from coming out. I wanted so badly to push my shoulder against his just to feel that warmth again, but I refrained.

"Dig in, guys," Opal said from her seat at the head of the table.

No one needed to be told twice; everyone scooped things on their plates and passed platters around, filling their plates to the brim. We all dug in, and as soon as the first bite of some weird baked vegetable thing hit my tongue, I moaned in pleasure. *Holy shit, that's delicious.* I moaned again when I took the next bite. So good.

Ailin froze beside me, so I swallowed my food and looked at him. "What?"

"Nothing," he said quickly, then turned to his food. *Is he blushing right now?* At that thought, his cheeks turned a deeper shade of pink. *Oh my god! He is blushing! What the hell is he blushing about? Ailin doesn't blush!*

Ailin cleared his throat, then said to the whole table, "I have to call Emrys."

Everyone froze and stared at him with wide eyes. Opal asked, "Are you sure that's wise?"

Ailin shrugged. "I don't have a choice. It's either that or call the assembly. And as much as I hate asking Emrys for help, the assembly is even worse."

Opal sighed. "That's true. Just... be careful."

"Always am."

Everyone went back to eating, including me, but I couldn't stop thinking about this Emrys person. I was pretty sure this guy was bad news, and I really didn't think having someone like that helping us was a good idea.

"Don't worry, Seb, I'll protect you," Ailin's hot breath whispered in my ear, sending shivers down my back.

I ignored the strange sensation and turned a little in my seat to look at him. "It wasn't me I was worried about. I don't want something to happen to you."

Ailin's smirking expression changed to a small smile, his eyes softening. "I'll be okay, I promise."

"I hope you're right."

Before he could respond, I felt something rub against my leg. I was so used to the feeling by now that I didn't even jump. I bent over and put my hand out so Seraphina could walk so her belly was in my hand, and I could pick her up. I brought her up to my chest and pet behind her ears, kissing the tip of her nose. When I realized there were eyes on me, I looked around the table to find almost everyone—minus Basil and Thayer—staring at me. "Oh, I'm sorry, you probably don't want her up here. I can put her back on the ground."

Ailin put his hand on my forearm to stop me, that warm feeling seeping in again. "That's not it. They're just surprised that Sera let you pick her up."

I frowned at that. "What are you talking about? She's the sweetest cat ever. She always lets me pick her up." The others started eating again, ignoring us.

He smiled at me and pet the cat. "I know, but she doesn't let anyone else hold her. She lets the rest of them pet her, but never pick her up like that."

"Really?" I looked at Sera and kissed her nose again, then whispered to Ailin, "Should I put her down while everyone is eating?"

"No, she's fine at the table. Most Bonded Ones sit here at some point with us." He nodded in the direction of Jorah, who had a bird of some kind sitting on his shoulder. The kid had green eyes, so I had a sudden thought.

"Do only nature witches have a Bonded One?"

Ailin shook his head. "No, almost all witches are bound to an animal, and it can happen at any time, although Jorah bonded very early. It usually happens after we go through puberty and our magic grows. Jorah is very strong already, just like my brother."

"Does Basil have a Bonded One?"

He shot me a grin. "Wait till you meet Blaze. I can't wait to see your face." He chuckled.

"Why? What kind of animal is it?"

Ailin shook his head. "I'd rather you be surprised."

I glared at him. "You're an asshat."

He shrugged and smirked at me before taking a bite of his food.

Arrogant ass. He snorted and I couldn't help the small smile that quirked up at that. It was annoying as hell to have him in my head all the time, but it paid off occasionally.

Chapter Twelve

"So you can have this room for the night," Ailin said as he swung a door open, revealing a huge bedroom with a bed made out of the living tree, of course, and several dressers. I walked past him and took the large room in. The bed had dark grey sheets and big pillows, and was probably at least as big as a king-sized bed, probably bigger. "There's a bathroom right through there." He pointed at a door across from the bed. "Help yourself to whatever clothes you want. There should be some sweats and tees in this dresser that fit you." He patted the tall dresser near the door.

"Thanks, A."

He grinned at me. "Make yourself at home, okay? Help yourself to anything up here, anything in the kitchen, whatever. I'll be on the couch in the living room if you need anything, though, 'kay?"

"What do you mean you'll be on the couch? Aren't you sleeping in your room?"

"This is my room, Seb."

I blinked at him. "I thought this was a guest room. I can't take your bed, man. I'll sleep on the couch."

Ailin's mouth curved up on one side. "It's fine, detective. I'll be okay, and you're my guest, so you get to sleep in the bed."

"I... I thought you'd have a guest room in this huge house." *Shit. Was that rude?*

Ailin snorted out a laugh. "All of our rooms are taken by my coven members. But you can stay here, I promise it's fine."

I cringed. I didn't want him to sleep on the couch. He'd had a long day, too. It'd been the longest day ever, the longest week, really. It wasn't fair to throw him on the couch while I got the bed.

"Well, you're not sleeping on the couch, that's for sure. You need the rest after healing twice in a row."

I wanted to argue, but I knew it was true. I was still sore and my body was worn out.

"The only other solution is to share the bed, Seb, and I know you don't want to do that." Ailin's voice was quiet and a little hesitant.

I thought about what it'd be like if he was in the bed, too, and I thought about what it'd be like if he was on the couch. I probably wouldn't sleep very well if he was on the couch because I'd feel guilty. But could I handle having him so close? Was it really that big of a deal? I took a deep breath. "Just sleep in the bed with me."

Ailin's eyes went up into his hairline. "You sure?"

I nodded. "Yep. It'll be fine." I walked over to the dresser and pulled out some sweatpants and a t-shirt. "Will these fit me?"

Ailin put his hand on top of them, and I felt the clothes grow warm before he nodded. "Yep, they'll fit you fine."

"Thanks." I ran into the bathroom and quickly changed, brushed my teeth with a new toothbrush he'd left on the counter for me with a little note, peed, then looked into the mirror at my neck. I moved around at different angles looking for the mark or whatever, and I didn't see it at first. But on closer inspection, I found a circular mark that looked golden against my dark skin. There were swirling patterns inside it so intricate and tiny, I couldn't tell where one line ended and another started. *What the fuck? What the fuck did he put on me? Holy fuck! Is this permanent?*

I went back out, set my folded dirty clothes on top of the dresser, then stood there with my arms crossed. He was sitting on the edge of the bed looking unusually vulnerable, like he was awaiting my verdict or something. I almost felt bad for him for a split-second, but then I remembered the fucking mark he put on me, and my anger rose even higher. "What. *The. Fuck.* Did. You. Do. To. Me, Ailin? What the fucking fuck is this thing? Take it off of me right now!"

He took a deep breath. "Please don't freak out."

"Saying that is only going to make me freak out even more!"

He stood up and put his hands out like he was approaching a wild animal he thought might attack him. He'd be lucky if I didn't. "I can't take it off of you."

I stared at him for several seconds before my anger exploded. "What the fuck is the matter with you? How could you put something on my skin like that without my permission? I don't care what you have to do, just get it the fuck off of me, Ailin!"

He closed his eyes and swallowed thickly. "I can't take it off. I'm sorry, but it's there... permanently."

I screamed and walked away from him, pulling on my hair a little. "What the fuck is it?"

I heard him mutter under his breath, "Thank the Mother the room is soundproof."

I turned to look at him. "How could you do this to me?"

"I had to."

"No, you didn't, you asswipe!"

"You bear my mark now, Sebastian Cooper Fitz. My mark has become *ours*. Any supe that comes near you will know that you fall under my protection. They'll know if they attack you, it's a direct attack on me. If they hurt you, I'll know. If they touch you, I'll know. If they harm what's mine, I. Will. Hunt. Them. Down." His eyes looked stormy, his voice was so cold it gave me chills. His skin was glowing green, just faintly like he was struggling to keep his power inside, and it was threatening to pour out all over him. The non-human part of him was showing, and I didn't know whether to be afraid of him or in awe. If I didn't know him, I'd be terrified of whatever it was he kept locked inside. But I did know him, and his little power display was pissing me off.

"If they harm what's *yours*? I'm not a possession, Ailin, you possessive fucking supe! I thought it was the other supes I had to be afraid of, not you! I'm a person.

You can't just say I belong to you and think I'll be okay with that!" *What the hell have I gotten myself into?*

Ailin didn't answer me, he just stared, his green energy swirling around him more forcefully.

"You warned me that your… people were possessive. I didn't think I had to worry about you."

"You don't… I would never hurt you."

"Maybe not, but apparently, you think it's okay to mark my skin!"

He stared at me and the energy around him swirled faster, making me take a step back before I got knocked on my ass. Fucking dick with his fucking powers.

I tried another tactic so he didn't go all green blasts on my ass. "What do you mean, you'll know if someone hurts me?"

He took a few deep breaths, and his energy finally calmed, though I could see it just below the surface. "You and I are forever linked. If… if someone harms you, I'll feel it. And… if I'm harmed, you'll feel it, too."

My heart began to race, and I shook my head. This was too much. It was all too much. I backed away from him until my butt hit the closed door. We were forever linked? What the fuck did that even mean?

Ailin walked a little closer and pulled his shirt collar down a bit to reveal his neck. He turned and angled himself so I could see that on the same exact spot the mark was on my neck, a mark was on his.

"Wh-what is that?"

"It's your mark, Seb. *Our* mark," he said quietly. "We bear the same mark. We're linked. I put your hand on my neck, too, remember?" I nodded very slowly. "I did that to link us both together. I know you're pissed, and for that I'm sorry. I should've talked to you about it beforehand, but there wasn't time, and I sorta panicked with Nikolai looking at you like he was going to eat you, especially after that fucking incubus tried to take you from me. I didn't have time to explain. But I *had* to do it. I'm... I'm sorry I didn't ask for your permission first."

"You're... sorry?" I asked in disbelief.

He nodded. "I am. I'm sorry I didn't ask you first, but... I'm not sorry I did it. I... we needed to be linked." He looked completely sincere. He actually believed what he was saying.

But it was a hell of a lot to take in, so I didn't know what to say or what to do. He linked us together? I didn't even understand what the fuck that meant. *And forever? Was he serious about that shit?*

Ailin walked closer and touched my arm, then slid his hand down to my palm, holding my fingers tight. "It's going to be okay, Sebastian. I promise."

I shook my head, in a daze.

"Let's go to sleep. I'm sure you have questions, and I'll answer them, but you've had a lot thrown at you today. You need to rest; your body is still healing." I nodded and he gently pulled me to the bed, then pushed me until I laid down. He covered me with the soft blanket and whispered, "I'll see you in the morning." Then he walked toward the door.

"Wh-where are you going?" My voice cracked a little. *I think I'm in shock.*

"Downstairs to sleep on the couch."

My brow furrowed. "I thought you were sleeping in here."

He looked surprised for a few seconds, then a small smile spread over his face. "Okay, sure."

I watched as he whispered something under his breath, and his jeans and tight black shirt turned into sweatpants and a casual t-shirt. I blinked a few times and shook my head. This magic shit was going to take a lot of getting used to.

Ailin walked around to the other side of the bed and climbed in. "Sorry. I can stop doing that in front of you if you're uncomfortable."

"No, it's fine, it's just... weird."

He smiled a little, then held his fingers up and flicked them. The lights instantly went out, and he settled into the bed about a foot away from me. After a few silent and awkward minutes, Ailin said, "Goodnight, Sebastian."

I swallowed and whispered back, "Goodnight."

***

I followed the path through the trees and wasn't surprised to find the mouth of a cave. I looked around and didn't see anyone following me, so I picked up my pace and headed inside, following the long tunnels deep inside the cave. I knew where I was going, I'd been here many times before. I just needed to find the right opening.

I blinked a few times. *What am I doing? Where am I?*

When I finally saw the place I needed, I headed through the small space between rocks and took a deep breath. I was hidden away deep enough that I was safe here, at least for a few minutes. They wouldn't find me. I opened my cloak and pulled out the small bundle—*I recognize that, what's going on?*—then walked through a small passage to the back of a cave and pulled out an old wooden box covered in etchings. I ran my fingertips over the etchings, then carefully lifted the lid and gently set the small bundle inside. I placed my hand on the bundle and knelt.

When I began speaking, I didn't understand the words, I didn't know what was going on. It was like I was stuck inside my body, but someone else was controlling my movements and my voice. "Elita le mehi elmirai sel eh. Elita le mehi elmirai sel eh," I said over and over and over in a voice that wasn't my own.

I cut myself off when I heard a loud bang coming from the cave entrance. I shut the box and carefully placed it in a crevice in the rocks, then swiped my arm over the crevice and the hole closed, leaving only rock in its place as if the hole and box had never been there. *What the actual fuck?*

"Where issss it," a man in red hissed as he entered the cave. His voice sounded more reptilian than human.

"In a place you'll never think to look," I answered, my mouth moving of its own accord.

"It belongs to me!"

"Not anymore." I swirled my arms in a circle, and the air began to whip around me. *I can do magic! What the heck is happening?* "Leave this place. You do not belong on sacred ground."

The man in red threw his head back and laughed. "You really believe that, don't you, old wench?" He lifted his arms and inky black smoke poured out of his hands, filling up the cave and shrouding me in complete darkness.

I screamed in pain as the smoke filled my lungs, veins, and bones. I coughed out, "You'll... never... find it."

The red man hissed, "You led me straight to it, old wench."

I screamed in agony as the smoke finally reached my heart. I was dying. I was dying and it hurt, everything hurt.

"Sebastian!"

I coughed myself awake and looked around the strange room.

"You're in my home, Seb. You're safe."

I nodded and sat up, moving my arms and legs to make sure I was in control of myself. That dream had freaked me out, it felt so real. I swear I felt the pain of that inky black smoke filling me up. "I... it was a dream."

"Do you always have these... nightmares?"

I stretched my arms above my head, then shook them out. "No. I don't know what's going on. I usually don't even remember dreaming, let alone waking up screaming from such a vivid dream."

"Was it the same nightmare as before?"

"No. This one was just weird. It wasn't the demon or anything." I yawned. "Sorry I woke you up again. You can go back to sleep. I'm okay."

He nodded, and I laid back down. Sera walked over and laid down in between us, licking my nose and putting her ass in Ailin's face. I chuckled. "That's a good kitty."

Ailin snorted. "Watch it or I'll bring George inside and tell him to sleep on your chest."

I wrinkled my nose. "I'd kick your ass if you did that."

He snorted again and pet Sera a little. "Wake me up if you need anything, okay?"

"I'm fine, but... thanks."

I saw him nod before I closed my eyes and yawned again.

***

When I woke up, I had no idea where I was, but I could tell I had my face plastered against a soft fabric. I went to move my arm and hit something solid beside me, so I blinked a few times, then froze. *Oh my god, my head is on Ailin's chest!*

I tried to gently and quietly scoot away, but Ailin's arm was firmly around my shoulders, holding me tightly to him. I looked him over as I lay there and noticed the mark on his skin. At this angle, I could see it a lot more clearly than I could see my own in the bathroom last night. The mark was a gold color, which was kinda light on his skin, so it was harder to see than his other tattoos that were done in blacks, silvers, dark greens, and yellows—oh! They were the same colors as the witches' eyes. The swirling pattern inside the circle was quite elaborate, and if I were being honest with myself, it was actually pretty cool looking. Too bad I hadn't had a choice in getting mine. It looked like the swirling pattern intersected with a flower-like symbol in the center of the circle. I wanted to get a closer look, but I was afraid to move. Underneath the mark, there was another tattoo peeking out from beneath his shirt collar. Seeing just that little bit made me wonder how many tattoos he really had and if they all meant anything to him.

I tried to move out from under him again, but his arm was even tighter around me, so I held my breath as I waited for him to wake up and freak out that I was using him as a pillow. I could feel my cheeks heating up in embarrassment. I couldn't believe that I'd scooted closer to him like this. I'd never really shared a bed with someone all night, except the one long-term boyfriend I'd had years ago. Before that, I'd been at the academy and in the military where all I'd ever had was a little bunk not made to hold two people. My ex had stayed the night a bunch of times, but he hadn't been a cuddler, and I didn't think I was either. My ex and I had *never* woken up like this, not even once.

Ailin was going to be so mad when he woke up.

"I'm not mad." Ailin's grumbling, rough morning voice startled me enough that I jumped.

"How long have you been awake?" He still hadn't released me.

"I woke up before you."

I glared at him even though his eyes were closed. "Why didn't you let me move off you?"

He shrugged, making my head move with him. "You're kinda comfortable there."

I didn't really know what to say to that, and I couldn't tell if he was joking or not. "Are you making fun of me?" I wouldn't put it past him.

He tightened his hold on me. "No, vitmea, I'm being honest."

"Did you just call me a vitamin?"

He chuckled, his chest moving me with him. "No, you're my vitmea. The mark? My chosen one? Vitmea."

"Ch-chosen one?"

He froze and I heard him curse under his breath. "Uh, yeah. The whole mark thing, that's all I meant."

I had a feeling there was more to it than that, but I could tell he wasn't going to answer, so I let it be. *For now.* "I still don't know what to think about that."

"I know. I'm sure you'll forgive me eventually, though."

"Are you that confident in your persuasion skills?"

"Yep."

I snorted. "Whatever. Let me get up so I can piss and take a shower."

He gave me one last squeeze before releasing me, so I scrambled out of bed and ran for the bathroom. Right before I shut the door, I asked, "Why do you have so many tattoos that look like weird symbols?"

"They're runes. Sort of like spells. Each one does something different, like protection from being glamoured by a vampire or whatever."

I nodded and shut the door, a little surprised he'd actually given me a straight answer for once.

When I came out of the bathroom, he was sitting on the edge of the bed petting Sera. "We're going to have to make a pitstop."

"Okay... where?" I leaned against the wall.

"We need to find Emrys."

"You keep mentioning him. And that is...?"

"He left my coven a while ago. He's... my ex."

"The human asshat?"

One corner of his mouth lifted. "No. He's a witch."

"Why do you need him when you have a house full of witches?"

"I think I figured out a way to track the demon, but I need more power. He's a Prime."

"What the hell is that?"

"It's the... level below Sage, which makes him incredibly powerful. Basil's a Prime, but the Supreme Assembly doesn't know that, for his own protection. They think he's a High-Marrow, which is a higher mid-level witch, and I plan on keeping them in the dark on that one."

I waved him away. Too much hierarchy bullshit that I didn't understand. "Why can't you use Basil, then?"

"I need three powerful witches to help me, one from each affinity, so Basil is already going to help since he's shadow. Thayer will help, too, because I don't want him to feel left out. Opal's affinity is light, and she's about the same level as Thayer, so it doesn't matter which of the two I use. So now I just need to get Emrys on board because my other sister is pregnant, and I don't want her involved in this."

I stared at him for several seconds as I absorbed that before a memory of something he'd said a long time ago popped into my head. "Is this the guy that tried to burn you at the stake or something?"

He scrunched up his face a little, like he was afraid to answer. "Uh... not at the stake."

I waved him away. "So we have to hunt down a witch that tried to burn you alive?"

"Actually, I think I know where he is."

"Ailin! Did he try to set you on fire?"

He looked at me out of the corner of his eye, then huffed out, "Yeah."

"For fuck's sake." I walked over and pulled on my holster, then checked my gun. "If he tries to hurt you, I'm going to shoot him."

For some reason that made him smile really big.

"What?"

He stood and walked into the bathroom, then looked over his shoulder. "You're sexy when you're being protective of me." He shut the door, leaving me gaping after him.

Is he making fun of me again because he knows I think he's hot?

"I'm not making fun of you," he yelled through the door.

"Get outta my head, witch!"

"Stop thinking so loudly!"

I groaned in annoyance and sat on the bed while I waited for him to finish up. I pulled out my phone and checked my messages. Or I would have if I'd had any. *No one would even miss me if I disappeared.*

"I would miss you."

Ailin made me jump when he walked out of the bathroom, freshly showered without a shirt on. He absentmindedly ran his hand over his chest and stomach, and I followed the movement with my eyes, looking at all that exposed skin that was covered in tattoos.

I forced my gaze off his appealing body and looked into his green eyes. "Stop reading my thoughts."

"You need a better vision of yourself, Seb. I don't like all these dark thoughts floating around in that head of yours."

"It doesn't matter if you like them or not, it's my head, not yours, so stay out!"

He smirked at me and walked over to his dresser, pulling out a dark green t-shirt and shrugging it on. I watched as he strapped his arm bracers onto his forearms, and when he strapped on the second one, I caught a glimpse of the inside.

"Do you have gems inside your bracers?"

"Yep."

When he didn't elaborate, I sighed, exasperated. "Why do you have them in there?"

"They're an emergency energy force. I store up energy inside the stones and gems all over my body in case I'm ever out of resources or I need an extra boost."

"All over your body?"

He grinned at me. "In my bracers, my boots, my necklaces, and my thigh straps."

I stared at him for several minutes while he finished getting ready. "Is your life really so dangerous that you have to have that many backup plans in place? All the time?"

He stopped what he was doing and looked at me, leaning against the wall. "I am Sage. I'm the protector of the world, of our country, of my coven. When dangers enter our world, I'm the one that has to deal with it. I could forget about my responsibilities and live a peaceful life here on my land, and leave the others to deal with it, but that would only last so long. Many of the... dangers that crossover are too much for the average witch. If I don't take care of it, sooner or later the monsters will arrive at my front door, and by then, they'll be too powerful to stop."

Wow, that was way more serious an answer than I was expecting.

"I take my responsibilities very seriously, Seb."

"I can see that. I wasn't... questioning your motives, I just... wanted to know how dangerous your life is."

He flashed me a small grin. "I know, vitmea."

I blinked at him several times, and his grin grew.

"Come on, let's eat so we can get on the road. I have something I want to talk to you about on the drive."

I opened my mouth to ask him what the hell he was talking about, but he opened the door and walked out before I had the chance. Smug bastard. He knew I wouldn't ask him outside of this room because of all the little ears in the house. Jerkface.

I heard him laugh down the hall. With a sigh, I headed out of the room and made my way to the kitchen where I found Ailin and Opal talking quietly. They both froze when I walked into the room.

"Great. Now you're talking about me." I was too frustrated with this whole situation to let it go.

Opal looked a little embarrassed, but Ailin grinned at me. "We talk about everyone, especially family, so you should feel special."

I rolled my eyes. "Do you happen to have coffee?"

"Yep." Ailin walked over to a weird leaf thing and started messing around, so I looked at Opal with a small smile.

She smiled back, and I couldn't help but notice how young she looked. Ailin had said once that he was the oldest of his siblings, so if he was only twenty-six, how old was Opal? She had to be early twenties, yet, I was pretty sure the responsibility of all those kids landed on her shoulders. I really wanted to ask them both about everything, but I didn't want to be rude and intrude.

"Here you go, vitmea." Ailin handed me a cup. "I added cream and sugar for you already."

I lifted a brow at him. "Thanks." I took a tentative sip, and when the deliciousness hit my tongue, I closed my eyes. "Mm, this is really good. Thanks, A."

"You're welcome. Let's eat breakfast so we can be on our way."

I nodded and followed him to the table. Ailin waited for me to sit down, and I was surprised that he sat down right beside me instead of at one of the other chairs since no one else was at the huge table with us. I was even more surprised that he scooted close enough to press his shoulder against mine. *What the heck is he doing? Why does he keep touching me?*

Not that I was complaining, because I kinda liked it, but... he was being weird. Weirder than usual.

We started eating, and slowly the rest of his coven or whatever they were called woke up and joined us at the table for breakfast. Ailin stayed pressed to my side the whole time we were there, and the warmth he always exuded seeped into me, settling somewhere deep in my chest until I found myself pressing back against him, too.

Chapter Thirteen

Once we were finally out the door, and Ailin had said goodbye to all of the kids, we walked over to my car. He held up his hand and said, "Keys."

"I'm driving." I mean, really, who did he think he was trying to drive my car all the damn time?

"Can you open the trunk, then? I need to put my bag in the back." He lifted the duffle he was carrying.

I hit unlock on the key fob, then walked around to the driver's side and slipped in. A few seconds later, Ailin slid into the passenger seat, and I started the car. "So where are we going?"

"He lives a couple miles west."

My brow furrowed. "I didn't think there was anything farther west than this?" We were supposed to be in the farthest western town before the forest. Well, technically, Ailin's house was on the outskirts of the forest, but the Brinnswick Forest was protected land. No one was supposed to build on it.

"There's not any humans out west, but a few supe towns are out that way."

I drove through the trees on the dirt road that led to the bridge to get off his property as I tried to comprehend what he was saying. "There are whole entire towns of supes in the forest?"

"Only a couple. They're deep in the forest and well cloaked so humans can't wander inside by accident."

"I don't even know what to say to that."

He shot me a grin. "I want to ask you something before we drive over there."

"Uh, okay?"

"I know you have the one tattoo on your wrist, so you must not be opposed to tattoos, and I didn't see any others on your torso when I healed you the first time. But... do you have any other tattoos beside the wrist chain?"

That's what he wants to talk about? "Uh, nope."

"Why do you have the one around your wrist, by the way? I meant to ask you before."

My brow furrowed at the weird and personal questions. Usually Ailin wasn't one for small talk while we were on the road. "Uh, it's just a family thing... like from my parents before they were killed or left me at the Academy or whatever happened to them."

He was silent for a few seconds, but then he rested his hand on my thigh and gave it a little squeeze. Embarrassingly enough, my cheeks heated at the thought of his palm being so close to my cock. *Shit, did he hear that?* My cheeks heated more.

If Ailin had heard my thoughts, he didn't point them out, thank god. "I'm sorry you had to grow up there, Seb. I truly am."

I shrugged, too keenly aware that he hadn't removed his hand from my thigh yet. He left it there for a good five minutes of driving through the woods on small dirt roads I didn't know existed before now. He didn't say much except to point out directions.

"Okay, I need you to pull over. There's a little opening up here where you can park the car. It should give us enough room."

"What the hell do you want to do now? In the middle of the woods?"

"You'll see. And I think you're forgetting something."

I pulled the car into the clearing he pointed out. "What's that?"

"My affinity is nature. Being out in the middle of nowhere is where I'm at my strongest, which means the magic I do out here will be stronger than if we went back to the house to do it."

"And what magic would that be?"

"You'll see."

I rolled my eyes at that. "Whatever." I turned the car off, and Ailin grinned at me before hopping out. I shivered at the loss of contact. I'd felt weird about having him touch me there, but now that his hand was gone, I wanted it back. *Ugh. Pathetic.*

"I need to give you some protection," Ailin said to me as soon as I exited the car.

"Um... what do you mean?"

He walked over to the trunk and started digging around and muttering under his breath. I sighed and folded my arms over my chest as I leaned against the side of my car.

"Take off your shirt," he called out to me from behind the trunk door.

"Excuse me?" *Who the hell does he think he is trying to boss me around like that? And why the fuck would he want me to take off my shirt, anyway?*

He huffed and muttered again before saying, "I need to draw a couple runes on your chest, arm, ribs, and shoulder blade. It'll be easier if you're shirtless."

I thought about what that might mean and sighed. "Fine." I pulled my shirt over my head.

He slammed the trunk closed, then set a duffle bag on top of it and began pulling shit out. I watched him pull out a few bottles of ink, a marker, and some kind of weird metal contraption. When I realized what I was staring at, my eyes widened. "Oh, hell no."

"Seb, don't make this difficult." He sounded exasperated.

"Difficult? Are you serious? You want to tattoo me, in the middle of the fucking woods, drawing heaven knows what on me without even asking me first. You always just assume that I'll go along with whatever asinine plan you come up with, and you never even consult me! What the hell, A? Don't you think I might have an opinion on what's permanently drawn on my skin? You'd think you would've figured that out after what you did to me yesterday, you asshat. You can't just go around making those kinds of decisions for me. We're supposed to be partners." He opened his mouth to argue, but I quickly added, "And I have no idea if you even know how to use that thing, not to mention whether you can even draw! You really fucking expect me to let you tattoo me? I'll end up with a dick drawn on my forehead. *Permanently.*"

He winced. "I'd never do something like that to you."

I glared at him. "No, but you sure as hell don't mind making decisions about marking me and claiming me or whatever the hell this weird-ass supe shit is you did yesterday." I pointed at my neck. "So excuse me if I don't trust you with a tattoo gun."

He looked a little hurt, but I wasn't going to feel bad about what I'd said. It was true, and he knew it.

"In general, would you mind getting a few more tattoos?"

"I've never thought about it."

He pointed at my wrist. "Well, clearly you've thought about it a little."

"This isn't about me and the stupid-ass tattoo I've had forever."

"Remember when you asked me if there was something we could do to keep you better protected from the demon?"

"Yeah."

"Well, I can tattoo runes on your body to help with that."

"You seriously want to put *more* permanent marks on my skin?"

Ailin sighed. "That's why I'm asking you. I don't need you even more pissed at me, and this is the best way I know how to protect you."

I sighed and rubbed my eyes with my thumb and forefinger. "Will I be able to help fight this demon with the runes?"

"Yes, it should help with that."

I thought about it for a few seconds. It'd be nice to be able to do something, and I wanted to have Ailin's back while he tried to vanquish this thing. "How many do you want to give me?"

"Between two to four. I gotta check your skin first."

I had no idea what that meant, but whatever, it wasn't the weirdest thing to come out of his mouth. Not by a long shot. "Fine."

"You're still mad at me."

"You think? You need to ask me about this shit before assuming I'll just do whatever the hell you want. I get that *You. Are. Sage.* And you're in charge of like the entire world or whatever the fuck, but with me, that's not how it should be. I'm not one of your... your subjects or whatever."

He opened his mouth for a moment, but snapped it shut and stared at me. I was pretty sure he'd never been at a loss for words before, which made me feel a little proud that I maybe got my point across. Finally. After another minute, he said, "I'm not used to needing to run things by anyone else. This is new for me, too. I've been trying to be better at it."

"I know you have."

"I'm good at tattooing, I swear. I've been doing it for years. Well, I'm good at runes, I don't know about anything else. The runes will only work if they're tattooed because they become a part of you and mix in with your blood, unlike a pen mark on top of your skin that you can wash off. I also have to warn you that it will hurt like a normal tattoo." He stepped around the car and slowly walked toward me. "I can't use magic to take away the pain or the bleeding or even just draw them into your skin with magic at all because it will interfere with the integrity of the rune. It must heal and become a part of you naturally in order to have the most powerful result. There is no cheating where this is concerned. But it will help protect you for the rest of your life if you let me do it the right way." He stopped right in front of me, so close I could feel his breath brush across my neck. "What do you say? Can I give you the runes?"

I swallowed thickly at his closeness and tried not to let him see how much he was affecting me, then I nodded, but still asked, "What are the runes for?"

He smiled a little, then placed his palm on my chest over my heart, his touch sending a shiver down my spine. He whispered, "A protection rune here that will make you harder to hex, though not impossible, it only works to deflect simple spells. I could easily get past this rune, so the demon most likely can as well. *But* most importantly, this rune will make it impossible for the demon to possess you, so it's worth it for that alone." He put his other hand on my ribcage on the other side of my body, another shiver shooting through me. "A healing rune here so you'll heal more quickly and efficiently." Without removing his hand from my skin, he ran it from my chest, under my arm and around my back so his palm was flat against my shoulder blade. The movement had him stepping even closer to me. "The rune I place here will be for power and," he slid his other hand up my side, over my shoulder and to my bicep, "the one here is for strength. These two work together to ensure you hit harder and keep your energy up for a longer period of time. I don't think I should do more than four at a time. I don't want to overwhelm your system."

He was so close to me he had to tilt his head up to look me in the eyes. For once, he actually seemed a little unsure being so close to me. I didn't really understand it, he could be such a complete dick, but I kinda liked him sometimes, and I really couldn't deny my attraction to him. My body was reacting to his touch on my bare skin, and I could only pray that he didn't notice. I took a shaky breath when his fingers started gently rubbing my skin, making goosebumps pop up. I flexed my hands, fighting the urge to grab him and pull him even closer.

Ailin whispered, "Can I tattoo the runes on you?"

I swallowed audibly as I stared into his bright green eyes, seemingly at a loss for words myself now. I nodded and he grinned up at me, then took a shuddered breath before stepping back. I instantly missed the heat of his body at the small distance. He fumbled a little with the items on the trunk, and if I didn't know better, I would've thought he seemed rattled.

After a couple minutes, he prepped the four areas of my body, cleaning them and shaving the skin, then he grabbed an orange marker and drew the four runes on me, and prepped the tattoo machine. When he turned it on, I almost asked how he had electricity for it considering we were in the middle of nowhere, but then I realized what a dumb question it was since I was standing in front of a man that could shoot someone with a lightning bolt if he wanted. Or at least I assumed he could.

"I can, so you might want to think about that the next time you yell at me."

I glared at him. "Get out of my head, Ailin."

He just smirked at me, then moved closer to me, examining my skin.

When Ailin started the first tattoo—the one over my heart—I was a little surprised by how much it burned, but I just tried to ignore the small pain and concentrate on something else, like all the beads in Ailin's hair and where they'd all come from. I made up stories in my head to distract myself, and I made a mental note to ask him about them later. It didn't take too long before he finished the rune, and as soon as he did, I felt a weird surge of energy pulse through my body, making me a little dizzy.

I grabbed my head. "Whoa... is it supposed to do that?"

Ailin held my elbow, and in a softer voice than I was used to him using, said, "That's completely normal. It's the magic filling your veins. It'll level off shortly. I'll give you a minute before I start on the next one."

I nodded my thanks and squeezed my eyes together as pulses of weird energy flew through my system.

The same thing happened after Ailin finished the next two runes, but when he finished my fourth rune—the strength one on my arm—I felt such a huge surge of power and dizziness, I almost tipped over even though I was leaning against the car.

Ailin grabbed my shoulders and said, "It's okay... come here." He surprised me for the millionth time in the past couple of days by pulling me into his arms and pressing my forehead to his shoulder. He gently rubbed my back, being sure not to touch the rune on my shoulder blade. "It'll pass, I promise. Just rest until it does, okay?"

I didn't respond, I just let him comfort me. If I hadn't felt like I would either fall over or throw up, possibly both, I would've been humiliated by my reaction. As it was, I soaked up the attention from him. When I finally felt like I could stand without upchucking, I pushed off him and crossed my arms over my chest, leaning against the car again, feeling awkward.

Ailin didn't call me out on letting him hold me—again—he simply said, "Alright, let's get you in the car to rest for a bit. And honestly, we should probably head home so they can settle further. We'll pick up the case later and head to Emrys's place after you rest for a few hours and we eat lunch."

I nodded. "You sure it can wait?"

He wrinkled his nose. "I think waiting a couple hours to get your strength back would be better than trying to go now. I should've done this last night, but I didn't want to do it at home since there's so many wards and things in place there. Anyway, you need to get home to rest for a bit."

"You want to meet at your place after lunch or at the office?" I asked as I walked around to the passenger's side. I didn't feel comfortable driving with a dizzy head.

Ailin looked at me in confusion over the top of the car. "Why would we need to meet somewhere? You're already with me."

My brow furrowed. "Aren't you dropping me off at home?"

"Do you mean that apartment where you've been sleeping?"

"Uh, obviously, that's where I live..." I shrugged at him. *What the hell?*

"I guess you'll have to give them your notice or whatever. Do you need money to break the contract?"

"What the hell are you talking about?"

"It's not safe there, Seb."

I shrugged. "It's perfectly fine." *Yeah, maybe the demon broke in a couple times, but where the hell else am I supposed to go? That place is the only place I've got.*

"The kuma mali demon is out there, and it knows what you look like, it has your scent, Seb. It threatened you with a damn body. On. Your. Bed. It's not safe there by yourself." He rested his arms on the roof of the car with that glowing eye thing going on. *Great. He's ready for a fight.*

"Are you suggesting I stay with you while we're working this case?" I was completely surprised and flabbergasted.

"No, I'm suggesting you stay with me for this case... and all of the others."

I stared at him for a long moment, not entirely comprehending what he meant. "You want me to what? Live with you? Indefinitely?"

"Obviously. Where else would you go?"

"To *my* home..."

"It's not safe there, Sebastian. The last time you were there, you were almost killed!"

"It's my home, A. What exactly are you suggesting here? You want me to move in with you?"

"Yes. Move in. Never go back to the tiny, lonely apartment again."

"You don't even have a room for me in your... your tree-house! You said all the rooms were taken!"

His brow furrowed. "You slept well in my bed last night."

All I could do was blink at him. I opened and closed my mouth several times, completely at a loss of words, but finally they came back to me. "You want me to share a bed with you for the rest of my life!" It was more of a shout than a question.

He lifted a shoulder. "Yes. I liked you there."

What. The. Actual. Fuck.

"Come on. You know deep down that you can't go back to your place."

"So what? It's still my home."

"Why does everything have to be so difficult with you? My coven has welcomed you in. You stayed last night, and I know you like the house."

"I'm a human."

"I'm well aware of the fact." He tilted his head. "Is that why you're being weird about this right now? Is this a human thing? It's not a big deal, detective. You need a home, I have one, so you need to move in with me. Problem solved."

"Yes. Yes, it is. It's a huge deal. A ginormous deal!"

He stared at me. "Witches always live with their coven and their vitmea. It's natural to stick together."

I didn't know what to do with that. "Seriously, you want me—a human—to just live in your fucking house with a million other witches. Not only in your house, but in your fucking bedroom? *In your bed!* Ailin, you can't be serious. You're just joking with me, right? What the hell are you thinking? I don't like being the butt of the jokes all the time, A."

Ailin walked around the front of the car to stand beside me as he stared into my eyes. He took a small step closer, looking up at me, and I pressed my back against the car door, trying to put some space between us. Ailin seemed to have other ideas, though, because he crowded into me, then caged me in, resting his hands on the car on either side of me. "I'm not joking, I'm not making fun of you. You are my *vitmea*. We belong together, Seb. I know you don't understand it, but I can't have you sleeping somewhere else." He moved his face closer so his nose was almost brushing mine. "I'd go out of my mind."

My voice sounded shaky to my own ears. "What do you want from me, Ailin? I don't understand *any* of this. How can you be asking me to move in with you? You hardly know me. I don't even understand what any of this means? You want me as a roommate? A partner? A l-lover? A friend that happens to sleep in your bed? Wh-what? What do you want from me?"

Ailin removed one hand from the car and gripped the back of my neck as he whispered, "You, Sebastian. I only want you."

Then the bastard did the unthinkable and slammed his lips into mine. Every nerve ending in my body came to life, and a surge of power shot through me, stronger than any of the runes' powers. I gasped against him and gripped his hips. *What the hell is he doing? Why is he kissing me? Since when does he like me like this? What's happening?*

He leaned back a millimeter and whispered, "Shut up and kiss me back, detective. Stop thinking so loudly and just feel."

He slowly pressed his lips to mine again, and when I parted my lips a little to give him access, he smiled against my mouth and flicked his tongue inside. When his tongue brushed my own, another surge of energy shocked me, and we both moaned at the same time. My body started quivering as he leaned into me and buried his fingers in my hair. His hands were roaming my neck and back and tugging my hair while he pressed his entire body against me. I could feel him everywhere, and the heat in my body started growing into an inferno, spreading through my entire being. I felt his growing hardness against my thigh, and I had no doubt he could feel mine against his stomach.

I finally let myself go and decided to let him in a little, to let this wonderful feeling fill me up the way I truly wanted it to. But the energy in my body suddenly started building at a more rapid pace, and I found it hard to breathe. I started gasping for breath, my lungs constricting, and my body quaking with power. I felt like I was going to explode. I'd never felt anything like it before. It was exhilarating and frightening at the same time. And it was all too much.

I gasped out, "Ailin."

He leaned back and took me in, his smiling face turning into a concerned one. The strange feeling inside of me kept growing and growing. My skin was buzzing, my insides on fire—and not the good kind of fire from a moment ago. I felt like I was burning up from the inside out.

My ears were thundering, but I still heard Ailin say, "Shit. Magic overload. It's okay, baby, I got you." *Baby?* "Don't be scared."

Hearing him tell me not to be scared had the exact opposite effect, and I started panicking more than before.

"Seb. It's okay. Take deep breaths, baby. Breathe. I got you, I promise."

My vision started to blur and everything was getting darker by the second.

I thought I heard Ailin whisper, "You're mine, Seb. Forever. I'm not going to let anything bad happen to you," but I couldn't be sure if it was reality or a dream because a moment later, I blacked out.

Chapter Fourteen

I groaned without opening my eyes. My entire body felt... like I had electricity running through it while also feeling like I could sleep for an entire day straight. I felt weird as hell. What the actual fuck? I stretched my muscles out and groaned when I realized I was lying on some grass. Fucking Ailin and his fucking grass beds. I held back a moan when the memory of what his lips felt like pressed against mine flashed through my mind.

I snapped my eyes open to see where he was, and also to cut off that train of thought before I embarrassed myself because I knew he'd pick up on my thoughts. He always heard the embarrassing ones.

"You're awake."

I turned my head to find Ailin lying beside me, staring at me. I pinched the bridge of my nose and closed my eyes. "Yeah, I'm awake. What happened? I feel like I have a bad hangover."

"You sort of do, only it's a magic hangover, not an alcohol one. The runes I placed on you were a lot at one time, and I guess when we... it was just too much."

I dropped my hand and looked at him. He was on his side, leaning on one elbow and looking down at me. I searched his face for any hint that he'd been messing with me with that kiss, but he just looked like his normal self.

There was no shit-eating grin on his face, no knowing smirk. He was just looking at me with a furrowed brow.

He suddenly lifted his hand and tentatively brushed something off my forehead. "I wasn't messing with you, Seb."

My eyes involuntarily flicked down to his lips before meeting his green eyes and whispering, "Why would that... I mean, did you like... spell me or our," I cleared my throat, "our kiss? Did you do something to make it... magic?"

His lips twitched, and I was pretty sure he was biting back a laugh at my expense, so I narrowed my eyes at him as he spoke, "I didn't do anything except kiss you. But we're connected now, so I think our connection just reacted to the new magic running in your veins."

"So it was because of the mark?"

He lifted a shoulder in a shrug.

"You suck." I looked up at the sky and noticed the sun was starting to set. "How long was I out?"

"A while. But the magic should be pretty settled in your system by now."

"But I feel off."

"I meant that it should be working. The magic should be in your system and ready to help protect you. Your body just isn't used to having my magic in its system. That will calm down soon."

"What about finding Emrys? We need to get going before it gets dark, don't we?"

Ailin shook his head. "It's too dangerous to take you west in the dark. We'll go in the morning."

"What about the demon?"

"It will have to wait. We're not risking your safety any more than necessary. And... meeting Emrys in the dark isn't something I want to do, anyway. I called Alec earlier, and there haven't been any new bodies found or any reports that could be linked to the demon, so we're fine for the night."

I glanced at him, then looked back at the pink and orange sky. Were we just going to pretend the kiss didn't happen and move on? Didn't he like it? Would he want to do it again? He said he wasn't messing with me, but maybe he had been. Or maybe I'm just a bad kisser. If my body was still adjusting to this magic or whatever the hell, I guess I couldn't kiss him again, anyway.

He whispered, "I did like it, vitmea." He moved closer to me so his face was only inches from mine. "I liked it a lot." He cupped my cheek with his warm hand and slowly lowered his lips to mine.

The kiss was unhurried and tentative at first, but when his tongue gently flicked out, and I opened my mouth, he groaned deep in his chest and my entire body lit up. I didn't know if it was his magic or just the fact that this sexy, crazy guy was kissing me, but I'd *never* been kissed like this. He was devouring my mouth in the best way possible, and my body was melting into goo while my cock hardened in my pants. I grabbed his elbow with one hand and rested my other on his upper back. I was a little worried that he wasn't enjoying this as much as I was. Ailin moved closer to me and ground his groin against my thigh, and I felt his erection pressing into me.

I guess he is enjoying it.

He groaned again and moved his knee in between my legs, and I couldn't help but rut against him. Ailin slid on top of me and ground his hips against mine as he deepened our kiss further. I moved my hands down to his hips, then flattened my palms on his lower back. I wanted to grab his ass, but I wasn't sure if I should.

Ailin broke our kiss and sat up so he was straddling my hips. He was panting and out of breath and looked absolutely gorgeous with the sunset behind him.

"Seb, do whatever the fuck you want to me." He reached for the hem of his shirt. "Don't hold back, baby." He whipped his shirt and necklaces off before falling over top of me again, catching himself with his hands on either side of my head and his lips crashing into mine.

He rutted his hips, so I slid my hands around and finally grabbed his ass, pulling him to me and making our cocks rub together through our pants. He moaned and moved his hips back and forth, slowly torturing me. He ran his hand down my side to the hem of my shirt and pulled it up so his fingertips brushed my skin, making me light up even more. He slipped his whole hand under my shirt and everywhere his hand touched felt like electricity was running between us, leaving goosebumps in its wake.

He tugged on my shirt, so I held his hips and sat up so he could yank my shirt over my head. He looked at my chest for a few seconds, then into my eyes with a hunger I'd never seen before. His eyes flashed with his green magic, and I suddenly felt like prey that'd been lured in by a predator.

He grabbed the back of my head and dragged me in to kiss me hard, making me moan and pull his ass tighter against me. I slowly lowered my back to the ground, and he came with me, not breaking the kiss. When he moved his entire body against mine, we both moaned as our skin brushed together. Little tingles of pleasure spread over my body, and all I could think about was getting him closer to me.

I grabbed ahold of him and rolled us so he was on his back, and I was covering his body with my own.

Ailin smiled against my lips. "Mmm. Taking control, detective?"

"Shut up." I captured his mouth again before he could laugh, but I felt the rumble against my chest.

I ran my hand down his side to his waistline and brushed my fingers along it. He made a sound that was close to a whimper, and I broke our kiss to lick and nibble my way down his jaw and neck. When I reached his mark, I leaned back to look at it for a few seconds before I bent back down to suck the skin between my teeth, a little thrill shooting through me knowing he bore my mark. Ailin hissed and bucked under me as he gripped my back and dug his fingers into my hair. I used my tongue to trace a tattoo on his pec and unbuckled his pants.

A small part of me thought that maybe I shouldn't sleep with my work partner, but I tried to push it away.

"There's no rule that says you can't," Ailin said breathlessly.

"Get out of my head, A." My voice held none of the anger it usually did when he invaded my privacy.

Ailin ran his hands down my back to my ass and squeezed it, making me groan, before moving his hands around to the front of my jeans. "But this is the perfect time to be in your head." He unzipped my jeans and pushed them down just enough to slip his hands in the front. He grabbed my cock through my boxers, and I moaned loudly as he whispered, "I can tell exactly what you like."

He squeezed and stroked me through my underwear and ran his other hand around to my ass, kneading it. I bit and sucked on his chest, then focused on his nipple, and he hissed and arched his back under me. I put my weight on one elbow so I could pull his pants down and shove my hand inside. I almost whimpered when I grabbed his cock through his briefs. My other hand was near his head, so I couldn't help but grab his hair, pulling on the non-braided side as I sucked on his neck again, on his mark.

He suddenly let go of my cock, but before I could complain, he yanked my pants and boxers down to my thighs, then pushed my hand out of the way and lifted his hips to pull his own pants and briefs down to his thighs as well. He grabbed my dick and pulled my hips down to his so he could wrap his hand around his cock, too. He used his other hand to pull my hair a little so I would lift my head up.

We stared into each other's eyes for several seconds before I slowly moved my hips, and we moaned together. Ailin pushed my head back toward him. "Come here, baby."

I wasn't sure how I felt about this *baby* thing he kept doing, so to shut him up, I covered his mouth with my own. He chuckled a little against my lips until I rutted my hips again, and his laugh turned into a deep moan. He tightened his grip on our cocks and his hand felt warm. When I shifted my hips again, our cocks felt slick. I almost asked where the lube came from, but then I realized that Ailin must've done some weird magic thing or whatever. Not that I was complaining because it felt fucking amazing; slick and warm and tingly in a way that was making my cock ache and leak all over, even more than it had been a moment ago. I moved again, and Ailin rutted his hips underneath of me as he grabbed my ass with his other hand. I tweaked his nipple with one hand and kept my grip on his hair with the other—I was still leaning on my elbow—as we sped up our thrusts.

Ailin moved his hand, twisting it with each thrust and soon my entire body was filled with ecstasy unlike anything I'd ever experienced.

"I'm... gonna come... Seb."

Hearing the desperation in his voice sent me over the edge, and I cried out into his mouth as my body tightened and shuddered, and my cock shot out streams of cum onto our stomachs and chests. Ailin tensed under me at the same time. He yelled out and moaned, his body was quaking beneath me, his cum shooting between us.

As we both calmed, and our bodies trembled and jerked a little, Ailin kept kissing my lips softly. He ran his hand up my spine to the back of my head and held me there to kiss me over and over and over. I rested more of my body weight on him, but tried to keep most of it on my elbows and knees.

As our kisses slowed even more, a slither of fear trickled in. *What did I just do?*

"Shh," Ailin hushed me in between a couple of slow kisses. "Don't overthink it, Seb."

He kissed me again, but I couldn't concentrate on how good it felt because I was too worried about what I was supposed to do next. *Does he want me to leave right now? Was this a one-time thing? Did he get what he wanted, so he'll just send me on my way now?*

"Shh..." He pushed my head until I let him press my forehead against his neck, and he pulled his hand out from between us so he could hug me to him. "I don't want you to leave. I hope it's not a one-time thing, and no, I won't send you on your way because I didn't get what I want yet."

I swallowed loudly, but I was too nervous to ask him what he wanted.

"I want you, Sebastian. I'm never going to send you on your way because I just want you."

I squeezed my eyes shut because I didn't know what to say to that.

"You don't have to say anything. You just have to stay. Can you do that for me? Can you stay the night? We'll take it one day at a time, okay?"

I blew out a breath and nodded against his neck. He wrapped his arms tighter around me and kissed my temple, rubbing his fingertips up and down my back. We lay there for a long time. I never liked cuddling after sex, but it seemed that Ailin was making me like a lot of things that I never enjoyed before.

"Let's go inside and get cleaned up. We can sleep in the bed together again."

I blew out a breath, then leaned back and rolled off him. I stood up and pulled my pants and underwear up, then grabbed my shirt, shrugging it over the dried cum on my body. When I turned around, Ailin had pulled up his pants, but was still shirtless. He walked closer to me, grabbed the back of my neck, and pulled me down to kiss me gently on the lips again.

"Let's get you cleaned up, vitmea," he whispered, and I nodded, then followed him inside his house.

I was beyond grateful that we didn't run into anyone on the way up to his room, and I was surprised that he didn't insist on showering together. But I was glad; I needed a little space.

He let me shower first, and once I was done and dressed, he walked into the bathroom, but pointed at the bed. "I grabbed us some food. I know you're starving, so help yourself while I shower. I'll be right back, baby." He winked at me before he closed the door.

I was pretty sure that wink was on purpose to make me uncomfortable. I heard Ailin chuckle in the bathroom, so I yelled, "Stay the fuck out of my head, A!"

His laugh deepened, but he didn't say anything back. When he came out a few minutes later, I had eaten almost everything on the tray, and he grinned at me. "Go ahead and finish it off. I ate while you showered."

"Thanks, A." I scooped up the last few bites and finished them off.

Ailin put the tray on a dresser, then crawled into bed. "Come on, let's get some rest."

I nodded and slipped between the covers.

He flicked his fingers and the lights went out. We lay there in silence for a few minutes on opposite ends of the bed, but I felt Ailin moving around until he was close to me. He gently placed a hand on my chest and let out a sigh. He wasn't touching me anywhere else, just on my chest. After another minute, I put my hand over his, and he threaded our fingers together, but otherwise didn't react. I was grateful, and I closed my eyes and let sleep claim me.

Chapter Fifteen

My eyes were heavy, but I knew I needed to wake up. My body was thrumming under its skin. It must've been the runes making me feel like my insides were twitching while the outside of me was exhausted.

"I promise that sensation will pass, baby." Ailin's voice was husky as he woke and spoke. I looked down and sighed. He was lying across my stomach, using my chest as a pillow.

I didn't know what to do. We... made each other come last night, then we slept together in his bed. But what did that mean for today? For tomorrow?

Ailin reached up and put his hand on my neck over the mark. "It means that you're mine forever, Sebastian Cooper Fitz. It means that I want you here with me."

I blinked at him several times. "As... what?"

Ailin grinned at me and rubbed his fingers over the skin on my neck, tickling me and somehow relaxing me at the same time. "As whatever we want it to be."

I huffed out a breath and rolled my eyes. "You're a pain in the ass."

He shrugged against me. "I *could* be a pain in your ass." He waggled his eyebrows.

Heat spread through me at what he was suggesting. I wanted that. I wanted him inside of me, but there was no way I was letting him get away with that idiotic comment when I was trying not to freak out inside. So I pushed him off me and sat up. "You wish, asshole."

He chuckled and shrugged again. "You could always be a pain in my ass, if you wanted."

The heat spread further, so I jumped out of bed and headed toward the bathroom. "Again, you wish!"

"I'll win you over one day, detective. I know I will."

I slammed the door shut and leaned against it, taking deep breaths. I needed another shower. A cold shower. I walked over and the water turned on by itself, then I stripped and jumped in. As soon as I pulled the curtain shut, the bathroom door opened up, so I popped my head out to find Ailin walking in.

"Wh-what are you doing?"

He smirked at me. "Don't worry, Seb, your ass is safe. I just need to piss."

"And you couldn't wait till I was done?"

"Nope." He unzipped his pants, so I quickly shut the curtain and pretended my cheeks weren't blushing profusely.

"There's other bathrooms you could've used."

"Yeah, but none of the others have a blushing, sexy man in the shower, so I picked this one."

My jaw clenched, and I chose to ignore him and his chuckles. I put my head under the water so I couldn't hear him peeing, and I started to wash.

"You sure you don't want some company in there?" Ailin called out loud enough for me to hear.

"Ailin." I closed my eyes, unsure of what to say or even how I felt.

"Hey, Seb?"

"Wh-what?"

"Don't freak out. We'll figure everything out together, okay? Just know... I... like you... I... care."

Before I could respond, the bathroom door opened and closed. I peeked out again, but he was gone, so I went back to washing.

He cared? *And* he liked me?

I was a little worried that he was messing with me, but after last night, after the way he'd kissed me, the way he'd held me, the way he'd laid on me while we slept, I really didn't think he was. I was pretty sure he was telling the truth. And I was pretty sure I felt the same way about him. And I had no idea how to tell him or what the hell to do with it.

After my shower, Ailin took his own, and the two of us headed downstairs without saying anything else about what'd happened between us. His entire family—coven, whatever—was down there already eating. They'd saved us two seats, the same two seats we'd sat in yesterday.

When we joined them at the table, they all greeted me as if they were used to me being in the house, and Ailin pushed his shoulder against mine again. As soon as he did it, I closed my eyes and after a deep breath, I leaned into him, too. He shot me a little smile, then passed me a roll.

All the witches turned their heads toward the front door, and a second later, I heard people walking into the house. A couple of the younger kids got up with huge smiles and ran to greet the newcomers. Ailin nudged my shoulder, then got up and I followed his movements with my eyes as he hugged someone before pulling a woman into the room. A very pregnant woman that looked a lot like Ailin, Opal, and Basil. I assumed she was his other sister, Aspen. My eyes widened when my chief walked in behind Aspen. *Holy shit, Chief Gillman is here! I totally forgot he's married to Ailin's sister!*

Ailin sent me a little smirk. "Seb, this is my sister, Aspen, and I believe you already know Alec."

I stood, held out my hand to shake, and nodded as Aspen took it. "Nice to meet you."

"You too, I've heard a lot about you," Aspen said with the same smirk Ailin always wore.

I smiled, then held my hand out to my chief. "Chief."

Chief Gillman took my hand in a tight shake. "It's Alec when we're not at work, Fitz. I have a feeling we're going to be seeing a lot of each other."

"Um... okay, Alec. I guess you should call me Sebastian, then."

"Or Seb," Ailin said with a grin.

I rolled my eyes and backed away as more of the teens came over to greet Aspen and Alec.

Opal walked over and hugged Aspen. "You're looking gorgeous, big sis."

Aspen smiled and put her hand on her belly. "I'm looking fat."

"Nonsense," Ailin said. "You look perfect. Sit down for breakfast." He led his sister to the table, and a few of the teens brought more chairs over to make room for Aspen and Alec.

Ailin pulled me back to my seat and leaned against me again as soon as everyone was settled. I leaned in and asked, "So you're the oldest, then it's Aspen, Opal, then Basil?"

Ailin grinned at me. "Yep." He pressed his shoulder harder against me. "After Aspen and Alec got married, we built them a house on the other end of one of the trails in the forest. They're still on the property and still part of the coven, but they needed some privacy, especially with the baby on the way. But they come down for meals at least once a day."

I nodded. This whole family or coven thing was completely new to me, but I had to admit that it seemed wonderful.

We ate, then said our goodbyes to his family. Little Jorah even gave me a hug, which was really cute, even if I was super awkward at hugging back. Thayer walked over and gave me a hug, too, before hugging Ailin and whispering something to him that made Ailin chuckle and both of them look at me.

I narrowed my eyes at them. "What?"

Thayer grinned, and Ailin shook his head. "Nothing, detective. Don't worry about it."

My eyes narrowed further before I turned on my heel and headed out of the house. Ailin followed behind me, and surprisingly, he didn't try to take my keys away. I hopped in the driver's seat, turned on the car, and as soon as he was buckled in, I drove down the long driveway.

When I didn't speak for several minutes, Ailin sighed. "Don't be mad."

"Who says I'm mad?"

"Your tense as hell shoulders, your clenched jaw, and the fact that you're going fifteen miles over the speed limit."

I looked down at the speedometer and sighed as I pulled my foot off the gas a little.

"All he said was that he likes you, and he thinks you're good for me."

I glanced at him, then back at the road as I headed toward the weird entranceway into the Brinnswick Forest that we'd taken yesterday.

"Seb?"

I sighed. "What?"

"What happened last night? I hope it happens again. Does that answer your questions? I want you in my life, okay?"

I glanced at him again and sucked in a breath. "Okay. Um... me too."

I saw him grin out of the corner of my eye, and he set his hand on my thigh again. "Good. That's good, baby."

"Will you quit it with the baby thing?"

He chuckled. "Nope. I like when you're flustered."

I shook my head. *Asshat.*

He laughed.

***

"What the fuck are you doing here, Ailin? Get off my property. Now." A voice I didn't recognize yelled from a distance as soon as I exited the car.

Ailin slammed the door with a sigh, then yelled, "Let's talk inside, Em. I need your help. You know I wouldn't be here if I had another choice."

A big muscular guy with dark skin walked out of the small cottage we'd parked in front of with a huge-ass rottweiler beside him. The guy, Emrys, I assumed, eyed me with silver eyes—*what affinity is that again?*—for a moment before looking at Ailin. "A human? Really, Lin, I didn't think you'd stoop that low." *Lin?*

"Do *not* disrespect Sebastian, Emrys." Ailin's entire body tensed, and I saw a flash of green in his eyes. "You don't want to see me pissed off."

Emrys snorted and his dog growled a little. "I've seen you pissed off plenty of times."

Ailin's whole body suddenly looked like there was an electrical current running through and around him. It almost looked like there was power below the surface waiting to explode. He tilted his head and narrowed his eyes. "No, you haven't. You've only see me irritated."

The ground rumbled, and Emrys's voice came out deep. "You don't need to put on a show, Lin. I know how powerful you are." He took a deep breath and placed a hand on his dog's head. "Why are you here?"

Ailin's chest heaved, and I had the urge rub his chest and calm him down, but I refrained. Ailin shot me a little smirk before speaking again, "Inside. We can't talk out in the open."

"Fine."

Ailin walked and I followed, but he sent me a reassuring smile over his shoulder. I was on edge meeting with this man—this witch that tried to kill Ailin. I didn't trust him for a single second, and I hated that we had to ask this guy for help. I wanted to shoot him so he could never hurt my Ailin again.

Ailin froze in front of me, and slowly turned around to look at me with wide eyes. He searched my confused face, then brushed his fingertips over my cheek and down my neck over my mark, sending flutters around in my stomach. I suddenly wanted to pull him to me and press his body against mine. This wasn't exactly the time for that. He smiled softly, then turned back around and walked inside the cottage.

What the fuck was that about? I shook off his randomness and followed him inside.

Ailin said, "Emrys, meet Detective Sebastian Fitz. Seb, this is Emrys Vinbloom. The dog's name is Zrak."

Emrys sneered and crossed his arms over his chest as he glared at us walking into his living room, the dog right beside him, looking angry.

"Real friendly guy," I muttered.

Ailin chuckled and walked over to a couch, so I sat beside him and he put his arm on the back of the couch behind me. He put his hand on my shoulder, and I caught myself leaning into his touch, and I did nothing to stop myself. I liked having him touch me so casually. *What the hell is happening to me? What did he do to me last night?*

Emrys sat in an old-looking armchair glaring at us like he wanted to murder us both. Zrak laid at his feet. "What are you doing here, Lin?"

"I need your help."

He huffed and sat back, crossing his arms over his chest. "I don't owe you a thing."

"You tried to burn me alive, Em. I'm pretty sure that justifies a favor."

"How many times do I have to tell you that it wasn't my intention to kill you?"

"You left me for dead, and you know it. If I die, you're next in line to become Sage. And we both know how much you've always wanted it."

Emrys glared at Ailin, and his eyes flashed with silver smoke. "If I wanted you dead, you wouldn't be here today."

Ailin waved him off. "There's a kuma mali demon that's been gaining power for over sixteen months unchecked."

Emrys's stance changed. He dropped his arms and suddenly looked interested in the conversation. "How did it get past the wards set in place? Why weren't we notified when it crossed over? Anything that big should've set off our securities."

"I know. I'm not sure why it didn't. I've only run in to it twice. But it's strong; the strongest I've ever fought. I'm going to need help to locate and vanquish it."

"What kind of energy are you sensing?"

Ailin let go of me to stand and walk closer to him. I tensed as Emrys stood as well, but the dog remained where he was, and Ailin shot me a small glance that I knew meant he'd be okay. I didn't trust this Emrys guy at all. He'd tried to kill my Ailin before, there was no way in hell I'd trust him not to do it again. I'd shoot the bastard if he made one wrong move. I put my hand over my gun and stood, but stayed by the couch.

Ailin held his hand out as he stepped right in front of Emrys, and I heard him whisper, "May I?"

Emrys nodded and leaned his head forward a little. I wasn't sure what he was doing, but when Ailin put his palm on Emrys's forehead, I figured he'd leaned down so Ailin could reach him. Although, I had no idea why Ailin would be touching some guy's forehead, some ex-boyfriend's forehead.

Emrys covered Ailin's hand with his own and sucked in a breath as he closed his eyes for a few seconds. When he snapped them open, he whispered, "Ailin, that thing is..." He swallowed and his eyes went wide. "We have to stop it."

"Does that mean you'll help me?"

"Of course, I will. You know that."

When Ailin dropped his hand, Emrys surprised me by pulling Ailin into a hug. *What the actual fuck?* He whispered something to Ailin that I couldn't understand, and Ailin smiled as he hugged the other witch back. I was so confused by their... relationship. One minute they hated each other, the next they were old friends. I narrowed my eyes when Emrys looked at me over Ailin's shoulder and smirked as he reached down to grab Ailin's ass, squeezing it as he said, "I've missed you, Lin."

Ailin pushed Emrys off him and stepped back. "Don't go there, Em." I expected Ailin's voice to hold anger, but it didn't. It was soft and almost sad—no, it wasn't sad, it was *hurt,* which made me frown. Ailin missed that asshole? My eyes narrowed further at them. There was obviously a past here I wasn't privy to, and I didn't like it one bit. I didn't like the way it was making my chest tight, making my jaw clench, and my muscles tighten in anger. I didn't even understand why I was so angry, but nothing would've made me happier in that moment than walking up to that asshole and punching him in the face.

"We're going to go back to Seb's station. We need to grab a few things and see if anything new has turned up. Maybe you and I can work on a tracking spell so we can hunt this thing down. Can you meet back at... my house afterward?"

Emrys looked out the window, then back into his kitchen. "I'll meet you there in an hour. I need to take care of a few things here first, anyway."

"Sure." Ailin walked back toward me, then stopped and looked at Emrys again. "Thank you for helping, Em."

Emrys sent him what looked like a genuine smile. "Anytime, Lin." Then he walked us out of his cottage, and Ailin and I got into my car.

Once I pulled back onto the little dirt road, Ailin blew out a long breath and put his feet up on my dash, leaning his forehead on the window. A few seconds later, I jumped when Sera suddenly popped up on my dash. I shook my head, then scratched her neck as she hopped down and crawled onto Ailin's lap. Ailin pet her with one hand absently and picked up one of his necklaces with his other. He brought the necklace up to his mouth and left it pressed to his lips. He looked so defeated, and I had no idea how to help him. He was clearly reliving some memories that the douche back there brought up.

After several minutes of silence, I cleared my throat. "Are you okay?"

Ailin startled a little and turned to face me. "Not really, but I will be."

"That guy's a dickhead."

He snorted. "I won't argue with you there."

"You actually dated him?"

"Yeah. He was there for me through some shit and we... connected. But he was always jealous that I'm Sage, and I think his jealousy got the better of him." I wanted to ask more details about that, but Ailin changed the subject before I could. "I think I have an idea of how this demon has grown so powerful without being noticed."

"Oh yeah? What's that?"

"I think it's being controlled by someone... someone very powerful."

"Someone powerful like the second most powerful witch on Earth?"

He blew out a breath. "Yeah. And if he had a fae involved, or somehow got ahold of an object that came from Faela, he'd easily be able to hide everything from me... and from Talon."

"You think Emrys is involved?"

"I hope not, but he set up those wards at the demon gate with me. If anyone could get a demon past them, it'd be him. We both used our energies to seal the wards. No one else should be able to bypass them."

"Well, shit. Are you telling me we just asked for help from the mastermind himself?"

"I hope I'm wrong, but yes, we very possibly did."

"Shit."

"He's not setting foot inside my home. We'll have to stay outside on the grounds where I'm at my strongest, and he can't get to the others. We can just grab the files from the bodies. I need to get my spell books somewhere safe. In a place he's never been before. The station has had wards for years, I placed them before I was even officially working there, so they've seeped into the foundation of the building. And I set extra wards up in your office, so they've been safe there, but I don't want to take any chances." He pulled out his phone and dialed a number. "Basil, I need you and Thayer to do me a favor." After speaking to his brother for a few minutes, he hung up. "Will you wear one of my necklaces?"

"Sometimes you ask the most random shit. Why?"

"I want to tattoo more runes on you, but I can't so soon after the ones I did yesterday. They're settled now, but they're not healed. For now, can you wear this to help protect you from Emrys? It will keep him from being able to penetrate your mind."

"Don't you need it?"

"I have two runes to protect my mind."

"Then why do you have the necklace in the first place?"

"I like my backup plans to have backup plans. You never know when something could go wrong. Plus, it's kind of a deception. When other witches and supes see my necklaces, they think they're my only protection, so sometimes they try to go after my necklaces instead of realizing my entire body is covered in protections and spells. If they get my necklaces, they think they've won and let their guard down making it the perfect time for me to strike."

"You know, you're quite terrifying."

He chuckled. "Thank you."

"It wasn't a compliment."

He laughed a little harder. "It was for me." He gently pushed my shoulder, and the touch made me smile. "So how 'bout it? Will you wear my necklace?"

"Sure." I held out my hand, and he put one of the necklaces in it, so I threw it over my head.

"I really thought you'd put up more of a fight."

I snorted. "Just be grateful I'm not."

He grinned. "Hey, Seb?"

"What?"

"I'm really glad you're my partner, and my vitmea."

I didn't respond because I was too busy trying to get the flutters in my stomach to stop.

He reached over and placed his hand on my thigh again, and I fought the urge to close my eyes and lean into him. *Jesus, what the hell is happening to me?*

When I finally parked the car at the station, I went to get out, but Ailin squeezed my thigh, so I turned to him. He was leaning close to me, so close I had to blink him into focus. "Wh-what?"

He reached his free hand up and gently cupped my cheek. "What are you doing to me, Detective Fitz?"

My brow furrowed. What was *I* doing to *him*? What the hell was *he doing to me?*

Ailin smiled softly, then ran his hand down my neck, brushing his fingers over my mark.

"I-is that mark making me...?" I didn't know how to phrase what I wanted to ask.

He shook his head and his brow furrowed. "No, it's not the mark." He abruptly let me go and jumped out of the car, so fast Sera hissed and jumped off his legs and onto mine.

I blinked a few times and shook myself out of the weird daze Ailin seemed to always put me in, then I looked at Sera and patted her head. "What the hell is going on with your... what's it called? Bonded One?"

She meowed at me, then rubbed harder against my hand. I was pretty sure she thought Ailin was just as crazy as I thought he was. I scooped her up and followed my weirdo, witchy partner.

I ignored all the strange looks I got from the other detectives as I walked through the station. At this point, I was used to it. They'd been looking at me weirdly ever since I started working with Ailin. Apparently, they thought I was crazy because I'd been working with him for more than a few days. No one else had ever lasted as long partnering with him. Not that I could blame them, he was a prickly bastard at times.

"Gee, thanks." Ailin's voice made me jump when I crossed the threshold of our office.

"Stay out of my head... *Lin*."

He glared at me. "Don't call me that."

I tilted my head and was about to throw in his face that he always called me Seb despite my protests, but something in his eyes stopped me. There was something about that nickname that upset him, almost like it hurt to hear it, so I shrugged. "Whatever. Let's get this shit cleaned up before your ex-boyfriend gets to your house."

Ailin looked at me with an odd expression, then turned and picked up a few of his books. "Put these in a pile on the desk. Basil and Thayer should be here any minute to pick them up and hide them."

I nodded and set Sera on the ground so I could help. "Where are they going to hide them?"

"In a place on my property that only Basil, Thayer, and I know about. We kept it well hidden, but I'll show you where after Emrys helps us."

I tilted my head. "You trust me enough for that?"

He stared at me with a stern expression. "I trust you completely, Sebastian."

The intensity of his stare along with his words was making those flutters go off in my stomach again. I could tell from his expression that he was telling the truth. He really did trust me enough to show me some secret place he had with his brother. I whispered, "Thanks, A."

He grinned at me. "Basil's here."

Seeing Basil and Thayer and their unusual eyes when they came to grab the books, I was reminded of Emrys's weird silver eyes, so after they left with the spell books, and we were back in my car with the files, I asked Ailin, "What's Emrys's affinity?"

"Death."

"Excuse me?"

Ailin put his booted feet up on my dash. "Emrys uses death magic."

What in the fuck is death magic? Thinking about what that meant was giving me the willies.

"Have you ever heard of necromancy?"

"Uh, like when someone raises dead people and makes zombies?"

He grinned. "Yeah, except it's not usually that... dark. He pulls his energy from dead things all around him. And there's always dead things; animals, plants, whatever. Sometimes they're deep in the ground, but that's what he uses. And yeah, he could use bones and things like that more easily than I could."

"Can he bring people back from the dead?"

He shook his head. "No. He can animate them for however long he wants, but they're not the same person as they were when they were alive. Their soul would've moved on, so really, it's like he uses their bodies."

I wrinkled my nose. "I don't know what to say about that."

He shrugged, and we rode the rest of the way to his house in companionable silence, then waited in his living room for Emrys to arrive. Before there was even a knock on the door, Ailin jumped out of his seat. "He's here." The two of us headed outside. Ailin told me that people he didn't trust couldn't get past the wards set around the house. He'd lowered the wards on the rest of the property so Emrys could come on the land, but he refused to let him inside.

Emrys got out of his car with his dog and took everything in from beside his vehicle. Sera immediately ran over to me and rubbed on my leg, so I scooped her up and let her settle on my shoulder as I pet her neck, and she rubbed my cheek. Emrys narrowed his eyes at me, then looked at Ailin as a cold expression washed over his face. "Your vitmea?"

Ailin nodded once and his eyes flashed bright green—brighter than his normal green. I was learning that when his eyes did that, he was holding his power back and making sure he didn't lose control.

Emrys didn't react to that other than to glance at me one last time as Ailin handed him the files. Ailin came to stand beside me as Emrys looked everything over, and he pressed his shoulder against my arm. He was a good four inches shorter than me, so his shoulder was against my biceps. Sera leaned over and rubbed against Ailin's face before settling on me again.

Once Emrys was through, he turned to us. "Are you thinking that someone is controlling this demon?"

I narrowed my eyes at this, but Ailin said, "We're taking that into consideration. It could have only crossed over with help from this side. But you know as well as I, that once he makes his last kill, he'll surpass anyone that's controlling him. We need to stop it before it becomes more powerful."

Emrys nodded, but I asked, "What do you mean its last kill?"

"Remember the pentagram on your palm?" I nodded, so Ailin continued, "Well, he's been killing a human on every point, cross section, and open space. There's twenty-one spots it needs a kill in. We know of eighteen bodies, although he may have drained enough blood from the officer he tortured, depending on what spell he's using. But since the officer lived, he likely had to kill another in that area. Mother help us if there's more bodies we haven't found." He turned and looked at Emrys. "It's saving Seb for last right in the center."

"Ailin, you don't know that."

He looked at me. "I do, vitmea. There's no doubt in my mind."

I shivered at that. What the fuck? Why didn't he tell me this before?

Ailin turned to me and put his hand on my cheek so I'd look at him. "I didn't want to scare you." When I opened my mouth to protest he cut me off, "I realize that was wrong, that's why I'm telling you now. You deserve to know, and I shouldn't keep secrets from you."

I blew out a slow breath and nodded. I had the sudden urge to pull Ailin closer to me and kiss him again. God, when he'd kissed me, he'd kissed so thoroughly and with so much intention and passion. I'd never been kissed like that in my life. Not even by Zane. And I wanted to explore what that kiss meant, I wanted to kiss him and hold him close, I wanted to rip his clothes off and feel his skin against mine again. I wanted him. I wanted Ailin more than I'd ever wanted anyone in my entire life. But I couldn't do that. Not here. Not in front of Emrys. So I took a deep breath and stared into his green eyes that looked like they were filled with the same hunger mine were. When Ailin smirked at me, I had no doubt that he knew what I was thinking about. I lifted a shoulder, embarrassed by my thoughts, but unable to do anything about it.

Ailin leaned up on his toes and put his mouth by my ear, his hot breath making goosebumps show up on my skin. "I want to feel your naked skin again, too." Then he pressed his soft lips to my neck right below my ear, and I shivered again. "Soon, detective." He placed one more kiss to the same spot before dropping his hand and putting some space between us.

"Are you two finished yet?" Emrys's voice held anger in it. "Let's do this tracking spell so we can vanquish this fucker, and I can get the hell away from you two."

Ailin looked at Emrys with a tilted head. "You okay, Em?"

Emrys huffed and rolled his eyes. "I'm perfect. I've always wanted to stand around and watch my ex seducing some fucking human. It's a dream come true." Wow, sarcastic much?

Ailin crossed his arms over his chest. "You have no right to be hurt right now. Not after what you did."

Emrys groaned loudly and pinched the bridge of his nose. "How many times do I have to tell you it wasn't what it looked like? How can I get that through your head?"

"You left me there to die."

"That's not what happened!"

"Care to explain, then?"

"I... I can't."

Ailin glared, then waved him off. "We don't have time for this. Let's go to the circle, and I'll get Basil and Thayer to meet us there for the tracking spell."

"Fine."

Ailin pulled out his phone and sent off a text as we walked to the side of the house and started down a trail to god knew where. The circle? Whatever the hell that was. Sera jumped off my shoulder and ran into the woods, probably to hunt or whatever it was that cats did, but I caught a glance of Emrys's dog running after her, so who knew what they were doing. Neither witch seemed concerned, so I figured they were fine. After Ailin pocketed his phone, he reached over and grabbed my hand. I tensed in surprise before relaxing a little as he threaded our fingers together. This whole touching thing was so completely new to me. Zane and I had been in the Special Forces together, so we'd never been able to hold hands or anything like that. Our relationship had basically been stolen moments in between missions when no one else was around. Having Ailin hold my hand and touch me casually wasn't something I was used to, but I had to say that I'd love to get used to it.

We walked along the path for several minutes before the trees finally opened up to reveal a perfect circle with stones lining the trees and several other pathways going in every direction. Ailin released my hand and began arranging some rocks and different herbs and things he pulled out of his pockets in the center of the circle.

Emrys walked over and stared at me for a few seconds. I was pretty sure he was trying to intimidate me, but I wasn't having it. I was sick of witches and supernatural creatures trying to use their magic or whatever to make me feel like a weakling human. I was frustrated and annoyed as hell at them all. *Asshats.*

He suddenly moved so quickly, I didn't have time to react. He grabbed my shoulder with one hand and my forehead with the other. I sucked in a breath as I felt his weird inky energy floating on my skin. I tried to push him off, but it felt like his energy was almost gluing him to me. I closed my eyes and concentrated on not letting him in my head. Wasn't that what Ailin had said before? That the supes would try to get into my head. I pictured a vault around my brain, and hoped it would work.

I could hear Ailin's angry voice yelling at him, but I blocked it out and concentrated on the vault. It was bad enough having A in my head, I didn't need this asshat. *Nice, big, steel vault.*

Emrys just as suddenly let me go, and I sucked in another deep breath when his inky energy left me. Ailin was standing between me and Emrys by the time I opened my eyes with a green bubble around me. No, actually it was around me and him. He'd put himself inside with me. Sera appeared on Ailin's shoulder hissing at Emrys just as the rottweiler appeared beside Emrys, growling.

"I didn't hurt him," Emrys said as he pulled up his own silver shield. "I was merely checking to make sure he hasn't been tampered with."

"Don't you think I would've noticed if he had?" Ailin's energy was swirling around and sparking. "He's clean."

"I can see that."

"Do. Not. Touch. Him. Again."

Emrys clenched his jaw. "I was only looking out for you. I wanted to make sure. You know how humans can be. You know that they're easily manipulated. I wanted to make sure he wasn't put with you to hurt you."

"He wasn't. And he's *mine,* so you better watch yourself, Emrys. I don't want to have to hurt you." I didn't even bother to comment on the damn possessiveness again.

Emrys was quiet for a long time as he stared at Ailin, but eventually, he blew out a breath and dropped his shield. "I'm sorry. I can see what he is to you. I'm sorry, it won't happen again, and I promise to look after him like one of my coven."

I wrinkled my nose at that. *Witches are weird as fuck.*

Ailin must've liked what he said, though, because he dropped the green bubble shield and walked forward to grab Emrys's forearm. They whispered something in a weird language—*do witches have their own language or is that like Latin or something? Where's a notebook when you need one?*—and when they released their arms, Sera hissed at Emrys.

Emrys held his hands up in defeat. "I understand. Sorry, Sera."

Sera nodded—or it looked like she did, anyway—then she leapt from Ailin's shoulder to mine and wrapped around my neck. I scratched her neck and watched the dog trot over to a trail and lie down, watching us with his head on his paws. I glanced at Emrys; I felt a little violated, and I didn't really understand what the hell they were talking about.

Ailin looked at me. "He wanted to make sure you weren't a spy from another coven or sent here by some other devious source."

I blinked at that and my eyebrows lifted. If Emrys was such a bad guy that'd tried to kill Ailin before, why the hell would he care if I was sent here as a spy? I narrowed my eyes at the guy. He was an enigma, that was for sure.

Before I could contemplate it anymore, Basil and Thayer walked into the clearing. They both gave Emrys wary expressions, but Emrys looked happy to see them. "You've both gotten so tall."

Basil narrowed his eyes, but Thayer sent Emrys a hesitant smile. Ailin looked up from whatever he was doing in the center of the clearing and said, "Go greet him properly." Ailin's green energy was swirling around over the rocks he was touching.

Basil didn't look happy with that command, but Thayer looked relieved. Thayer walked over to Emrys first and hugged him tight, both of them speaking in that witch language or whatever it was. When Basil walked over, he did that weird handshake thing with him, but he was stiff and unhappy. Although, I wasn't sure if Basil was ever happy about anything. He was always pouting like a typical teenager.

Once he released Emrys, Basil walked over to me and surprised me by hugging me. I blinked a few times before tentatively patting his back. I whispered, "You're just doing this to rub it in Emrys's face, aren't you?"

He chuckled. "That's my main reason, but you're my brother's vitmea, so you may as well get used to the hugs now. Ailin's prickly and an ass, but my family hugs. *Your—our* family hugs."

"Our?"

"Yep. You're a part of our coven now, whether you like it or not."

Thayer walked over and grinned at me before pulling me into a hug, too. "He's right."

"I just saw you twenty minutes ago."

"Get used to it, Seb." Basil grinned at me, sending me that same cocky smirk that Ailin always had on his face. He was being a brat, but I'd take it over the pouting.

I frowned at the use of my nickname. I'd always hated when people shortened my name, but for some reason, I didn't really care too much when Ailin or his family members did it. Ailin shot me a smile. He must've heard my thoughts.

"Okay, everything's set. I put the essence of the demon in the center. Now we just need to call on our affinities to help us locate this creature. Go stand on the path with Sera, Seb."

I nodded and walked over to the path we'd come from with Sera on my shoulder. She snuggled in closer as I stepped out of the circle.

Ailin looked over at me with his green eyes shinning and smoke moving through them. "Do not move from that spot. If I'm worried about where you are, I'll lose concentration. Sera, stay with him."

I nodded again, not arguing with him for once because I knew he was right.

Ailin turned back to the other three witches and said, "You know the words, right?" All three nodded. "Grab hands and let's begin."

Emrys was across from Ailin with Basil and Thayer on either side of each. They grabbed hands and began chanting. After the third time repeating the same strange words, I couldn't help the bile that started coming up my throat. I'd tried to ignore it, but hearing them chant brought back memories of Zane, of how he'd been killed during a ceremony that sounded a lot like this one. Of how he'd been killed and tortured right in front of me. Of how I couldn't get through that damn barrier to save him.

I closed my eyes and held my breath as Sera rubbed on my cheek. I didn't want to throw up. I needed to focus on something that would make the memories go away. But the chanting was so loud, I couldn't escape it. I promised Ailin I'd stay right here while he performed the tracking spell. Ailin. Yes, Ailin. Maybe if I concentrated on his voice and his voice alone, I'd be able to keep from losing my breakfast.

I squeezed my eyes shut tight and tried to filter out the sounds of the others' voices. I focused on the sound of Ailin's deep, warm, soothing voice and only on his voice. He was chanting, yes, but I knew deep down that he was nothing like the horrible creature that had killed Zane.

Ailin's voice filled me up until, finally, the uneasy feeling was pushed away completely, and I was able to open my eyes. When I did, I gasped. Holy shit. The entire circle looked like a swirling wind tunnel. The energy coming from the witches was zooming around and around in a circle, all four colors mixing together seamlessly. Each witch had energy coming from their chest as they chanted away; Ailin had green, Thayer had yellow, Emrys had silver, and Basil had black. Their affinities were coming together, floating around and dancing together as they spun in a circle. I squinted my eyes to see through the wind energy, but when I did, my eyes widened in surprise. I could see a picture floating in the center, almost like a hologram of the demon. It was inside some kind of room. Then suddenly, the wind tunnel froze, the energy floating in mid-air, but not going anywhere. The hologram demon shrunk to the size of a dragonfly, and small tendrils of the energy around the witches floated toward the hologram demon. When the tendrils touched it, they formed a line, and the hologram became more and more detailed until I realized we were looking at a map, and the tendrils had become a line we needed to follow.

Once the witches had examined the map thoroughly, Ailin said, "Let your energy go. We know what we need to do now."

All four witches blew out deep breaths, and the energy in the circle began to fade away, the natural breeze rushing into the circle to carry the energy away.

I blew out the breath I hadn't realized I was holding, and Sera nuzzled against me again. That had been... intense. But also really amazing. I'd never seen anything like it before.

Ailin walked into the center of the circle and moved the rocks around again, so I waited as the other witches passed me to walk down the path toward the house. Sera hissed at Emrys when he looked at me, so he held up his hands again and scooted past me with the dog trotting behind him. I held in a chuckle. It was kinda funny that the big man was scared of a little kitten.

Ailin finally finished and walked over to me, and before I could say anything to him, he grabbed the back of my neck, pulling me down to press his lips to mine. It was a brief kiss, one that I wanted to deepen and explore, but didn't have time to. He released me almost as soon as he grabbed me. But he pulled me to rest my forehead against his and closed his eyes.

"I don't understand what's happening, but... we're connected. You and I are connected."

I closed my eyes as well. "I can feel it, too."

He nodded against my forehead. "I could feel your... pain. I'm sorry we scared you."

"It's okay."

He moved away, so I opened my eyes to look at him, and he tilted his head. "Are you ready to take out this demon?"

I nodded.

"I'm afraid to let you come with us, but... I know you'll be safer with me than without. That demon has it out for you, and I'm afraid as soon as you leave my side, it will come for you."

A chill ran through me at the thought. "I can handle myself."

He nodded. "I know you can, but demons are tricky. I have something that could help us in this fight. Follow me." He took off down the path, so I followed behind, and he pulled out his phone to dial a number. "Hey, Alec, we managed to track it down." He paused. "Yes, he'll be with me." Pause. "Uh huh. In the Brinnswick-Eastbrook Caves. We'll keep you updated." He shut the phone, then looked over his shoulder at me. "Alec knows what's going on, so you don't need to check in with your chief until after we take this thing out."

I nodded. "Thanks, A."

When we reached the house, he spoke to the other three that were standing outside, almost looking like Thayer and Basil were guarding the door to the house and not allowing Emrys inside. "Emrys, you're coming with us, right?"

"Yes."

Ailin nodded at him, then looked at the teenagers. "You two are staying here."

"Ailin," Basil groaned. "We can help."

"You're too young."

Basil crossed his arms over his chest. "You were battling demons when you were twelve."

"I am not the example you should be following."

"Come on, Ailin, we can help," Thayer said, looking just as upset as Basil at the prospect of staying home and away from a fucking demon.

"That may be true, but you could also be killed. You're staying home."

Basil huffed and clenched his jaw. "You can't protect us forever, you know."

"Maybe not, but I sure as hell can protect you now. You're staying home. Help Opal with the younglings. Maybe teach them a little something."

"I hate you," Basil said before stomping into the house.

Thayer glared at Ailin for a moment before stomping in after the other teen.

I looked at Ailin. "You've been raising them for a long time, haven't you?"

Ailin glanced between me and Emrys. "Yeah, I have." Then he turned around and yelled, "Stay outside, Em. Seb, follow me, I have something for you."

I followed him inside, but not before I heard Emrys muttering curse words under his breath. Ailin led me to a door that revealed a staircase going into the ground. Apparently, there was some kind of basement in this house. *There's probably secret passageways and all kinds of shit in this place.* Ailin looked over his shoulder and smirked at me. "Follow me, baby." I rolled my eyes at the *baby*, and he disappeared down the very dark, very creepy staircase.

"If you're taking me down here to kill me, I am so going to haunt your ass."

He chuckled. "Wouldn't dream of it. I like arguing with you too much to off you."

I snorted. "That doesn't surprise me. You just keep me around for my mouth."

I heard a little bang, then Ailin's voice traveled to me, "Shit, my toe. Don't say shit like that without warning."

I thought about what I'd said and how he could've taken it, and my cheeks heated with embarrassment. The staircase was uneven and windy, so we were walking really slowly. "Did you stub your toe?" Totally avoiding the mouth thing I said.

"Yes, thanks for that."

"It's not my fault you have a perverted mind."

"It's not my fault you have a gorgeous mouth that I want to shut up by kissing and filling it."

My blush deepened, and I suddenly felt sweaty all over. "Is it hot in here?" Shit, I didn't mean to say that out loud.

Ailin chuckled. "It is now."

I came to the bottom of the steps and ran into Ailin's back because it was so dark down here. Ailin muttered under his breath, and a green ball of light lit up above his hand. He casually threw the ball in the air, and I ducked. I expected the little ball to come back down, but it floated above our heads, lighting up the entire room in a green glow. Well, room was being nice. It was more of a weird cave-like hole in the ground. But it was pretty big with rows of shelves lining the entire floor.

"What is this place?" I asked as I followed him down an aisle. There were all kinds of things on the shelves; books, sticks, gems, swords, strange objects I'd never seen before, all kinds of shit.

"It's a place of secrets."

I rolled my eyes. "Very mysterious, A."

He chuckled. "This is a place where my coven hides magical objects that we find. We also keep our spell books and anything else we don't want in the hands of our enemies down here. It's more secure than any other place. Only coven members are granted access. The trees won't let anyone else through. They have their own magic from being one with our coven for so many centuries."

"But... they let me down here."

Ailin turned to face me. "You may not be a witch, Seb, but you're a part of our coven now. You'll never be alone again." He ran his hand down my arm before turning and heading down the aisle again.

His words were simple, but they meant more to me than any words I'd ever heard. I'd never be alone again? I was a part of his coven? These people, these witches wanted me here with them. I didn't understand why they would want me, but they did. I was a part of something that was bigger than myself. I'd never truly had that before. Not even close.

"Come on, baby, I want to give you something."

Did he just call me baby again? Asshat.

I heard his chuckles as he turned the corner up ahead.

With a deep breath, I followed and found him in front of a shelf that held a bunch of... branches.

Ailin laughed. "They're not branches, they're staffs."

"Staffs?"

"Yes. They hold magic, some hold specific abilities." He picked up a smaller one that was only two feet long. "This one was cut in half by a powerful ogre a long time ago—"

"Ogre?"

He waved me away. "Not important. Anyway, it's meant to freeze a being in place, no matter what form they're in, so it should work well with Mr. Gassy Demon. I want you to hold on to it. It's your best defense against this thing. If you get the chance to freeze it, take it, and Emrys and I will do the rest."

I frowned at the mention of Emrys, but I didn't say anything. "How does it work?"

"You just have to stab it. You don't need to do anything else. If it's in gas form, you stab the gas and it will solidify as it freezes. And you can let go of the staff once it's in place. But you can't pull the staff out or it will unfreeze, and you'll have a pissed-off demon after your ass."

"Okay, good to know."

He passed me the staff. "Can you put this in one of your holsters? It should stay hidden until you're ready to use it, otherwise the demon will have time to prepare, and it won't let you close."

I nodded and put the staff in my holster on the opposite side as my gun. It was a weird fit, but I was confident it wasn't going anywhere.

Ailin brushed by the next staff, and all I could do was stare. The staff was leaning against the shelf since it was tall enough to come up to my shoulders. It was a long windy branch, but at the top was a white opaque ball. The ball was mesmerizing, so I moved closer to examine it. It looked almost smoky, almost like the smoke was swirling inside of it. I wanted to run my fingertips over it, but I'd learned my lesson about touching magical objects without asking first, so I refrained.

"That's a very powerful staff, Seb." Ailin's voice surprised me.

I turned to find him giving me a curious look. "What does it do?"

Ailin licked his lips. "That staff was meant to enhance one's powers. It's... very powerful and belonged to a very powerful man a few centuries ago. But it has laid dormant since its owner died. We put it down here in case someone was able to get it working again. If you... want it, we can take a look at it, but I'm a little unsure about it. I'd rather let you inspect it when we have more time."

I stood up straight. "Let's look another time."

"Sounds good." He held out his hand, revealing another necklace. "This will prevent you from getting any residual magic blown your way from coven members, including Emrys."

"Okay." I put it over my head, and a little tingle went through me.

"And these will help protect you as well." He passed me some bracers. "When you're wearing them, you can use them as a shield against spells. They only work on the lower level spells, but they'll help deflect or catch the magic, kind of like a shield."

I nodded and strapped the bracers on my forearms. "Is that everything we need?"

He nodded. "Yes, let's go find this demon. It's out in the cave systems in the Brinnswick-Eastbrook Mountains. It will take a bit to find him in the tunnels."

"Let's get going then before it leaves the area."

Ailin grinned at me, then headed toward the staircase. This time when we walked up, the green ball of light followed us, lighting the way and making it easier to see the steps formed of tree roots.

When we reached the top, I couldn't help but glance back and think about the staff we were leaving behind. I didn't know why, but I was really curious about the staff, and about its owner. I shook off the strange feeling and followed Ailin outside to our car. *Our car.* When the hell had I started thinking of it as *ours*? That car was *my* baby.

Ailin grinned at me and walked to the driver's side. "I know where we're going, you don't, so let me drive."

"Whatever." I unlocked the car, then threw the keys to him as I climbed in the passenger seat. Emrys climbed in the back, and when Ailin settled in the driver's seat, we set off to find us a demon to vanquish.

Chapter Sixteen

Ailin hadn't wanted anyone at my back but him, so he was behind me, Sera was on my shoulder, and Emrys was in front with his dog—his Bonded One—leading the way. As we walked through the tunnels, I furrowed my brow. Everything looked so familiar, like I'd walked these caves before. What the hell? I knew this place. I'd dreamt of it before.

"You have?"

"Get out of my head, A."

"Sorry."

"No, you're not."

"Will you two quit bickering?" Emrys's voice was filled with anger as he looked over his shoulder at us. "Shut up."

Despite his attitude, he was right, we needed to stop talking. But I needed Ailin to know what I saw in my dream. Maybe I could use his mind-invasion to my advantage. *Tap my back if you can hear me, A.* I felt a tap on my back. *Can you see a picture if I think of it clearly enough? Tap once for yes, twice for no.* He tapped my back once. I brought up a picture of the weird dream I had where the woman was being attacked by that hissing man or thing or supernatural being thing.

Ailin grabbed my shirt to stop me from walking, then reached around me and tapped Emrys, who turned around with a questioning gaze. Ailin held up a finger, then faced me and put his palm on my forehead and whispered almost under his breath, "Play the whole thing for me."

I nodded and thought about the whole dream. About the woman going through the caves, about her pulling the bundle free and putting it in the box, chanting, then hiding it in the cave wall, the reptilian man coming and threatening her and killing her. And after I finished going through the whole thing, I couldn't shake the sickening feelings off right away. I closed my eyes and shook off my body trying to get the feeling of being suffocated out of my head.

I looked at Ailin; he was staring at me with wide eyes filled with fear.

"What's wrong?" I whispered.

He shook his head a little. "Seb... you're... how are you connected to this?"

I lifted a shoulder. "Maybe it's just because of my connection with you? Or because I touched that red stone?"

"Maybe." He glanced at Emrys, then back at me. "At least we know it's not Emrys."

"What?" Emrys hissed. "You really thought I could do something like this? You *know* I would never do that!"

Ailin narrowed his eyes at him. "Apparently, I don't know you as well as I thought I did."

Emrys jerked back as if he'd been slapped.

I really didn't like the tension between them, I didn't like Ailin staring into Emrys's eyes one bit, so I whispered, "You know what that was all about, A?"

Ailin turned back to me and took a deep breath. "I know what the plan is. He's trying to open a portal to the demon realm. A two-way portal so demons can come and go as they please. Or at least, that's what I'm guessing is in the bundle. There's a story, a legend of a stone that connects the realms. It was guarded by the enchanters for millennia, but..."

"But what?"

"Enchanters are no more. There haven't been enchanters for a century." He turned to Emrys. "There's a warlock connected to this."

"Shit." Emrys ran a hand over his face. "Shit."

"Why is that so bad?"

Ailin took a deep breath. "Remember I told you they let spirits pass through their bodies? They do it so they can steal a piece of the souls. They use blood magic which makes them very powerful. Blood magic is extremely potent, but it doesn't last very long, so they... tend to murder many victims. Combine that amount of evil with the kuma mali demon, and we're looking at some very powerful beings." He looked at Emrys. "We need to call Basil and Thayer."

Emrys nodded. "Okay." He looked around, then put his hand on the cave wall and closed his eyes. "I can block your voice from traveling any farther than this. Make it quick."

Ailin pulled out his cell phone and dialed Basil's number. "We need your help. Bring Thayer to the Brinnswick-Eastbrook Caves. We'll meet you outside. Hurry. Bring all of your gear, both of you."

When he hung up, Emrys said, "I know you're worried about them, but I promise I'll do everything in my power to protect them. I may not be a part of your coven any longer, but I still care about all of you." I didn't know him well at all, but despite the fact that I knew he'd tried to kill Ailin before, I believed him.

Ailin put his hand on Emrys's shoulder, and when Emrys did the same thing, Ailin said, "Allallisse ala endomea nahire."

Emrys whispered back, "Endomea nahire ala liayalla."

It made me a little uncomfortable with how... overly friendly they were, but I tried to shake it off. We retraced our footsteps and met Basil and Thayer at the cave entrance. They both looked way too excited to be invited on this mission, and I frowned at them. This was dangerous. I didn't want anyone getting hurt.

Basil had some kind of a freaking lizard riding on his shoulder. Who brings a lizard to a demon fight?

Ailin grinned at me. "That's Blaze. Want to pet him?"

I wrinkled my nose and shook my head. I so did *not* want to get any closer to that thing.

Ailin chuckled at my reaction, then gave them all a quick rundown of my dream, and we headed back inside.

Emrys was in front again, then me, then Ailin with Basil and Thayer behind him.

When I knew we were about halfway to our destination, I stopped walking and turned around to face Ailin. It was dark in there, but my eyes had adjusted enough that I could see him with the faint green light he'd supplied. He searched my face with a furrowed brow, and I knew he was worried that something was wrong. I couldn't shake the feeling that something bad was coming, and I knew we had to keep pushing forward, anyway. But there were so many things that I hadn't said to Ailin before now, so many things I wanted to say. He'd changed my life in the short time I'd known him, and while it was really fucking crazy now, it was also a million times better. But I'd never thanked him. I'd never thanked him for choosing to be around me every single day since we'd met. I'd never thanked him for being my friend when I hadn't had any in a long-ass time. It was too late for words now, but I knew I would regret it if I didn't show him how much everything had meant—even all the arguing—before we went into a dangerous situation.

I swallowed down my nerves, then quickly leaned down and pressed my lips to his. I could tell I shocked him, but he only took a few seconds to recover before he grabbed my shirt, fisting it and holding me in place to elongate the kiss. I hadn't meant for it to last this long, but there was no way I was complaining about it. His lips were warm and soft and made me melt. As much as I wanted to pry his mouth open and taste his tongue, I held back because I knew this wasn't the time nor the place. But we held our kiss for a long time, and when we finally broke apart, I wanted to pull him into my arms more than ever.

He sent me a sweet smile—the kind he didn't let most people see—then he leaned up and placed a small chaste kiss to the corner of my mouth before he released my shirt. I sucked in some much-needed air, then nodded at him and turned around to follow an obviously pissed-off Emrys. I licked my lips, and smiled a little when I tasted Ailin on them.

Emrys started heading the wrong way, so I tapped his shoulder and showed him which tunnel to head down. Finally, we made it to the small opening, and we could see a light flickering inside.

Ailin whispered into my ear, "You stay by my side no matter what. The only reason I'm even allowing you in there is because I know if you're not with me, the demon will find and attack you. It's been waiting for you. Do. Not. Leave. My. Side."

I ignored the conceitedness and took his words for what they were; he was worried about me getting hurt. "I won't."

He nodded, then stepped in front of me and gave Emrys a nod, then looked a Basil and whispered, "A little cover, Bas."

Basil shot his brother a smirk that looked so much like Ailin's cocky *I got this* smirk, that I had to shake my head. The Ellwoods were a cocky bunch, that was for sure. Basil pulled shadows from the walls until we were enclosed. It was kinda freaky seeing our shadows come to life and surround us, but I had to admit that it was badass.

Emrys nodded, and as a group, we entered the small cave.

I wasn't sure what to expect when we went inside, but my eyes widened at the sight before me. There was a fresh body covered in blood and symbols in the center of a large pentagram that was likely drawn with blood. At each point on the star, there was a small red flame burning over a cup of blood. As we stepped closer, I realized there were bones all around the pentagram, human bones all over the cave. Just how many people did this thing kill?

The red demon was standing over top of the body right in the center of the pentagram. It was... feeding on the person, although there was no way the person was still alive. I could hear it swallowing, and the sound made me sick.

But what got my attention was the fact that a cloaked figure stood off to the side near the small area where the woman from my dream had hidden the box. As if the figure sensed our presence, it turned toward us and opened its arms wide as it spoke, "I sssee you brought my sssacrifice. Sso nice of you to join usss, Sssebastian Cooper Fitzzz."

My eyes widened as the thing's reptilian voice filled my ears and brought back the helpless feeling of choking to death on smoke.

It chuckled. "You are no match for me, Ssage. Even the lasst of the enchanters couldn't sstop me."

Ailin grabbed my wrist and shoved me behind him. "Send the demon back, and maybe we will let you live, warlock."

The thing laughed, and I glanced at the demon. It hadn't even stopped feeding, in fact, it looked like it was eating the human's skin now. Oh god. It was completely oblivious to us. Maybe this warlock really did have control over that thing. I turned away before I vomited from the sight.

"You are no match for me, Ssage. You should ssave your lossses and leave Sebastian with me. Take your coven home. Just like old times, fighting Ellwoods. I'd hate to have to kill any more of your family members."

Emrys whispered, "Is that Trevin the fae?"

"He's turned warlock," Basil muttered. "Explains how he got past the wards."

Ailin's entire body ignited, and I had to take a step back so I didn't get electrocuted.

A weird rumbling sound echoed along the walls, and the fae-warlock's mouth grew into a smirk. "Just in time to meet my horde."

Ailin didn't even flinch, but I was kinda terrified about what the hell was making all of that noise; of what was coming for us. Ailin glanced at Sera on my shoulder. "Take care of that, will you?"

Sera nodded, then jumped off my shoulder before I could stop her. Emrys's dog and Basil's lizard both ran out of the cave with Sera.

Ailin muttered, "They're connected to our magic, Seb, they'll be more than okay against a few goblins."

My eyes felt like they were going to bug out of my head, but we didn't have time for that. We had a demon and a warlock to kill.

"You smell even better than I expected, Sebastian. I can hardly wait to get my hands on you." The warlock shot some of that inky black smoke at me, but Ailin blocked it with his green shield.

Basil and Thayer stepped around me, and suddenly all four witches shot energy out of their hands. Emrys had his silver energy, Basil his black, Thayer his yellow, and of course, Ailin had his green. They were protecting me, and as much as I appreciated it, I wanted to help, but I couldn't really do anything with all the energy flying around.

The green, silver, black, and yellow energies swirled together in front of them, but right before they could hit the warlock, he threw an arm up and a burst of inky black energy shot through the entire cave, pushing everyone back a step and effectively cutting off their energy. I'd barely registered what was happening before Basil and Thayer were thrown through the air, hitting the cave wall and sticking to it. The warlock twisted his hand and rocks covered Basil and Thayer's hands and torsos, holding them against the wall, unable to use their magic.

"I see you want to do this the hard way. Just like your parents." The warlock stepped closer to us.

"I can't get out of this, Ailin," Basil yelled. The more he struggled the more the rocks covered his body.

"Stop moving," Ailin said to both of them. "The more you move, the more it'll grow. Stay completely still, and I'll get you out shortly."

The warlock cackled. "This day will mark the death of Sage and the beginning of the warlocks' reign."

Ailin spoke under his breath as his energy began swirling around and around. Emrys knelt down, putting his hands on the floor and muttering as the ground shook beneath us. The bones in the room started flying through the air, aiming for the warlock, but he easily dodged them or threw up a tiny black energy shield to block them as he walked closer.

Ailin yelled out and a huge surge of energy flew out of his chest, making me stumble back from its force even though it was aimed in the other direction. The green energy met up with the black, and I saw both Ailin and the warlock stumble. Ailin's green energy pushed a little harder, and the warlock stumbled further as he struggled to block it. The demon suddenly let out a loud roar, and in a flash, he tackled Emrys.

I pulled out my gun and aimed for the demon since I couldn't see around Ailin to aim for the warlock. I shot the demon a few times, and Emrys punched and scratched at it as the bones in the cave flew at the demon, scratching and puncturing it. I unloaded my gun into the demon, hoping it would help Emrys be able to contain the damn thing, and as I reloaded my gun with another clip of bullets, I looked at Ailin. He and the warlock were sending balls of energy at each other. Ailin dodged a few, but he hissed in pain when a black flame singed his shoulder.

"Motherfucker," I said. I needed to get to that fucking warlock and take him out.

"Don't you fucking dare, Sebastian," Ailin yelled. "Stay behind me or so help me, I will kick your ass."

I snorted, but before I could respond, the demon roared again, standing up to its full eight-foot height as it towered over Emrys. Emrys had his hands in front of him, shooting silver light, but the demon was unaffected. The demon bent over and shoved his hands through Emrys's stomach, and the witch yelled, then coughed as blood splattered out of his mouth.

"No!" I yelled, then popped the clip in and cocked my gun, shooting my bullets into the demon's head. It screamed and released Emrys, grabbing its own head where I'd shot it. Emrys continued coughing, but I saw him using his energy to try and stop the bleeding. I couldn't do anything to help except draw the demon away to give Emrys a chance to heal himself, a chance to maybe live.

"You ugly, no good, asshole demon! What the fuck is the matter with you?" I yelled as I loaded my gun yet again. "I'm going to kill you, you fucker."

"What are you doing, Seb?"

I ignored Ailin. "Why don't you go back to your own realm, you good for nothing... demon!" *God, I'm terrible at yelling threats!*

The demon turned its black depthless eyes on me. "Sebastian Cooper Fitz. I will taste your blood before the night is through!"

Its voice gave me the creeps. "Gross," I muttered.

I spared Ailin a glance and noticed that he was looking worse for the wear. His clothes were burned, his hair was a mess, and he was covered in ash. The warlock was in the same boat, but I was worried that Ailin didn't have enough energy to finish him off.

"Seb, use the staff I gave you!"

Right, the staff that should lock the demon in place. I pulled it out of my other holster and held it with my gun as I unloaded another clip on the demon, this time I aimed for its chest. Maybe it had a heart and I could hit it. Who knew?

The demon roared and came at me. I bent my knees and prepared to fight. I knew the runes that Ailin gave me would help, but I braced myself for impact. When it threw its fist, I was able to dodge under its arm and punch it in the ribs. The demon wailed. *Holy shit, I'm strong. Holy fucking hell.* I threw another punch to its gut, and it bent over a little from the force before punching me again. It hit me in the stomach, and I stumbled back a few steps. Jesus, that hurt.

I gasped for breath as I threw another punch, but before I could make contact, the damn thing turned into that weird gas. "Fuck! How do I fight gas?"

"Use the staff!" Ailin sounded out of breath.

I knew what he meant in theory, but trying to stab gas was fucking difficult. The gas separated, so I didn't hit it, and before I could try again, it flew over to the warlock and solidified into its beastly shape again.

"No!" Basil yelled at the top of his lungs.

Ailin suddenly screamed, and I turned to see him fall to one knee as inky black smoke fizzled around him.

"Ailin!"

I started to run to him, but the warlock threw a black fireball at my feet. I tried to jump out of the way, but the energy ball hardened into rock around my feet and held me in place. I tried to break free, but I couldn't move.

"Ailin!"

He didn't turn around. I could only see his back, see him heaving in heavy breaths like he was having trouble breathing. "Ailin!" Something was wrong. Something was very, very wrong with him. I could feel it in my bones.

The warlock stepped closer to Ailin and said, "You can't beat me. You witchesss destroyed yourselves when you warred with the enchantersss." The warlock looked over his shoulder at the demon. "Bring it to me."

The demon disappeared out of view, and a moment later, it returned with a box in its hands. The bundle was inside, I'd seen it.

"No!" I didn't know what the bundle was, but I knew they shouldn't have it. I knew it couldn't fall into the wrong hands.

The warlock looked at me and pulled his hood down revealing his green, ugly face. "Finally. Everything isss in place."

"Ailin! We have to stop him!"

The warlock laughed. "Ailin can't hear you right now. I'm afraid hiss earss are bleeding almosst as much as hisss neck and eyess."

I narrowed my eyes at the warlock. Whatever he did to Ailin was not gonna fly. He was not going to kill my Ailin.

The warlock wiggled his fingers, and Ailin was spun around to face me. I gasped and tears filled my eyes. Ailin's neck was bleeding, blood gushing out and down his chest. His ears had blood coming out, and his eyes... I couldn't even see the green in them anymore, they were pouring blood. "Ailin," I choked out.

The warlock laughed, and the demon opened the box, but I ignored them so I could take Ailin in. His beautiful face was covered in blood and scratches and bruises. But I couldn't give up on him. I needed to save him. *Ailin, it's going to be okay.*

Run, Sebastian. Please run. Save yourself! I heard Ailin's voice in my head for the very first time, and more tears sprung to my eyes. He was dying, and I couldn't do anything about it.

I will never leave you, my little witch.

No, Seb. Get out. I can't move. I can't save you. Please. You have to run.

I ignored him and refocused on the warlock behind him. "You have me, let the others go."

"Oh, but my friends will need to feed as sssoon as they're freed. And witchesss make the tasstiest of sssnacks." The warlock reached around and grabbed Ailin's head, yanking it up, and making Ailin whimper. The warlock reached down and swiped his finger across the blood pouring out of Ailin's throat, then lifted his finger to his mouth and sucked on it. "Mm... deliciouss." He looked over his shoulder and dropped Ailin, who fell on the ground.

"Ailin," I whispered out.

The warlock grabbed the box, and I caught a glimpse of a weird yellow stone inside as he chanted, "Elita le mehi elmirai sel eh-estra. Elita le mehi elmirai sel eh-estra," over and over again.

The stone began to glow, and the symbol on the ground around the dead body glowed with it. I struggled against the rocks covering my feet. I had to get out, I had to stop this. They couldn't open that portal. Earth would never be the same again. Nowhere would be safe.

Sebastian, I'm sorry I couldn't save you. His voice was weak, even in my head. I looked at his body lying on the ground. The rise and fall of his chest was slowing down. He was dying before my eyes, and I couldn't even reach him. *Not again!*

Don't give up on me now, Ailin.

I'm sorry. I watched as his chest lifted one more time, then stilled. I waited a few beats before I realized that he'd stopped breathing. Ailin stopped breathing. Ailin was...

"Noooo!" I screamed and something inside of me broke. I felt that warmth that was usually reserved for Ailin suddenly explode from my chest and spread throughout my entire body. I was shaking with rage and grief, my body filling with adrenaline. I screamed out, and the rock around my legs broke. Without a thought, I ran at the warlock. He was so surprised, he didn't have time to brace for impact, and the two of us fell to the floor as I tackled him down. The stone flew out of his hand, and the glow around it started to fade.

I punched and screamed before the warlock finally pushed me off him using his black energy to send me flying back. But I didn't care. I was too pissed and grief-stricken to give a shit about him and his damn powers. I could hear Basil and Thayer yelling, but my blood was pumping so hard, my ears were pounding.

I ran at the warlock again, but he put up a shield that sent me flying backwards. I hit the wall near Ailin, and as I sagged down and coughed up a little blood, I reached out, my fingers just barely grazing his leg. He was really gone. A new energy filled me at the sight of his lifeless body.

The demon and warlock were both walking toward me, so I looked around for something to use as a weapon. The only thing close enough was that stupid yellow stone, so I reached for it.

I heard Basil yell, "Don't touch that, Sebastian!" But I was too far gone.

I grabbed the damn thing, but as soon as my fingers touched it, I inhaled at the amount of energy I could feel inside of it. When I looked up, the warlock and demon were both completely still, staring at me, and if I wasn't mistaken, the warlock looked fearful.

The stone's magic was racing through my body, and I felt invincible. They could no longer hurt me. They could no longer hurt anyone I loved. But I could hurt them. Oh, I could *really* hurt them. I could kill them. I could destroy them.

Destroy them. I heard a deep, strange whisper in my head. *Destroy them all.*

I stood and slowly took a step toward them, and they both stepped back. A slow smile formed on my lips. They were afraid of me. They should be, I could destroy them in a heartbeat. I *would* destroy them. I took another step, and they stepped away again. My smile grew. They were my prey, and I was the predator.

"Not so tough now, are you?"

The warlock sneered at me. "You have no idea what you're doing."

I tilted my head and smirked. "I'm going to kill you." I held my hand out with the stone on my palm, and it ignited into a yellow flame. That strange feeling inside of me, the one that Ailin brought out of me, it filled my body and shot out of my palms. A weird blue energy emerged and mixed with the yellow flame, turning it green. The green flame traveled up my arm. I knew it should hurt, it should burn, but I was way past feeling anything at this point. I lifted my other hand and held my palm out toward the warlock. The green fire danced along my arm, over my shoulders, and down my other arm to my palm. I thought about Ailin lying dead behind me, and the green fire shot out straight at the warlock.

The warlock screamed and screeched as the green flame engulfed him. He tried to put the fire out with his inky black smoke, but I was too powerful for him. I was barely using a trickle of energy, and he was already burning. I should've slowed it down to make him suffer, but it only took a minute for him to turn to ash.

The demon was trying to escape, so I lifted my hand in its direction and shot the green fire at it. It screamed and fell to its knees as it slowly turned to dust.

When both threats were taken care of, I turned to the other three living creatures in the cave with me. I held my hand out toward a witch with black hair that was stuck to the wall. *Witches are our enemies. They turned on us, they killed us, they deserve to burn.*

"Sebastian. We're on your side. You know us. Sebastian, come back to us."

I tilted my head when the witch's voice penetrated a memory.

"It's me, Basil. You need to put the stone down, Seb."

Hearing my nickname snapped the memory in place. He was Basil. He was a friend. I looked him and Thayer over. They were both still stuck to the wall, so I lifted my hand. I heard Basil yell, "No!" But I ignored him and aimed for the rock holding them both captive. The green fire burned the rock over their hands and bodies until they both fell free.

I looked down at Emrys lying on the ground, knocked out, but still breathing. He'd be okay.

"Drop the stone, Sebastian," Basil said in a voice that sounded a lot like his brother.

I shook my head and walked over to Ailin's body. I didn't want to let go of the stone because I knew the pain of losing him would engulf me the moment I did. The stone was keeping it at bay.

I walked over to Ailin and knelt beside him, placing my free hand on his chest and rolling him onto his back. "You weren't supposed to leave me, A." I dropped the stone, and a huge sob came out. I wrapped my arms around Ailin's back and dropped my forehead to his neck, not caring that his blood was getting all over me.

I'd finally found someone that wanted me, someone that actually cared what happened to me and wanted to keep me close, and I'd already lost him.

I pulled him tighter to me and cried, heavy sobs escaping my chest. I rocked him in my arms, my chest tight with pain. "You promised we... were connected... forever... you big asshole." I hugged him to me and buried my face against him to breathe him in. He smelled like blood, but I could still smell his rosemary scent underneath. "You weren't supposed to leave me." My tears poured out and ran down the skin of his neck. There was so much blood, such a huge gash. "Ailin... you can't be gone." *Come back. Please come back to me, Ailin.* I knew I was too late, but I didn't want to live in a world without him. "You're my vitmea. Come back, vitmea," I whispered through my tears.

I cried into him for a long, long time.

"Sebastian," a soft, teary voice said from behind me. "We need to get out of this cave. We need to take him home."

I shook my head and refused to look at them. "P-please don't take him away f-from me."

Basil placed his hand on my upper back, and I felt him kneel behind me. "I'm not taking him away, okay? But we shouldn't stay in this cave any longer. The energy here is... unclean."

"You... you'll let me come with you?"

"Of course, we will. You're one of us now, Sebastian. You're an Ellwood, and we take care of each other."

I nodded into Ailin's neck and finally lifted my head to look at Basil. He was crying, so was Thayer. Even Emrys, who was finally awake, was crying. He even had his arm around Thayer, letting the teenager cry on his shoulder.

Basil put his fingertips on Ailin's forehead and whispered something I didn't understand before kissing his skin, then he looked at me. "Do you want to carry him out, or would you like some help?"

"I-I'm not ready to let him go yet."

Basil nodded at me and stood, so I refocused on Ailin, cupping his face and wiping a little dirt off his cheek. I trailed my fingers down to his neck where my tear tracks were in the blood so I could touch our mark. I ran my fingers over his skin and gasped.

"What? What's wrong?" Basil was at my side again.

"The gash... it's... it's smaller than it was before," I whispered as I tried to clear away more of his blood.

I glanced up at Basil and saw his doubtful expression, but I didn't care. I knew the truth. Ailin's wound was closing up.

"Sebastian I really think that—"

"It's smaller, Basil. Look." I ran my fingers over a pink line, like the scar of an old wound.

Basil leaned in and stared at Ailin's skin, then looked back at me with wide eyes. "Let's get him outside near the trees."

I nodded and gathered Ailin up in my arms, following Basil out through the cave tunnels. I knew it was stupid to hope, but I couldn't help it. Ailin wasn't alive, his heart was no longer beating, but why would his skin be healing itself if he was really dead?

Once we exited the cave, I ran over to the nearest patch of grass and laid Ailin's body in it, then I leaned over him and cupped his cheek. "Come on, A. Come back to me. Please. You have to come back to me."

At first nothing happened, but then the grass around him started to move and grow, clinging to his body. Seraphina suddenly appeared beside him and climbed on his chest, licking his wounded neck. She was covered in gunk, so I guess she attacked some goblins, but maybe if she was able to appear here now, there was a little more hope. Could a Bonded One appear beside their dead bonded?

"Come on, Ailin," I said as I moved near his head, knelt down and cupped both his cheeks. "Come back, A."

As if on cue, Ailin's chest rose, and he took a shaky breath.

I let out a small laugh. "That's it, A. Come back to me."

He took another shaky breath and his eyes opened. They were bloody, but I could see the green a little. He looked around, confused until he saw my face and focused on me.

"It's okay, Ailin. You're okay. I'm right here."

He took a few more shaky breaths, then rasped out, "Seb?"

I nodded. "It's okay. Just rest so you can heal."

I went to move my hand, but he snapped his eyes to mine. "Don't leave me."

"I'm not. I'm never leaving you."

He sighed and closed his eyes.

I looked at Basil, Thayer, and Emrys. They all looked relieved, although Emrys looked a little worried, but I wasn't sure why.

I ignored the others for the time being and rested my forehead on Ailin's, breathing in his scent that was mixed with blood. "You died."

His hand grazed my elbow. "I know."

"How... how are you here?"

"I don't know, Seb."

A little sob escaped me, and I buried my face into his neck again. Ailin's arms came around me, but I could feel how weak they were. But he was here. He was alive. He wasn't leaving me.

"It's okay, baby. I'm okay now."

I nodded into him. "I thought I'd lost you."

"Shh... I know. I know."

We stayed there for a long time, but Basil eventually said, "If you're healed enough, I think we should get to coven ground, Ailin. We don't know if there were other warlocks involved. I don't want to be here unprepared and injured if they come."

Ailin whispered, "Okay, but I need help walking."

"I'll help you," I offered as I leaned up, pulling him to a seated position. I stood and put my arms under his armpits, hauling him up to standing, then I wrapped his arm over my shoulders. "Can you walk? Or do you need me to carry you?"

He smiled a little. "I can walk, I think."

I nodded and before we set off, Basil grabbed Ailin's other arm, putting it around his shoulders as he said, "I'll help too."

Ailin looked at his brother. "Thanks, Basil."

Sera trotted beside us with Blaze the lizard riding on Zrak the dog's back. I didn't even know what to do with that, so I just looked away.

Basil took a deep breath. "I'm just glad you're okay."

"Me too."

Basil leaned forward a little, and I saw the tear tracks on his cheeks, but he sent me a small smile. "Thanks for bringing him back to us, Seb."

I blinked at him. "I didn't... I didn't do anything."

"I saw what you did. You saved us all. And you brought Ailin back."

"That wasn't me... that was... where's the stone? We can't let anyone else get it."

Thayer held up the box, and I saw the stone wrapped up inside. "I have it in here. It's wrapped so it can't harm anyone. We didn't think it was safe to touch."

"What is that thing? Why did it... it almost felt like it was alive when I held it—"

"You held it," Ailin cut me off. "Why the hell would you do that? You could've been killed."

"I thought... I thought you were gone, A. I didn't have anything left to lose. It was either try it, or all of us would've been killed anyway."

Ailin fell quiet, but I could tell he was thinking things over.

"It felt alive?" Thayer asked.

"Yeah, it felt like another energy took me over and invaded my mind, my whole body, really. It was... a weird sensation, but also kinda... powerful."

"It's an enchanter's stone."

"Wh-what's an enchanter?" I didn't ask earlier when Ailin had mentioned them.

Basil answered, "They're extinct. But they were very powerful. They had magic of their own."

"What do you mean? You guys have magic."

"True, but we pull energy from our surroundings. Enchanters could pull magic from inside themselves. They didn't have affinities, so they weren't limited to the same physics that we are. They were the most powerful spellcasters in the world. Or at least, that's what we were taught." Basil shrugged.

"If they were so powerful, how'd they go extinct?"

Ailin answered this time, and his voice held a coldness to it that I wasn't used to. "They were hunted. They were used by other creatures to cast more powerful spells; their blood was spilled to do the most powerful and evil of magics."

"Tell him the truth, Ailin," Thayer said.

Emrys interrupted, "Enchanters and witches worked together to keep the balance of good and evil, of dark and light. They worked together for centuries until... until our great grandparents' generation turned on them. They got... jealous of the immense power enchanters held, and they handed them over to the warlocks. They... betrayed them."

For some reason, that made my chest constrict and my heart feel heavy. The witches were so power hungry, they betrayed another race so epically they became extinct.

"It's the worst part of our history, something I wish I could fix. Our great grandparents let the darkness into their hearts, and they became the exact thing we're supposed to protect our world from. They were evil, and I'm ashamed of what our people did," Ailin said quietly.

The others nodded. "Me too," Emrys said.

I knew they didn't have anything to do with it, I knew that we couldn't help what our parents or grandparents or great grandparents had done. Hell, my parents left me for dead in the middle of a parking lot, so I got it. But I couldn't shake the uneasy feeling I was getting about all of this.

We got to the car, and I debated where to sit. I wasn't ready to let Ailin go yet, but I needed to drive. Basil saved me from my predicament by grabbing my keys out of my hand. "I'll drive so you can sit in the back with Ailin."

"Didn't you guys drive here?"

"We rode Narenthea." He nodded into the trees, and I had to blink.

"You guys rode a horse here?"

Basil smiled. "Yep. Thayer and Emrys can ride her back. I don't want Thayer by himself."

I turned sharply to Emrys and glared at him. He held up his hands. "I promise I won't hurt him or whatever it is you think will happen."

Thayer added with an eye roll, "I'll be fine, Seb."

I nodded and helped a smiling Ailin into the back of my car while Basil climbed in the front seat, and Thayer and Emrys walked down to a freaking horse about a hundred feet away. Sera, Blaze, and Zrak all climbed in the front passenger seat together.

"What are you so happy about?" I slid in next to Ailin.

He surprised me by curling into my side and resting his head on my shoulder. "You were protecting Thayer."

I shrugged and put my arm around him. "I don't want anything to happen to him."

Ailin moved in closer and kissed my neck. "Thank you."

I looked down and noticed his eyes were closed. "Go to sleep, A. I'll keep an eye on things while you rest."

He nodded and grabbed my free arm, pulling it over him.

I was still getting used to the whole snuggling thing, but for Ailin, I'd do what he needed, and apparently, he needed me to hold him. The more I settled into him on the drive home, the more comfortable I became with him in my arms. In fact, when Basil parked the car, I was hesitant to let him go, so we stayed there for a few extra minutes. Thayer and Basil saw Emrys and Zrak out. I could see the longing in Emrys's eyes before he walked away. I was pretty sure he wanted to come inside with the rest of us, but we still didn't trust him. He'd lost the coven's trust when he'd left Ailin for dead.

Before we got out of the car, I used Ailin's phone to shoot a short text to my chief so I wouldn't have to worry about it, then I pulled A out of the car. As I helped Ailin through the house, I did a double take of the living room. Right in the middle of the couch there was a snake curled up in a ball with a freaking rat lying over its neck and head. "Is that George and Matilda?"

"Told you they slept in there," Ailin muttered.

"Aren't you afraid George will eat her?"

Ailin smiled a little even though he looked like he was ready to pass out. "They were both lonely. They're natural enemies, but they both needed a friend, so I guess they got over their differences because they're best friends now. They're together all the time, even out in the woods."

My eyebrows raised and I shook my head. Whatever. At least they seemed happy.

Ailin climbed into bed as soon as we entered his room, and I found myself following him in. He snuggled up into me again, and I kissed his forehead and relaxed as he fell asleep in my arms.

I didn't really know what happened in that cave. I didn't know how he was still alive, or rather alive *again* after what'd happened. But whatever force brought him back, whatever energy brought him back to me, I'd be forever grateful for it.

My life was already so entangled with Ailin Ellwood's that I didn't think I'd survive without him.

Chapter Seventeen

"Sebastian."

I blinked myself awake.

"Sebastian."

I looked around the dark room for the source of the voice, but Ailin was sound asleep on my chest, Sera was curled up on the pillow beside us, and no one else was in the room.

"Sebastian."

"Who's there?" I called out.

"Sebastian."

The voice was coming from outside of the bedroom. It sounded like someone needed my help. I looked down at Ailin again, but he was still sound asleep, and I knew he needed to rest after what'd happened. He needed time to heal, so I pressed my nose against his hair for a few seconds, then as gently as possible, I slipped out of the bed.

"Sebastian."

I walked out of the room, glancing back at Ailin and Sera asleep on the bed one last time before I shut the door behind me and made my way down the hall. I didn't see anyone else. The house was asleep, the moon was shining, everything was quiet.

"Sebastian." The voice was coming from downstairs.

"Where are you?" I muttered, not wanting to wake up the rest of the coven.

I made my way to the ground floor and searched the kitchen, living room, and dining room, but they were all empty.

"Sebastian."

I whipped my head in the direction of the voice and walked closer to the basement door. I hesitated for a few seconds, but if someone was down there, they had to be a coven member, right? So there was nothing to worry about. With a deep breath, I opened the door and called down the stairwell, "Hello? Is anyone down there?"

"Sebastian."

"Shit," I muttered under my breath. "Hold on, let me find a light."

Before I turned away, the basement lit up in a glowing white light.

"What the fuck?" I hesitated for a few seconds before walking down the steps. "Hello?"

"Sebastian."

Whose voice was that? They sounded familiar, but I couldn't place it. My brow furrowed when I reached the bottom of the stairs and still didn't see anyone. "Hello?"

No one answered, but the glowing white light was coming from one of the aisles, so I headed in that direction. The light was so bright down the aisle, I had to squint as I walked. I couldn't tell who was down there.

"Sebastian."

I turned around, looking in every direction for the source of the voice, but I still didn't see anyone. The white light suddenly brightened so much, I turned away from it and squeezed my eyes as I groaned a little from the change of intensity. With a small popping sound, the light went out, leaving me in darkness.

I blinked as I tried to let me eyes adjust, and I muttered under my breath, "Well, this isn't creepy at all."

"Sebastian."

What. The. Fuck.

Once my eyes adjusted, I walked a little farther down the aisle. I could've sworn the voice came from down here. When I reached the halfway point, I recognized where I was. This was the aisle with all of the staffs. I found that weird one I wanted to examine further, and I squinted as I moved my face right in front of it.

"Sebastian."

"Holy shit!" I jumped back in surprise. The voice was coming from the damn staff! I leaned in a little again. Something about this staff was calling to me. Well, besides the fact that it was actually calling my name. But I almost felt a... connection to it. I wanted to know more about this staff. I wanted to explore it, experiment with it.

"Sebastian."

I jumped again and wrinkled my nose. "Why the hell are you saying my name, you, you, you staff?" *Nice one, man.*

"Sebastian."

"What? I'm standing right here. What do you want?" *Okay, now I'm talking to inanimate objects in a creepy, dark basement.*

"Sebastian."

"What do you want?" I huffed out in frustration because I wanted to knock the stupid thing over, but I knew I couldn't touch it. I had just decided that I better run upstairs to grab Ailin since I was pretty sure a supposedly dormant staff shouldn't be saying my name out loud, but the staff wiggled a little. "What the hell?" The moment I went to turn around and run, the damn thing flew from its spot against the shelf, flying at me. I lifted my hands defensively so it wouldn't hit me, but my fingertips grazed the staff's wood. A strange buzzing shot through my body, and I wrapped my hand around the staff without a thought of what I was doing. It was like the staff was controlling my movements.

The staff's white opaque ball started moving around, the smoke inside was swirling around and around. I gasped in surprise when I felt a strange tingle running from my chest, down my arm and into my hand. It felt like the strange sensation was leaking out of my hand and into the staff. The longer I stood there, the stronger the sensation felt, and the white ball started turning blue. I was mesmerized by it.

But something changed, and suddenly, I wanted to let go. The tingling sensation started to hurt and my hand went numb. The staff was tugging at my energy, pulling it out, and I felt completely drained, yet it was still tugging. I tried to let go, but my fingers wouldn't listen to me. My ears started ringing, and when I went to call for help, my voice wouldn't work.

The tingling sensation burned, hurting my skin, and when I looked down, I realized a small blue and green flame was dancing over my hand. It began traveling up my arm until it was to my shoulder and spreading across my chest.

"Let go of the staff, Sebastian!"

I heard him, but I couldn't turn. I was frozen in place as my skin burned hotter.

"Holy fuck. Shit."

"We have to help him, Ailin!"

"Sebastian, let go!"

"Ailin, what do we do?"

"I don't know!"

I heard their voices, but I couldn't make myself turn to them.

"Seb, you need to concentrate. Please look at me. Don't think about anything else. Just look at me." Ailin's voice was soft, but I could hear the panic underneath.

With everything I had in me, I concentrated on Ailin's voice and finally, *finally* was able to turn my head just enough that I could see him.

He nodded. "That's it, baby. Concentrate on me." He stepped closer. "I can't touch the flames, Seb. They're creating a forcefield I can't seem to penetrate, and they're burning too hot. I'll melt before I can pull your hand off. So I'm going to need you to concentrate on letting go. Let go of the staff, Seb."

I tried to move my fingers again, but they wouldn't listen.

"You were able to move your head, right? So I know you can do this. Please... you have to let go." His voice broke, and I could see the worry on his face.

Seeing him like that, and hearing his panic, made me double my efforts. I closed my eyes and concentrated on my hand. I needed to let go. I just had to open my fingers and *let go.*

As soon as my hand opened, the staff fell to the ground, and the flame burning my body dissipated. I fell to my knees, but before I could faceplant, Ailin had his arms around me, holding me up.

"Shh... it's okay. It's going to be okay." Ailin's words were supposed to be a comfort, but all they did was bring worry. He was scared. I could hear it in his voice.

Ailin wiped my cheeks, and I realized I'd been crying from the pain.

He held me close again and called over his shoulder. "No one goes near that staff. I need you to do a perimeter check and lock down this room after I make sure he's okay and we leave. No one is allowed down here until I figure out what the fuck that was."

"Okay," Basil answered.

I didn't have the energy to look, but I knew Basil, Opal, and Thayer were all down here with us, but had started making their way upstairs.

"What happened?" Ailin whispered to me.

I took a few deep breaths before answering, "I was woken up when someone called my name. You were asleep, and I didn't want to wake you, so I got up and followed the voice down here. The... the staff lit up the whole room, and when it said my name again, I... I went to walk away from it, but it flew at me and it sorta grabbed me instead of me grabbing it."

"It moved by itself?"

I nodded.

"And the staff was calling you?"

I nodded into him. "It kept saying my name over and over."

He grabbed my wrist and rubbed his thumb over it in a soothing pattern. With each small touch, my skin was settling more, hurting less. He was healing me even though he should've been saving his energy for himself.

"Seb?"

"Yeah?"

"When did you get this tattoo?"

I was confused by the direction of his question, but I answered easily, "I've always had it. At least as long as I can remember."

"So... when you said it was a family thing, you meant...?"

"My parents—my birth parents, I guess, gave it to me before they left me at the Academy."

Ailin sucked in a deep breath, then pushed me up a little so I leaned back off him, but he didn't let go of my wrist. Ailin had a few glowing green balls floating overhead to light the room, and he brought one closer so he could examine the tattoo on my wrist, although, I didn't understand his sudden fascination with it.

"Holy shit."

"What?"

He pulled a necklace off his neck and looked at me with wide eyes. "This might hurt a little."

"What? What are y—"

I hissed in pain as Ailin used the sharp edge of his necklace's charm to slice open my wrist over my tattoo as he muttered a spell under his breath.

"What the fuck, A?" I tried to pull my arm away, but he held on tight.

"Just trust me."

I opened my mouth to yell at him again, but before I could, a weird sensation ran through my body before settling in my chest. "Whoa. That's weird."

"What? What do you feel?"

"It's,.. warm."

He dug a little harder, and the sensation shot out from my chest through my entire body to every single cell, then it shot out of every inch of my skin. A rush of wind flew out of my body, knocking Ailin over, rattling all of the shelves, and even blowing Ailin's green balls of light out so we were in darkness again. The strange wind was pouring out of me in waves. Wave after wave after wave. My whole body felt like it was filling up with energy and about to explode.

I looked at Ailin's wide green eyes, and before I could freak out too badly, I felt another calmer energy surrounding me. It was... Ailin. I could feel him.

It's okay, Seb, I'm right here with you. I heard Ailin's voice inside my head. *Just let me in so I can help you.*

I stared into his green eyes, and I knew without a shadow of a doubt that I could trust him. *Okay.*

As soon as the thought entered my mind, Ailin's essence filled my entire body, my entire soul until all I could feel was him in every piece of myself.

Chapter Eighteen

Ailin

As soon as Sebastian let his walls drop, I felt our souls connect so hastily, I almost got knocked over again. I could feel our connection growing with every passing second. He was everywhere, I couldn't tell where I ended and he began. Our souls were wrapping around each other, fusing together, and I could feel Sebastian's confusion. And his fear.

The energy was so strong, I couldn't speak, so I channeled my thoughts toward him.

It's okay, Seb. We'll be okay. I'm right here with you.

What's happening? Even his thoughts sounded shaky.

I didn't want to scare him any more than necessary, so I told him a half truth. *We're... connecting. Just calm down and let it happen. Stop holding back, baby.*

He finally let go all the way, and his energy came pouring out, pushing me back again, but I held onto his wrist tight. I would *not* let go of him. I wasn't going to let him go through this by himself. I fought against the power radiating off him and brought my free hand up, placing it on his neck. As soon as I touched his vitmea mark, his energy floated into me and started flowing from both of us instead of only from him. I heard him take a deep breath,

345

and I was glad I could take some of the power away and make him more comfortable.

With his power floating through us instead of against me, I was able to move closer to him until I rested our foreheads together. Our souls were still wrapping around each other, so I could feel how scared he was even though his face was fierce.

"It's okay," I whispered.

He looked surprised to hear my voice, but then he spoke back, "I don't understand what's happening."

"I know. But it will pass. Just try to relax."

"My body feels like it's full of electricity. How am I supposed to relax like this?"

I smirked. Hearing him give me shit was a good sign that the energy burst was starting to slow down and level off. "Maybe if you didn't sneak out of my bed in the middle of the night, we wouldn't be here right now."

He narrowed his eyes at me. "I thought someone was hurt."

I could feel the truth of his statement, so I gave his neck a little squeeze. "I know. Close your eyes, it's almost over."

He stared at me for a few seconds before following directions. I loved when he actually listened to me, but... I sorta loved when he argued back even more. Not many people talked to me the way Seb did. Most were too scared of me to say how they really felt, so I was always grateful when I came across someone with a mind of their own.

The energy surge finally came down until it was merely a trickle. Thank god Sebastian was okay. I didn't know what I'd do without him.

Seb's eyes flew open and he whispered, "I can hear you."

Shit.

"I heard that."

Fucking hell.

His eyes widened further and he smiled, but it was the *I'm gonna give you shit* smile I was so used to. "I can hear you. Oh my god, A. I can finally get you back for invading my head all the damn time, can't I?" When I didn't deny it, his grin turned up a notch. "Just you wait."

I rolled my eyes, but couldn't help but smile. He was okay, he was going to be fine. "Do you think you can stand?"

"I don't know. I can still feel the energy. I sorta feel like my skin is staticky."

I took a deep breath and pulled him to his feet. He was shaky, but I held him up. "I know. You'll get used to the feeling after a while. It'll sorta level off even more so it's kinda below the surface instead of fizzling on top like it is right now."

"Wh-what are you saying? Isn't it going to go away soon?"

I cringed internally. "Uh... no. No, it's not going to go away."

He narrowed his eyes at me. "Are you serious? Is this because of that stupid mark again? That thing is a pain in my ass."

"It's not because of the mark."

He looked down at the wrist I was still holding that was covered in blood. "What did you do to me, A?"

"I didn't do anything, baby. I simply took a spell off of you that's been there for years."

"Wh... what the hell are you talking about?"

I took a deep breath. "Sebastian, that tattoo your parents gave you? It was placed there for protection. It was there to keep you safe when you were a child so... so they couldn't find you to hunt you. Your parents probably planned on coming back to get you, but I'm assuming they were killed."

His brow furrowed. "What the hell are you talking about? What do you know about my parents?"

I sucked in a deep breath and blew it out slowly as I stared into his honey eyes that were filled with so many emotions, I couldn't make them out. "Sebastian Cooper Fitz, you're an enchanter."

He blinked at me.

"Your tattoo was a cloaking spell so strong I couldn't pick up your energy at all, even when we were close, even when I claimed you as my vitmea."

He just kept blinking at me.

"That energy you feel is your magic, baby."

He opened and closed his mouth several times. "But... but... but enchanters were killed. They're extinct."

I nodded. "I know."

"Then how...? I'm not an enchanter, Ailin. You must be mistaken."

I let go of his wrist and put my hand in the center of his chest. "It all makes sense now. That's how you were connected. That's why you were able to hold the stone, how you brought me back to life, baby." I didn't know how that demon and warlock knew what he was before I did, but maybe it was because they had the enchanter's stone. He still didn't believe me, I could tell from the look on his face. "Can you feel your energy here, baby? Can you feel all that power? It wasn't there before, was it?" He shook his head, and I smiled gently. "It's your magic."

"But I'm a human."

I smiled and pulled him close to me so our chests were touching. "It doesn't matter what you are. We can figure that out tomorrow. I only care that you're here with me, and that you're mine."

A tremble racked his body, and I smirked at the fact that I could cause such a reaction simply by being close.

"Ailin, I don't... why can I hear your thoughts?"

I cringed. "There's something I should've told you a long time ago."

His eyes darkened, and he looked guarded again. "What?"

"I only claimed you as my vitmea because you're my viramore. You're my... soulmate."

He opened his mouth, then snapped it shut and pulled away from me. "Why do you keep lying to me?"

My heart felt heavy as he put more distance between us. *Shit.* "I didn't lie to you. I just didn't want you to freak out, and honestly... I wasn't ready to admit it before now."

He closed his eyes and took a deep breath. "You're my vira-whatever? So what is a vitamin or whatever you call it? I don't understand."

"A viramore is a soulmate. A person that was made to be your other half. A vitmea is... well, it can be anything you want, I guess, but you can only claim one. Usually a person claims a lover, lucky ones claim their viramore, and some try to claim a... servant."

Seb's eyes narrowed further at that. "Your world has too many weird rules. What kind of person marks someone else as their servant? And you told me before that *that* wasn't what it was! Now you're saying it is?"

I shook my head. "You and I claimed each other. That's the difference. We are balanced out together. We are equals. We are vitmea viramore."

"We're vitamin viras?"

I bit my lips to keep from laughing. "Vitmea viramore."

He threw his hands up. "Whatever! I don't even care. I feel like my skin is going to explode."

I walked to him, but he backed away again. "Seb."

"Don't touch me."

My chest tightened again, and I felt like I got punched in the gut. "Seb, please?"

He wrung his hands out in front of him. "I don't... I don't know what's happening."

"I can help, if you'll let me." I stepped toward him.

"Don't come any closer."

That knocked the wind right out of me. "Seb, please don't do this." His chest was heaving, and all I wanted to do was pull him to me even though he'd probably kick my ass if I did that.

"Ailin," his voice broke. He was terrified of the energy inside him.

I held out my hand. "Please, baby, let me help you."

He searched my face for what felt like eternity before slowly putting his hand in mine, and I felt like I could breathe again. As soon as our fingers touched, I could feel him in my every cell again, and from the wide-eyed expression on Seb's face, I was pretty sure he felt it, too. I pulled him closer until I could wrap my arms around him and hold him against my chest. This man was pulling out my possessiveness, and there wasn't a damn thing I or anyone else could do about it.

Sebastian very slowly put his arms around me, too, and after several seconds, he rested his head on my shoulder, tucking into my neck. As soon as he relaxed in my arms, his energy leveled out completely.

"There we go, it'll take some getting used to, but I can help you. Our connection will help level you out."

"Just because you helped the weird energy, doesn't mean anything. I'm not an enchanter. That staff just did something weird to me."

I rubbed his back. "Whatever you say, baby."

"Don't patronize me, Ailin. I'll kick your ass."

I chuckled. "You can believe whatever you want. But I know the truth."

"What's that? That I'm some weird mythical creature that's been extinct forever?"

"Nope. That you're mine, and nothing else matters."

He sagged into me further and his voice cracked, "A."

I rubbed his back. "Come to bed with me. We both need our rest and... our connection needs time to grow."

"I don't want you in my head anymore than you already are."

"Too bad."

He groaned.

"At least now you'll be in mine, too, right?"

He groaned again. "Now I get to hear all the names you call me inside your head. Fun times."

I grinned at him and pulled him closer. "Come on, baby. Let's go to bed."

He sighed but nodded against me and whispered, "I'm scared, A." I knew that took a lot for him to admit.

"I know. But I'm here. You have nothing to worry about."

I didn't tell him that I was scared, too, because I didn't want to freak him out anymore than he already was. He didn't need to know that I was terrified for his life because if he truly was an enchanter, he was going to be hunted for his power... and for his blood.

There was no way that others in Brinnswick didn't feel that explosion of power. And many of the older creatures would know exactly what kind of being made that explosion. They'd know that the enchanters were back, just like the old prophecy foretold. And if Seb was the enchanter from the prophecy, his life was going to be filled with horrors I wish I could protect him from.

My vitmea viramore was going to be hunted.

But I would kill anyone that came after him without a second's hesitation.

He was mine now, and I was planning on keeping him.

Epilogue

Somewhere West in the Brinnswick Forest

The surge of energy knocked him back, and he sucked in a deep breath, then looked around the forest as he dropped the dead rabbit from his hands. He took a deep breath and gasped. He knew that scent of power; it'd been missing from this world for a long time, but he remembered it well. He walked in the direction the energy was coming from, breathing it in as he went. He filled his lungs with the long-lost scent, and his mouth lifted at the edges in a cruel smile, revealing his blood-soaked fangs. He would find the creature, and he would siphon that energy, suck it up, and use it for his own. Then he would consume its soul and slice the creature open bit by bit, piece by piece so he could eat its flesh and drink its blood.

"Klazog, is that what I think it is?" his younger brother asked, joining him in the trees.

"Yes, my dear brother. I believe the last enchanter has finally awoken. We have our chance, let's not waste it. Grab the others, and follow the scent."

"Where will you go?"

He turned and grinned at his brother, showing his mouth full of sharp teeth. "I'm going to wake the elder."

His brother's eyes went wide. The elder had been sleeping for hundreds of years, only to be awoken when the prophecy foretold.

"Are you sure, Klazog? What if this is a mistake?"

He tilted his head at his idiot brother. "Have I ever been wrong before, Ezegork?" His brother shook his head. "I know an enchanter's smell well. This is it, dear brother. Now go, you have your orders."

The younger ogre ran off toward their caves they called home, and Klazog continued his walk as he soaked up the fading scent of enchanter.

When the smell finally faded, Klazog smiled that cruel smile. "You can run, enchanter, but there's nowhere on this earth that you can hide. I will find you, and I *will* have you." He walked toward the ancient sacred tree.

It was time.

***

The End of The Enchanter's Flame

Sebastian and Ailin's stories will continue in The Enchanter's Soul: The Ellwood Chronicles II.
And if you want to learn more about Ailin, Emrys, and Alec, be on the lookout for the prequel, The Witch's Seal, coming out in October!

If you would like updates on my new books or to be notified when a new book is released, please join my mailing list:

http://eepurl.com/cseIXT

You can find me on Facebook here:
https://www.facebook.com/profile.php?id=100013432570194

I also have a reader's group on Facebook to talk about my books and others' as well. I share teasers, exclusive excerpts, a first look at cover reveals and more. If you're interested, feel free to join Notaro's Haven:
https://www.facebook.com/groups/NotarosHaven/

Feel free to contact me on Facebook. I'd love to hear from you.

If you enjoyed this book, please think about leaving a review. Every bit of encouragement is a huge help to authors, especially indie authors, so every review helps. Thank you!

Acknowledgements

As always, I'd like to thank my husband and our two boys. Kiddos, I love you more than life itself, and I'm so grateful that I get to call you my kids. Dom, you are the most amazing hubby I could ever ask for. Thank you for putting up with me. I'm the luckiest person in the world to have such a wonderful family. I love you, my incredible, amazing boys! <3

Brittany Cournoyer, thank you so much for being super supportive no matter what the hell I'm writing! Your encouragement means the world to me. I appreciate your friendship more than you know. Love you, girl! <3

Steph Marie, I could never thank you enough for your friendship. Thanks for being an ear whenever I need it, and for always having my back. Thank you so much for helping me make this book the best it can be. Love you!! <3

Steph & Britt, FDS, I love you guys! Hahaha. Thank you! :*

I would like to give my AMAZING team of beta readers a shout out: Kyleen Neuhold, Shannan Arnold, Melinda James Rueter, Abigail Kade, Ashe Winters, and Jacki James. You guys rock so hard. I love that I have such an amazeballs team behind me, and I'm incredibly grateful. Thank you so much!! <3

Tracey Soxie Weston, you have no idea how much I appreciate the hard work you put in for this cover, and I have to say that it's absolutely stunning. Thank you for another amazingly beautiful cover. I think this is my favorite one yet! <3

To all of my wonderful members in Notaro's Haven, I love you guys! You always manage to make me laugh, even when I'm having a bad day, and even when y'all keep torturing me with disgusting pickle concoctions! lol. Love ya all! <3

To my ARC readers. Thank you all so much for taking the time to read my books, write reviews, and let people know about them. I appreciate it, and I'm so thankful to have you interested in my many crazy stories. Your help is immeasurable and I'm so very grateful. Thank you!!!

To my readers, I wouldn't be doing this without you. Every time someone picks up one of my books, I'm incredibly grateful. It blows me away when people give me a chance, and I am beyond appreciative for every single person that reads one of my books. From the bottom of my heart, thank you.

Thank you for reading, and I hope you enjoyed it!!! As Orrean (from Taoree) would say, "Thrive and love, as bright as the stars!" <3

About the Author

Michele is married to an awesome husband that puts up with her and all the characters in her head—and there are many. They live together in Baltimore, Maryland with their two young boys and two crazy dogs. She grew up dancing and swimming and taught dance—ballet, tap, jazz, hip hop, & modern—for ten years before her kids came along. Now she stays home to write about the sexy men in her head and does PTA everything—as long as coffee is involved. Two other tattooed moms run the PTA with her, and though she wants to rip her hair out from it, she still loves it.

Books by Michele Notaro

Finding My Forever:
(Contemporary Romance)

Book 1:
Everything In Between
(Caleb and Reese's story)

Book 2:
A Little Bit Broken
(Harley and Theo's story)

Book 3:
Left Behind
(Levi and Andy's story)

Book 4:
A True Fit
(Declan and Trent's story)

More to come in this series...

A Finding My Forever Short Story:
(Contemporary Romance)

Falling In Time
(Jamie and Ezra's story)

A Valentine's Tail
(A Levi and Andy story)